on a *Whim*

Also by Robin Jones Gunn

Peculiar Treasures

KATIE WELDON SERIES

on a *Whim*

BOOK TWO

ROBIN JONES GUNN

ZONDERVAN®

ZONDERVAN.com/
AUTHORTRACKER
follow your favorite authors

On a *Whim*
Copyright © 2008 by Robin's Ink, LLC

This title is also available as a Zondervan ebook.
Visit www.zondervan.com/ebooks.

Requests for information should be addressed to:

Zondervan, *Grand Rapids, Michigan 49530*

Library of Congress Cataloging-in-Publication Data

Gunn, Robin Jones, 1955-
        On a whim / Robin Jones Gunn.
            p. cm.
        ISBN 978-0-310-27657-9 (pbk.)
        1. College students—Fiction. 2. Self-actualization (Psychology—Fiction. I. Title.
    PS3557.U4866O5 2008
    813'.54—dc22

                                                                    2008026366

Scripture quotations taken from:

The *Holy Bible. New Living Translation*, copyright © 1996. Used by permission of Tyndale
House Publishers, Inc., Wheaton, Illinois. All rights reserved.

The *Holy Bible, New International Version*®. NIV®. © 1973, 1978, 1984 by International
Bible Society. Used by permission of Zondervan. All rights reserved.

Internet addresses (websites, blogs, etc.) and telephone numbers printed in this book
are offered as a resource to you. These are not intended in any way to be or imply an
endorsement on the part of Zondervan, nor do we vouch for the content of these sites
and numbers for the life of this book.

Published in association with the Books & Such Literary Agency, 52 Mission Circle, Suite
122, PMB 170, Santa Rosa, California 95407-5370. www.booksandsuch.biz

Interior design by Michelle Espinoza

Printed in the United States of America

08 09 10 11 12 13 • 23 22 21 20 19 18 17 16 15 14 13 12 11 10 9 8 7 6 5 4 3 2 1

For my forever friend and amazing agent, Janet Kobobel Grant. Thank you for two decades of wisdom and grace every time I'm ready to go out "on a whim." What will the next two decades hold for us?

With deep appreciation to the team of God-Lovers I have the privilege of working with at Zondervan Publishers.

And to the best assistants on the planet, Rachel and Natalie.

W hich button do I push?" Katie stared at the panel of options on her best friend's microwave.

"The one that says 'popcorn.'" Christy's voice from her apartment's bedroom carried enough emphasis to communicate that Katie should have known the obvious answer.

"Oh. Got it!" Katie pressed the popcorn button and flipped her swishy red hair behind her ears. She was ready to work up some serious snackage for their Girls' Night In. Opening the door of the freezer, she called out, "Is it okay if I use all the ice? You don't have much in here."

"Use all of it," Christy called back. "You can always go down to Rick's apartment if you need more."

"Rick is in Arizona. I told you that, didn't I?" Katie stopped filling the blender with ice as Christy walked into the kitchen. She had changed into baggy flannel PJ shorts and a hooded sweatshirt belonging to her husband, Todd. Her nutmeg brown hair was pulled up in a ponytail, and her face was green.

"Whoa! That's more minty green than I had remembered," Katie said. "Does it feel tingly yet?"

"A little. My skin is tightening even as we speak."

"That's what it's supposed to do."

"Then I guess it's working." Christy picked up one of the frozen strawberries thawing in a bowl on the kitchen counter. "What did you say this was made from?"

"The smoothies?"

"No, this facial mask."

"Green tea powder, bee pollen, honey, egg whites, and some other organic stuff."

"And tell me again who gave this to you and said it was so great?"

"Nicole. She uses it all the time, and you've seen her skin."

"Her skin is flawless," Christy said. "But Nicole probably exercises regularly and eats right, so I'm guessing she has advantages going for her that you and I don't."

"We're working on the healthy eating even as we speak." Katie scooped some frozen strawberries and blueberries into the blender on top of the low-fat yogurt and ice cubes.

"Did we have enough ice?" Christy opened the freezer door. "I think our icemaker is broken."

"We have enough. It helps that the fruit is still frozen."

"If you do want more ice, I was serious when I said you could go down to Rick and Eli's apartment. Eli is probably there. As a matter of fact, he might be happy to be the one to give *you* the ice for a change."

"Very funny."

"So is this." Christy tried to open her mouth in the shape of an O and patted the side of her face. "Am I cracking?"

"Yes. And I won't add any further comment. I also won't add any comments to the topic of how supposedly rude I am to Eli. I hear enough about that from Rick. Eli makes me nervous, okay? That's all I'm saying. That's all I've ever said about him. The guy is ..."

"He's one of us, Katie. You just haven't given him a chance. He's your boyfriend's roommate, and he was Todd's roommate when they were in Spain. Eli is part of our circle. You really need to make peace with that. You're just not around the times that we hang out with him, so you haven't had a chance to get to know him the way we do."

"Okay. You're right. Peace on Eli. Peace on me when I'm around Eli. Any friend of yours really should be an instant friend of mine. I'll start being more normal around him. I promise."

The microwave gave a dull *bweep*, and Katie took advantage of the interruption to step out of the current conversational topic. "I think your microwave is in about the same shape as your icemaker. This popcorn bag is still flat as a pancake."

"It smells like popcorn in here, though. Popcorn and something else." Christy stepped over to the window that opened to the grassy courtyard and cement walkway.

"That would be the scent of the garlic butter that comes as a bonus with this popcorn." Katie pushed the popcorn button again on the microwave and returned to the blender, where she gave the waiting ingredients a whirl. "How blended do you like it?" she shouted over the sound of the ice being crushed.

"It doesn't matter to me just so long as it turns out sweet. I don't like smoothies that taste more like tangy yogurt than fruit."

"Why don't you work on the perfect blend while I paint my face green?"

Katie slipped into the small bathroom of Todd and Christy's one-bedroom apartment.The bathroom was the same configuration as the one in Rick and Eli's two-bedroom apartment a few doors down. The oval sink had the same brass faucets with the same sort of chipping, fading, and lime buildup at the base.

What made Todd and Christy's bathroom almost appealing was the matching rug, shower curtain, and towels. Katie had helped Christy pick out the colorful set with credit Christy had at Bath and Bliss after she returned a variety of mismatched wedding gifts. Now everything in her bathroom matched. The beachy shades of pale yellow, blue, and green stripes in the shower curtain were accented by the rug and towels and made the framed waterfall picture on the wall look even more inviting.

Katie could almost believe this was going to be the relaxing home spa experience she had hoped for. The long hours she had been putting into her studies were beginning to wear on her, as was the round-the-clock availability required of her as a resident assistant at Rancho Corona University.

This reconnecting time for Katie and Christy was long overdue.

Pulling her silky hair back and snapping it into a ponytail holder, Katie made use of the bobby pins Christy had left on the counter. First step was to wash her face. Next, she applied the earthy goo with two fingers. The cool, refreshing sensation prompted her to open her eyes and mouth wide and make a funny face in the mirror. She noticed that the green shade of the mask was the same shade as her eyes.

With a sniff, Katie called out, "Christy, is that the popcorn I'm smelling?" The words were lost in the blender's reverberating whir.

Trucking to the kitchen, Katie arrived just as Christy turned off the blender. With one look at the microwave, Katie screamed, "Fire!"

Lurching across the room, Katie slammed her fist on the off button for the microwave. She grabbed the blender, and opening the microwave's door, she doused the popcorn bag with strawberry yogurt smoothie.

"Katie!"

"It's okay. Look, it put out the fire. Don't worry. I'll clean it up. Man, what happened to this pathetic thing?" Katie pulled a pair of tongs from the top drawer by the stove and lifted out the popcorn bag. She held the scorched rectangular disk dripping with strawberry muck over the sink. Instead of puffing up and rising like a normal bag of microwave popcorn, the flat, unresponsive paper bag had self-combusted and burst into flames.

"What a mess! It smells awful. Katie, where did that popcorn come from?"

Katie dropped the barely averted disaster into the trash and reached for a kitchen towel to sop up the pink mess without responding to Christy's question.

"Do you still have the box?" Christy continued. "Because I'm thinking we should tell the store so they can recall the rest of that lot number."

"That won't be necessary." Katie avoided Christy's gaze. "I didn't buy it at a store."

Christy handed Katie a whole roll of paper towels and waited for her to finish her confession.

"I bought the popcorn at a garage sale."

"Katie!"

"I know, I know. You don't have to say anything. I'm making a note to myself at this very moment: 'Hey, Katie, from now on, don't buy food at a garage sale.' There. I got the memo."

Christy dumped the used wad of paper towels into the trash can and gave Katie a perturbed look.

With a pinched grin, Katie said, "I guess this means I shouldn't use the box of Hamburger Helper I also bought at the garage sale."

Even though Christy looked like she wanted to be mad, she began to laugh. Or at least try to laugh. Her mouth was drawn back in a tight, unnatural position.

Katie giggled at Christy's oddly slanted expression, thankful that her friend was once again extending grace to her.

Just then a loud thumping sounded on the door.

Katie and Christy stopped laughing and gave each other instinctive "caught" looks. Katie could feel the mask drying and tightening in the creases her laughing expression had just created.

"Are you going to answer the door?" Katie whispered.

"Not looking like this!"

The pounding sounded again.

"You answer it." Christy gave Katie a nudge.

"Me? This is your apartment, not mine."

A muffled male voice on the other side of the closed door called Christy's name.

"I think it's Eli," Christy whispered.

"He probably smelled the smoke out the open window. Come on. We should both go." Before Christy could protest, Katie pulled her to the entry and swung the front door wide open. Trying to play down the near disaster, Katie struck a casual pose as if she hung out every Friday night at her married friend's apartment, painting her face vibrant colors and catching unassuming appliances on fire.

Eli, or Goatee Guy, as Katie had dubbed him at Christy and Todd's wedding, stood on the welcome mat holding a large black trash bag. He was wearing the khaki shirt required for his campus security position. His light brown hair was much shorter than it had been the last time Katie had seen him driving around in one of the beat-up golf carts on campus.

As soon as the Kermit impersonators with their Pebbles Flintstone hairdos opened the door, Eli and his trash bag took an involuntary step back. His exclamation seemed to stick in his throat.

"Little early for Christmas," Katie quipped, nodding at the bag. She was proud of herself for acting "normal" around Eli, just as she had promised.

Eli put his chin up like a grizzly sniffing for campfires. "Is everything okay? I thought I heard someone yell when I left my apartment. Then I smelled … man, that is awful. What burned?"

"Microwave popcorn." To Christy's credit, she was keeping her composure even though Katie knew this sort of moment was more humiliating for Christy than it was for her. However, Katie was feeling her face grow warm beneath the mask and realized she too was embarrassed. That didn't happen very often.

"To be precise," Katie said, "the package was labeled microwave popcorn, but I believe the actual contents would need a DNA test to determine their true origin and identity. Or maybe the popcorn is a candidate for carbon testing. We have the petrified article in the trash, if you want proof."

"I believe you," Eli said, his composure returning. "I just wanted to make sure everything was okay. I knew Todd was with the junior high group tonight, but I didn't know if you were with him, Christy, or if your place was empty."

"Thanks, Eli," Christy said sweetly. "I appreciate your checking in on me."

"As I'm sure you've figured out by now," Katie added with a sweeping gesture toward their apparel, hair, and faces, "we're having an evening of extraordinary beautification since Rick and Todd are both gone tonight."

Eli tilted his head. "Rick is here."

"No, he's not. He's in Arizona."

"He hasn't left yet."

"Is he at your apartment now?"

Eli nodded.

Katie needed no further invitation to blast past Eli and blaze a trail to Rick and Eli's apartment.

Thinking through her actions had never been Katie's strength. She was much better going with the flow. At this moment, green face and all, she wanted to see Rick. She knew he wouldn't be surprised. Very few things surprised him about her anymore, including her on-a-whim spontaneity.

Last summer Rick was the one who told Katie her best decisions were the ones she went with on instinct. He made that statement during a difficult week when she was trying to decide whether to change her major just before her final year of college. At the same time she was thinking about taking the resident assistant position at the dorms. Her gut-level choices turned out to be good ones.

She tapped a rhythmic little number on the closed apartment door and considered briefly what she would say when he answered. Now that she and Rick had taken the next step in their relationship and officially called each other "boyfriend" and "girlfriend," they were finding their communication with each other needed more work than they had expected. Katie knew Rick would have a good explanation for why he wasn't on his way to Arizona like he said he would be. She just wanted to hear it from his lips.

Tall, dark-haired Rick stood in front of her with a barely amused look on his handsome face. He could cast an authoritative figure when he wanted to draw himself up to his full six-foot, two-inch height and square his quarterback shoulders. Katie had seen him stand like this at the Dove's Nest Café where he was the manager and where she had worked with him for eight months before starting her senior year of college.

"Trick or treat?"

"You're a little late for Halloween." Rick rubbed the back of his neck and gestured for her to come in.

"And you're a little late for your flight. I thought you would be on your way to Arizona by now."

"I would have, but Josh decided we should drive this time and use the airline award points for tickets next time. I'm waiting for him to pick me up. I told you all this in the message I left on your phone. Have you checked your messages during the past hour or two?"

"No. Christy and I were sort of, uh ... busy."

"So I see. Do you need a towel or something?"

"No. Well, actually, yes. I'm ready to wash this off. I'll be right back." Instead of using Rick's bathroom, Katie went to the kitchen sink and washed her face. She used paper towels to dry and rubbed hard to remove the hardened green goo.

Returning to the living room where Rick was watching TV with the sound on mute, Katie plopped down next to him and reached for his hand. Rubbing his fingers over her cheek, she asked, "What do you think? Is it softer?"

"Feels a little sticky."

"Yeah, it does, doesn't it? This stuff works like a miracle potion on Nicole's skin."

"Who is Nicole?"

"You've met her. She's the other RA on my floor. Nicole, the one with the beautiful dark hair and the glowy skin."

"Oh, right. I've seen her. I don't know that I've officially met her."

"Doesn't matter. The green mask is something she gave me to try. I'm supposed to have smooth, glowing skin now."

Rick put his arm around Katie and kissed her on the end of her nose. "To me, you look great just the way you are."

"Did it fade any of my freckles?"

"I hope not." Rick leaned closer just as the front door opened. He pulled back.

Eli entered and went into the kitchen without looking at Rick and Katie cuddled up on the couch. They could hear him replacing the trash can under the sink.

Katie realized she had left her wadded-up, used paper towels on the counter and called out, "Sorry, Eli, I left a small mess in there. Although, if it's any consolation, it's nothing compared to the mess I left in Christy's kitchen."

Turning to Rick she said, "I really should get back and help Christy to clean up. We had a small disaster."

"Do I want to know what happened?"

"Probably not." Katie grinned at Rick. "Do you want to come with me anyway?"

"I better stay here." He looked at his watch. "Josh is going to want to get on the road right away since it's a five-hour drive."

"When will you be back?"

"Thursday."

Katie had grown accustomed to Rick's treks to Arizona over the past few months. He and his brother were trying to open a café in Tempe. Many of the steps that were supposed to be a snap were taking more attention and time than they had anticipated. Rick was excited about the project, but his trips were turning out to be about equal to the number of times she had to turn down opportunities to be with him because of her RA responsibilities at Rancho Corona.

"You'll definitely be back in time for the Doubles Pizza Night on Friday, though, right?" Katie asked. She knew all too well how quickly Rick's plans changed whenever he went to Tempe.

"What time is that again?" Rick pulled out his new cell phone and brought up his calendar on the screen.

"Look at you, all organized. It's seven on Friday night, at Crown Hall, and we need to go with another couple because the pizza-making part of the event is for teams of four."

Rick entered the info in his phone. "Who are we going with?"

"I don't know yet."

"Hey, Eli!" Rick called out. "What are you doing next Friday night?"

Katie reached over and fwapped Rick on the arm.

"What?"

In a whisper Katie said, "Don't ask him."

"Why not?" Rick whispered back.

Eli stepped into the living room and took a seat in the recliner by the bookcase. "I have to be at work at eleven. Why? What's going on?"

"Katie was saying there's a pizza night going on at Crown Hall."

"Yeah, I heard about it."

"I thought you might want to find a date and go with us."

Katie turned away from Eli and gave Rick a can-I-talk-to-you-a-minute-in-private look. She rose from the couch still not sure what to say to smooth out the awkwardness of the moment.

Rick picked up on all Katie's nonverbals. "Well, just think about it, Eli. We can figure out everything later. I'm going to walk Katie back to Christy's. If Josh arrives, send him over there, okay?"

"Sure."

The worst thing at that uncomfortable moment was the expression Katie caught on Eli's face. She knew that expression and the feelings that lurked behind it because she had experienced them herself. Those feelings had followed her around for years, feelings of being left out and overlooked and never part of what was happening with the "in" group. For her, when she started to hang out with Rick almost a year ago, those feelings had dispersed. Now she felt as though she belonged with someone.

But then the expression on Eli's face shifted, as if he had settled into a place inside himself, a place with a different time schedule or different expectations from everyone else.

In a final effort to make good on her promise to Christy to act normal around Eli, Katie turned, ready to toss a final, flippant comment over her shoulder as she and Rick walked out the door. However, no words came to her. And that was not at all normal.

W hat was all that about?" Rick kept his voice low as he and Katie walked down the apartment complex trail toward Christy's apartment.

"I don't know. I mean, I do know about the pizza night. I didn't want you to invite Eli to go with us."

"Why not?"

"I don't know!" Katie's voice escalated.

"Hey, it's not that big a deal. I thought it would be a good idea for us to do something together so you can get past your phobia or whatever it is you have with him. Eli is a great guy. I want you to get over whatever it is that makes the room go weird whenever the three of us are together."

Katie took a deep breath.

"What about Nicole?" Rick asked.

"What about Nicole?"

"What about Nicole going with Eli on Friday night? Isn't she the one with the face you were talking about?"

"The *face*?"

"You know what I mean. Since she's your floor partner aren't the two of you supposed to do these social events together?"

"Yes, of course. Nicole and I love doing things together. But I'm pretty sure she already has a date. And aside from that, Rick, this isn't your event to plan or invite random people to."

"Whoa! What is with you tonight? I thought you and Christy were supposed to be relaxing. You're more amped up than you were when I saw you Wednesday after you bombed that quiz."

"Oh, that was good, Rick. Thanks for reminding me about the quiz. Now I definitely feel more relaxed."

"Hey, come here." Rick looped his arm around her and drew her close. "Forget everything I said. You'll do great on your next quiz. You always bounce back in your classes. And if you have your reasons for not including Eli, I'll back off. I know you needed to relax tonight. Sorry I made it more stressful. Do you think you can go back in there with Christy and find a way to ramp yourself down a few notches?"

"Yeah, I can do that." Katie drew in a deep breath. "Now, will you do something for me?"

"Anything."

"Can you tell Eli we don't have any doubling up plans that include him so that I don't have to tell him later? I don't want you to take off for Arizona and leave me with this tangle to undo."

"Okay. I'll tell him I spoke too soon without knowing the details."

"Whatever you say, try not to hurt his feelings, okay?"

Rick gave Katie an odd look, as if he didn't expect her to express such concern for Eli. They were standing in front of Christy and Todd's apartment. The front window was open, and the scent of the burnt popcorn still hovered in the air.

Instead of commenting on what Katie had said, Rick asked, "Do you smell something burnt?"

"It was our microwave popcorn. That was the disaster you didn't want me to tell you about. I probably should take the trash can down to the dumpster, or else the apartment is going to smell all night."

"Let me do that for you," Rick offered.

Katie tapped on the front door before turning the knob and going inside. Christy had washed the green off her face and was standing in the kitchen with a sponge in one hand and a bottle of spray cleaner in the other.

"Rick is going to take the trash out for us," Katie said.

"Thanks, Rick. That's the last evidence of the near catastrophe."

"Except for the evil smell that doesn't seem to want to leave," Katie said.

Rick took the trash can out the front door without saying anything.

Christy looked at Katie as if trying to gauge the temperature of what was going on between them. "Is everything okay?"

"I think it will be. We're just having one of our miscommunication discussions. He has one way of solving problems; I have another. We're figuring it out."

Christy gave her a hopeful smile. "How does your face feel?"

"Sticky."

"Really? Mine feels soft. Here." Christy came closer and turned her cheek for Katie to feel.

"Man, that's totally different from mine."

"I had to leave the washcloth on my face for a while. Did you use warm water?"

"No. Is that the problem? I just used cold water and a paper towel in Rick's kitchen."

"A paper towel? Katie, you probably still have some of the pasty stuff on your skin. Why don't you try washing it off with warm water and a washcloth this time?"

Katie returned to Christy's bathroom and let the water run a few seconds until it turned warm. She doused the washcloth and held it to her face, breathing in the steam. This certainly felt better than a cold splash and rough paper towel scrub.

The washcloth still was covering her face when she heard Rick's voice behind her. "I'm going to get going. I told Christy she should keep the waste can outside to air it out. I'll call you tomorrow."

Katie lowered the washcloth and turned to look at Rick, who stood in the doorway, ready to leave. "Okay. And you're going to talk to Eli before you go, right?"

"I said I would."

"I know."

"You can trust me to follow through."

"I know."

They looked at each other a moment. She was red in the face from the hot water and was dripping on the bathroom rug. He was looking slightly flustered and ready to jet out of there.

"I'll see you Friday," Rick said.

"Okay. Bye."

As soon as she heard the front door close behind him, Katie turned to look at herself in the mirror. *Can you blame the guy for not initiating a good-bye kiss? You look like a lobster fresh from the sea. How does Rick put up with you, Katie? What does he see in you?*

"So, is that better?" Christy asked, her image appearing in the reflection in the mirror.

Katie turned to Christy and asked, "What do you think Rick sees in me?"

"At this moment, I'd say he just saw a very rosy complexion."

"Seriously, what do you think he sees in me? Besides the opposites attract thing?"

"I'm sure he sees your heart, Katie. Your beautiful, generous, loyal, and loving heart. He also sees you. The real you. The fun and deep-spirited person you are. Why do you ask? Are you having insecurities again about your relationship?"

"Always." Katie caught herself. "No, erase that. I'm not supposed to use *always* when it comes to our relationship."

"Why not?"

"It's something that came out of an old argument. Something about how I shouldn't go to extremes and use *always* or *never* when I'm upset. Yeah, right. Like I'd ever go to an extreme or get upset."

Christy offered the knowing expression Katie was hoping for with her sarcasm.

Christy said, "Isn't *always* sort of like *forever*? Todd and I have been using the word *forever* in our relationship since almost the beginning."

"Ah, yes, the famous forever ID bracelet."

Christy held up her right arm when Katie mentioned the bracelet Todd had given Christy soon after they had met. He had had the word "forever" engraved across the top. The bracelet had gone through several near disasters during its history. One of them was during a brief season in high school when Christy dated Rick. He took the dainty bracelet from Christy without her knowing it and replaced it with a clunky silver bracelet with the word "RICK" engraved on it.

"Katie, all of us have lots of bumps along the way in our relationships. You know that."

By the look on Christy's face, the memory of Rick and the ID bracelet seemed to open a grace-filled part of her heart. It wasn't a happy expression that came over Christy's freshly revitalized face, but it wasn't a bitter one, either. For all the potential awkwardness of the overlapping relationships between Christy, Katie, and Rick, clearly Christy didn't harbor any regrets or bitterness about her short dating relationship with him. She had dealt with all that a long time ago.

"You know what's strange to me now," Christy said, as Katie patted her still-red face dry with one of the soft yellow hand towels. "So many things that happened in high school and at the beginning of college seemed traumatic and irreversible, as if they were the most intense things in life. But now they seem like a bunch of uniquely crafted experiences that God used to make me depend more on Him."

"What a nice-sounding, spiritually mature thing to say." Katie neatly folded the towel and returned it to the rack where it belonged, even though it now had a slight green tinge in the center of it.

"Are you making fun of me?"

Katie grinned at Christy. "Always."

"You're just trying to find ways to get in trouble tonight."

"Yes, I am. How am I doing so far? Don't answer that. I already know. If I'd been serious about wreaking havoc with the universe, I would have kissed Rick good and mushy right on the lips before he left."

Christy tilted her head and gave Katie a sympathetic look. "You guys are still in the total abstinence zone, I take it."

"We're not just in the abstinence zone; we're planted there. Permanently, I think. Eternally. I predict that I will be ninety-eight years old and still waiting for Rick to decide he is ready to kiss me. All I can say is that by that time, his big kiss better be really good, or I'm definitely going to break up with the guy."

Katie noted that Christy hid a smile by looking down.

"Don't you even start with me about the blessed bliss of waiting." Katie put her hands on her hips.

"Waiting has its definite benefits. Love is patient."

"So, tell me something." Katie leaned against the edge of the bathroom sink. "How do you know?"

"How do I know what?"

"How do you know when you're really in love? Or maybe I should ask how or when do you know you're with the guy you're going to be with 'forever'?"

Christy plunged her hands into the front pocket of Todd's sweatshirt. Her expression softened. "It takes time, Katie."

"I know. And then what?"

Christy laughed. "Time as in, it helps if you at least *try* having a little patience."

"Yeah, well, 'patience' is a ..." Katie counted on her fingers. " 'Patience' is an eight-letter word, and I make it a practice not to use eight-letter words whenever possible."

Christy counted on her fingers. " 'Possible' is an eight-letter word too. 'Possible' is a good word. With God, anything is possible."

"Possible, yes. I couldn't agree with you more. My question is when. When do you know? How long does it take?"

"It's not like there's a chart, and you can check off the required number of days you're together, and then on a certain day you know. It's different for every couple. You need time and enough experiences together to be settled in your own spirit."

Katie pulled the ponytail holder from her hair and gave her head a shake. "Well, at least you didn't give me that 'when you know, you know' line I've heard from other women."

"That line is true. Even though not every woman 'knows' in the same way, I think every relationship has a mysterious invisible line you cross. It's as if you're going along like you have for a while, just putting one foot in front of the other, moving forward. Then suddenly you take a step, and the path looks different. There's more light or something. And that's when you just know you're on the right path with this guy. No matter how many obstacles are ahead, you know you're supposed to keep going. It's like your first step into the forever part of your future, but you wouldn't have gotten to that one decisive step without taking all the other steps."

"I'm waiting for that moment when the fairy dust comes and sparkles on me so that whenever I smile I get one of those starbursts in the corner of my eye." Katie struck a pose sporting a cheesy grin with her shoulder up and her eyes open wide.

"So basically, you want to turn into a cartoon character."

"Sure. Why not?" Katie shifted her position against the sink and crossed her arms over her middle.

"Because that's a fairy tale," Christy said matter-of-factly.

"Do you mind if we sit in the other room?" Katie asked, realizing that this conversation could last a while and the apartment did contain better spots than the bathroom for a heart-to-heart talk.

They moved to the bedroom instead of the living room and stretched out on the comfortable bed the way they used to during their time of being college roommates. Christy handed Katie a pillow.

"So give it to me straight then," Katie said. "How is it being married? Is it like you thought it would be?"

"It's different than I thought. In some ways it's more wonderful, but in some ways it's a lot more difficult."

"How is it more difficult?"

Christy looked away for a moment and traced the quilted pattern on the top of the bedspread. "We fight a lot more than I thought we would."

"I can't picture you guys fighting."

"We had a ridiculous argument tonight right before Todd left. He assumed I was going with him for this bowling night, but I told him you and I already had made plans. I told him three days ago about our plans, and at that time he said, 'Great. Have fun.' But he forgot, and when he found out they had more kids coming than he expected, he assumed I would help out."

"You could have gone, Chris. I would have understood if you said you had to cancel."

"I know. And I told him that too, after I finally said I would go. But by then he said he had found someone else to chaperone. We came to a restless sort of agreement before he left. We're going to keep a calendar together so both of us can be reminded of what the other has coming up. I guess it was a useful argument, when I think about it. We should have put together a joint calendar a long time ago. I just hate the way we argue. We're not very good at it."

Katie laughed.

"It's not funny. You're good at arguing, Katie. You are fearless when it comes to speaking your mind and getting everything out in the open. I do most of my processing on the inside; so even though I only end up spitting out a dozen sentences or so before the conflict is settled, on the inside I've fought an exhausting battle with myself just trying to say what I think or what I want."

"You know what I think? I think you're too polite." Katie adjusted her position.

"Polite?"

"Yeah, you're too polite."

Christy furrowed her brow.

"Honestly, Chris, you're going to end up driving yourself crazy if you don't start speaking up."

Christy rolled over on her back and stared at the ceiling. Folding her hands across her middle she said, "How do you do it, Katie? How do you say what you're thinking and feeling without hurting other people?"

"Not very well. You know I'm horrible at holding my tongue. Maybe we can help each other find a middle place. You have to speak up, and I have to hold back. We can learn from each other."

Christy turned her head back toward Katie. "You're right. It's not a bad idea for you and me to try to adjust our extremes."

"I'll tell you something else that's not a bad idea."

"What's that?"

"Food. Eating is a very good idea right now. Do you have any food around here that I can eat without obliterating your appliances? Or better yet, we could go out for some food and then go do something."

"Like what?"

"Like roller skating or night skydiving or ..."

"We could go bowling with fifty junior highers. Todd's going to be at the bowling alley with them until midnight."

"Yeah, not exactly what I had in mind. I'm thinking something like flying to Arugula and riding a camel."

Christy narrowed her distinctive blue-green eyes. "I think arugula is a type of lettuce. It's not a country, if that's what you were trying for."

"Well then, *let us* — get it — *let us* find a country that has camels and go there for a midnight gallop. Do camels gallop?"

"I have no idea. Would you settle for watching a DVD that has camels in it?"

"Does the DVD also have lettuce in it?"

Christy laughed and shook her head. "We won't know until we go to the DVD rental store and review the options."

"I don't want to watch an adventure," Katie said, "I want to experience one. Maybe I should have gone to Arizona with Rick and Josh."

"Why?"

"The all-night road trip would have been fun."

"Katie, you have way too much energy for someone who has been keeping the kind of schedule you've been maintaining."

"Don't talk to me about my schedule. I have to be on front-desk duty tomorrow at 8 a.m."

"So you couldn't have gone to Arizona with Rick even if you wanted to."

"I know. I'm just dreaming. Dreaming is good for us."

Christy settled back. "I'm dreaming of cheesecake right now."

"Cheesecake?" Katie stared at Christy. "Are you pregnant?"

Christy bolted upright. "No. Why do you ask that?"

"Because you don't usually dream of cheesecake. Chocolate chip cookies, yes. An occasional chimichanga at Casa de Pedro, yes. I've just never heard you say that cheesecake was at the top of your dream list."

Christy shrugged. "It sounded good. Someone at work had a piece of cheesecake in the refrigerator for two days, and it looked yummy. If they didn't end up eating it by today, I was going to help them out, but it was gone when I checked this afternoon."

An odd sort of scratching sound came from the front door.

Katie asked, "Do you hear that?"

Christy went to the front door, and Katie trailed her into the living room, flinging herself onto the couch. She expected Todd to be on the doorstep without his key.

Opening the door a crack, Christy said in a firm voice, "Don't you have anywhere else to go? Todd isn't going to like it if he knows you're back."

"Christy, who are you talking to?"

"Mr. Jitters."

For a brief moment, Katie was certain her best friend had lost her mind. First the cheesecake wish and now a conversation at her front door with someone named Mr. Jitters?

As Christy stood at the open front door of her apartment, a large calico cat darted between her legs and scampered inside. He ran straight to the kitchen and made himself known with a hoarse-sounding meow.

"Mr. Jitters!" Christy cried, going after the intruder.

"When did you get a cat?"

"He's not ours. He just showed up last week."

"Tell me you haven't been feeding him."

"Come here, Mr. Jitters," Christy called in a singsong voice. She picked up the puffy culprit and scratched his head. The cat closed his eyes with a contented blink and purred so loudly that Katie laughed.

"Is that an animal or a fuzzy electric can opener? Christy, that thing is possessed!"

"Don't mind her, Mr. Jitters." Christy reached into the back of one of the cupboards and pulled out a plastic bag of cat food. She shook the bag in front of the contented cat. Mr. Jitters ramped up his rattling meow.

"He sounds like a chain smoker," Katie said.

"Hey, did I make fun of your goldfish last year?"

"How could you? Rudy and Chester didn't live long enough for you to come up with any sort of derogatory statements about them."

"Maybe you didn't feed them enough." Christy opened the front door and put cat food in a little bowl she had tucked behind the bushes.

"Maybe you're feeding this guy too much. That's why he feels free to run into your apartment uninvited."

"You sound like Todd. He's the one who named him because the first time the cat came to our door he was shaky."

"So why don't you guys adopt him?"

"We barely have enough money to buy food for us. If we kept Mr. Jitters in the apartment, we would have to take him to the vet. Do you know how much that would cost? I do. I used to work in a pet store, remember?"

As Christy and Katie stood by the open front door, they watched Mr. Jitters devour his midnight snack. The not-so-polite guest chowed down in record time and took off without so much as washing his paws or meowing his appreciation.

"And there he goes," Katie said. The cat disappeared in the bushes. "That guy is using you, Christy. He's playing on your sympathy."

"I know."

"Just so you know what's going on here."

"I do."

Katie looked across the well-lit path of the apartment complex area, trying to see if Mr. Jitters was going door-to-door with his sympathy act. He seemed to be staying out of the light and keeping to the stretch of low shrubs that lined the front of each of the single-story apartments.

"You know, if this same plot of land would be developed as apartments today, most builders would put two or maybe three times as many units in the same space," Katie commented. "I don't know any other apartment complex that has such a huge grassy area in the center or is so quiet."

"I think that's because when the apartments were first built they were on the outskirts of town, and land was relatively inexpensive," Christy said. "Now that the town has expanded so much, the location is great."

"Do you think you guys will live here a long time?"

Christy shrugged and closed the door. "You know Todd. About every two weeks he starts talking about signing up with some sort of ministry that would place us in one of the untamed corners of the world doing Bible translation or something."

"And how do feel about that?"

"Depends on what day you ask me. I knew early in our relationship that living in the jungle or in a tree house was part of Todd's dream. I don't know if that idea will ever entirely leave his mind." Christy reached into the cupboard and pulled out a bag of tortilla chips and handed them to Katie along with a few items from the refrigerator, including salsa, a bag of mini carrots, and a jar of peanut butter.

"So you would pack up and go with him to the ends of the earth if he asked you?"

Christy nodded. Her expression looked peaceful. Not resistant or resolved. Just content.

"Whoa." Katie spread the miscellaneous items on the small kitchen table and lowered herself into one of the chairs.

"Whoa, what?" Christy ran water in the sink, filling two glasses with water.

"I assumed Todd would feel settled now and want to stay in one place since you guys are married and he has a good job. It's a job as a pastor, even. That's ministry, right? I don't like thinking about the possibility of you guys ever moving far away."

"It's always a possibility. But don't freak out. We don't have plans to go anywhere in the near future."

They snacked and chatted for another hour before Katie decided she should head back to the dorm. Reaching for her shoulder bag and jacket, she asked, "Do you want to try to meet up for lunch on Tuesday at the Dove's Nest? I can be there at 1:30."

"Tuesday at 1:30 works for me. I'll ask for my lunch break then." Christy rose and gave Katie a hug. "This has been great. I really needed this. I hope you relaxed a little too, even though we didn't manage to fit in any skydiving or camel rides."

"There's always next time," Katie said brightly. "Say hi to Todd. And if Mr. Jitters comes back tonight, I recommend you send him away without food. Better yet, I'll bring over the Hamburger Helper I bought along with the popcorn at the garage sale, and you can feed him that."

"Katie, one of these days you're going to find an animal you really like, and you're going to turn into a softy too."

"Yeah, maybe. Do you have any kangaroos that come to your door for snacks? I like kangaroos."

Christy hugged Katie one more time. "The next kangaroo that comes to my door I'll save for you."

"You better."

With a wave over her shoulder, Katie walked briskly to the guest parking area and climbed into her 1978 VW, which she affectionately called Baby Hummer. Tossing her bag onto the passenger's seat, she turned the key in the ignition.

Nothing happened.

She tried a second time and a third time. Nothing. Not even a Mr. Jitters-type purr came from under the hood.

"What's wrong, Baby Hummer? Are you asleep? Come on, wake up. You have to take me back to school now."

When attempts four, five, and six produced not even a flutter, Katie pulled a flashlight from the glove compartment and got out. She unlatched the hood and flashed the light on the engine.

"Not that I know what I'm looking for ...," she muttered as she shone the light back and forth, here and there. She had the notion that some obvious tube had popped out of its proper connecting spot, or some wire would be dangling right under its corresponding plug-in spot.

Nothing revealed itself during Katie's random examination. Her brother was the one who fixed cars. He knew all about Baby Hummer; he would know what to do. However, Katie didn't have his number in her cell phone. Even if she did, she was pretty sure he wouldn't be eager to jump on the freeway and drive more than an hour to rescue her at midnight. She hadn't seen him for almost two years.

Because he was so much older, by the time she was grown up enough to get to know him, he was out of the house and in trouble regularly. It probably would be a good idea for her to find a different mechanic.

Katie flashed the light over the engine one more time in a final, futile fanfare. The light flickered. Then it dimmed considerably and flickered again.

"I'm a walking disaster when it comes to all mechanical devices tonight! What is my problem? Did the microwave meltdown turn me radioactive or something?"

Katie stood in front of the open hood, trying to decide what to do. If she went back to Christy's apartment, she would have to wait until Todd came home since Todd and Christy had only one car. But Katie knew she could count on him to give her a ride, so she started to close the hood, having made her decision.

But before she could act on her decision, she heard someone approaching behind her. Spinning around with the heavy flashlight firmly in her grasp in case she needed to use it as a weapon, Katie heard a guy ask, "Is everything okay?"

A number of Rancho Corona University students lived in this apartment complex. Katie knew a lot of them. Even in the shadowed lights of the parking area, she recognized the voice and the gait of the guy coming toward her. It was Eli.

"She doesn't want to start."

"Did you try pumping the gas pedal a few times and letting out on the clutch while turning the ignition key?"

"No."

Eli stood next to her and peered at the engine. Under his arm he carried a sleeping bag and a thermos.

"Are you going camping or something?" Katie asked.

"I'm going out to the desert."

"Now? Are you crazy?"

"Probably."

Katie looked at him more closely in the amber glow of the parking area. Eli's light brown hair always looked tousled. Tonight he wore a beanie that allowed only a few patches of unruly hair to escape in different directions. She usually identified him by his goatee, as if that were his most distinguishing feature. His eyes were actually more distinguishing. She had noticed his intense, examining expression before when he had stopped her in the cafeteria last August and tried to engage her in a conversation. But now, in the limited light, his focus on her seemed even more intense.

"So . . ." She tried to find a smooth way to finish out this conversation. "Do you go out to the desert by yourself a lot in the middle of the night?"

"Not often. I usually go with Joseph. Do you know Joseph Oboki? He goes to Rancho."

"Yeah, I know Joseph. Is he going with you tonight?"

"I'm on my way now to go pick him up."

"Fabulous! Could I catch a ride with you back to campus?"

"Sure, but I'm picking up Joseph at the gas station where he works."

"Is the gas station near Rancho?"

"It's not far. I can drop you off."

"Thanks." Katie closed the hood and grabbed her bag and jacket from where she had tossed them on the front seat. She followed Eli to his beat-up Toyota Camry. This seemed like her chance to work on being nicer and more "normal" around him.

When Christy and Katie had munched on chips and salsa earlier, Christy had mentioned how Eli had joined her and Todd off and on for lunch after church on Sundays ever since the semester began. Katie had been too busy to be a part of the lunch pack, but she realized now that if she had spent more time around Eli when he was with Christy and Todd or even when he was around Rick, she would have thought of him as truly being part of their group.

She slipped into the passenger's side, and the first thing she noticed was that he still had her hair wreath from Todd and Christy's wedding. The dried circle of tiny white baby's breath flowers had fallen off Katie's head at the wedding, and when Eli drove away from the site of the ceremony, Katie had seen it hanging from his mirror.

"Um, that's mine, right?"

"Yep."

"Why do you still have it?"

"You said you didn't want it."

"Yeah, because it fell on the ground. When you tried to give it back to me, I think my words were along the line of 'throw it away for me.' Not 'turn it into a creepy rearview mirror ornament for me and drive around with it in your car for the next six months.'"

Eli put on his seat belt and drove out of the parking area. "Do you want it back?"

"No, not particularly."

"Do you mind if I keep it?"

"Yeah, I do mind."

"Why?"

"There's no reason for you to have it there. It's strange."

"Stranger than running around with green stuff on your face?"

"There was a reason for that."

"And there's a reason for this," Eli said confidently.

"What reason?"

"It reminds me to pray."

Katie let Eli's declaration float in the air between them. She couldn't argue with someone holding onto something as a reminder to pray. But pray for what? Or for whom? Why would her dried-out wreath prompt him to pray? She decided she didn't want to know. The best conversation route at this point was to turn this awkwardness into a joke.

"Oh, well, if you're going to pull out the spiritual excuses and say it's your prayer wreath or whatever, I guess I can't exactly put up a fight."

Eli's expression turned into a satisfied, victorious sort of look.

Note to self: Don't ever try to play chess with Goatee Guy. His brain spins in circles you don't want to visit.

For the next five minutes, neither of them spoke. That was fine with Katie. As a matter of fact, it was more than fine. She was used to riding with Rick when he had the music on in his classic Mustang, and talking wasn't a part of how they related. Rick liked having the windows down so he could hang his arm out the window and keep time with the music by thumping on the side of his door. Lots of times Katie would sing along with the music, more to herself than to Rick.

Katie thought of how Rick would be glad she was making an effort to connect with his roommate. This was good. For a moment she considered bringing up the topic of the pizza night just to make sure Rick had explained to Eli that the earlier invitation was offered too hastily.

But she didn't bring it up. She trusted Rick. If he said he was going to settle things with Eli, she knew that's exactly what Rick would do. All she had to do was be polite to the guy. This was a chance to be a little more like Christy, just like the two of them had discussed earlier, each taking on some of the other's personality qualities.

Katie thought she was doing pretty well.

The silence lasted three more blocks before Eli turned into a well-lit gas station on a corner lot. He cut the engine and got out. With a look back at Katie, he said, "You know that you can come with us, if you want."

What surprised Katie as she watched Eli take long strides into the gas station convenience store was that she almost blurted out "okay" before he closed the door.

Why would I want to go out to the desert in the middle of the night with these guys?

Through the glass windows of the convenience store, Katie saw Eli and Joseph exchange an insiders' sort of handshake as they talked for a minute. Joseph looked out at the car and raised his arm to wave at Katie. She waved back. He had been in one of the orientation groups

Katie had shown around campus a year and a half earlier when she had volunteered to be on the campus hospitality team. The only thing she remembered about him from their first meeting was how shy he was. Later she found out he was from Africa, and she understood why everything seemed so overwhelming to him his first week on campus.

Katie had a soft spot for exchange students. She thought about how quickly she had been drawn to Michael in high school. He was from Northern Ireland, and the first lyrical sentence out of his mouth had charmed her. They dated long enough for Christy to express concern about where Katie had placed her values and priorities. But the relationship gave her a tender heart toward those who tried to make themselves at home in a new culture and country.

Katie leaned her head back and wondered how long it had been since she had thought about Michael. Months. Maybe a year. She and Rick had been doing things together for almost a year, and for all the obvious reasons, Rick had been at the forefront of her thoughts about guys.

With a hint of a smile, Katie remembered how intensely Michael had influenced her during their dating stint. The romantic Irishman had convinced her to radically change her eating habits. She turned into a vegetable-eating fan of all things organic and a consumer of garlic and tofu.

Her shoulders gave an involuntary shiver as she thought about some of the odd sushi combinations she ate when she was with Michael. She quickly said she loved his preferences in food even though most of the time she was swallowing each delicacy too fast to have any idea how it tasted. Looking back, she wasn't sure she shared his vegetarian-raw-seafood-slanted affections, but she did love the way he appreciated her for embracing his favorites. And she loved the adventure of trying something new.

Eli and Joseph came toward the car, and Katie's earlier surprising thought returned. *What if I went with these guys to the desert? Wasn't I just telling Christy I wanted to try something new? To go after some sort of mini-adventure? This certainly qualifies.*

Joseph opened the door to the backseat and greeted Katie with a warm hello. He was older than Katie by at least five years, she guessed. The few times she had seen him around campus, she had greeted him but not stopped to engage in any sort of conversation.

"Are you coming with us to the concert?" Joseph's speech pattern was a honeyed sort of tumble of words, with an eclectic accent that sounded slightly French sometimes and other times slightly British.

"Concert?" Katie said. "I thought you were going to the desert."

"We are. We have a place we like to go and hang out with the rocks 'n' stars."

"Really. Exactly which 'rock stars' do you go hang out with? I didn't know we had any that lived around here."

Eli laughed. Katie hadn't heard him laugh before. The earthy sort of rumble came from deep inside and was such a great, rolling happiness that Katie was surprised at the sound of it.

"Katie, we're going out to watch a meteor shower," Eli said plainly. "Those are the *rocks* and the *stars* Joseph is talking about."

"Oh. Okay. So which one of you is the president of the local Star Wars Club?" She wobbled her hands in the air and made space station beeping noises.

Neither of them laughed.

"*Star Trek?*"

Eli started the engine. "I'll drop you off at Rancho."

She bit her lower lip as Eli pulled out of the gas station and drove through the green light, heading west toward the campus. He went through three intersections before Katie cleared her throat and quietly said, "I'll go."

"Did you just say something?" Eli asked.

"Yes." Katie said with determination. She pressed her shoulders back and turned to Eli. "I'll go with you guys to your meteor-shower, rock-star concert."

"Good," Joseph said.

Katie leaned back as Eli turned the car around. This was the late-night adventure she had wanted to go on. True, no camels or leafy arugula factored into the trek, as they had in the adventure she had tried to conjure up with Christy. But the thrill of the unknown was waiting for her beyond the glare of the city lights, and that made her happy.

It had been too long since she had done anything on a whim.

This was going to be good.

The three unlikely amigos were about five minutes down the road when Katie took on the role of social director since both the guys were so quiet. She started by asking Eli how his campus security job was working out. That was the first fact that occurred to her about him.

"It's a good job. The hours don't conflict with classes, and as you know, since you're an RA, not much happens on campus to make security a huge problem. What about your job?"

"It's been great," Katie said. "I mean, I complain a lot about working 'round the clock, but the position covers room and board, and that's huge. All summer I worked ridiculously long hours at a different job, and everything I earned went to tuition. I don't know how I'm going to pay for next semester yet."

"This is the challenge for all of us, is it not?" Joseph said.

"Joseph, what part of Africa are you from?" Katie asked.

"Ghana."

"Is that near Kenya?"

"Opposite side of the continent," Eli answered. "Kenya is East Africa. Ghana is West Africa."

"Where is Zimbabwe?" Katie asked.

"South Africa." Again, Eli was the one answering her questions.

"Ding-ding-ding!" Katie said as if she were a game show host. "Eli … what's your last name?"

"Lorenzo."

"Really?"

"Yes, really."

"Okay." Switching back to game-show-host voice she said, "Eli Lorenzo wins for the 'Places in Africa' category. We apparently have a geography genius as a contestant this evening."

"He is not a genius," Joseph said with a chuckle. "He knows because he has been there."

"You've been to Africa? How cool. Did you two meet in Ghana?"

"No, we met here," Joseph said.

"I think it's pretty incredible that you went to Africa," Katie said to Eli.

He laughed. Joseph joined him.

"What?"

"You said that I 'went to Africa,'" Eli said.

"Yeah, I think it's cool. Traveling to other places in the world is such a great opportunity. Two summers ago I went to Europe with Christy and Todd. On a different trip before that, I went to England and Ireland. I think traveling is a privilege."

"It is," Joseph agreed.

"Christy told me that you and Todd lived in the same place when you were both in Spain."

"That's right," Eli said.

"Of all the interesting places you've been, which one is your favorite?"

"Here."

"Here? Southern California? You're not serious, are you?"

"Of course I'm serious. I like it here."

"But after being to Europe and Africa, are you saying that, honestly, this crowded, smoggy, traffic-jam corner of the world is your favorite place?"

"Yes."

"Well, I don't think I would ever say that. And I doubt you would say that if you grew up here."

"No, I probably wouldn't. But then, I didn't grow up here."

"And where did you grow up?"

Eli paused before answering. He looked over at Katie as if checking to make sure she wanted to hear his answer. "Africa. I grew up in Africa."

"Did you really? Wow. What part?" As soon as she asked the question, she laughed. "Not that I would know where, even if you told me, since we've already established my limited knowledge of African geography."

"I grew up in Zambia. It's in southern Africa just above Zimbabwe and Mozambique. When I was twelve we moved to Nairobi."

"Nairobi is the capital of Kenya, right?"

"Ding-ding-ding. Looks like we have a winner on the bonus round," Eli said with a half smile, imitating Katie's earlier joking around.

"So I suppose you've seen a giraffe."

"A few," Eli said.

Joseph laughed.

"And a zebra or two?" Katie asked.

"Yes."

"What did your parents do in Zambia?"

"They were teachers. Then my dad took over a mission organization at the headquarters in Nairobi. He scouts out villages that need a well dug to bring them clean water."

In the reflective lights of the oncoming cars, Katie saw Eli's jaw clench and unclench. She couldn't imagine that talking about Africa or where he grew up would be a tension-filled topic, but then she didn't know Eli. And she didn't know what the current political temperature was in Kenya. She knew things had been rough there off and on. She wondered if he was one of those missionary kids who felt more comfortable when people thought he grew up in suburban America with a knowledge of skateboards and familiar TV sitcoms.

"You know, if I grew up in Africa like you guys, I think I would be the biggest bragger on campus. Everyone would know how exotic I was."

Eli laughed, and Joseph joined him.

"I mean it. Do you have any idea how cool it is that you've lived in another part of the world?"

"And do you realize," Eli said, "that to us, *this* is another part of the world? Living here is what makes us *cool* to everyone we left at home."

"Interesting. I see what you're saying. So is this your final year?"

Eli nodded.

"And then what?"

"I don't know yet."

What struck Katie about Eli's response was that he was the first student she had ever heard that sort of answer from who didn't also sound panicked. A few months earlier she had to settle on a major before she could register for her senior year, and the stress of not knowing for sure was awful. She couldn't believe Eli was taking his future so lightly.

I wish I had the same deep confidence and contentment Eli has. I have no idea what I'm going to do when I graduate.

As she had done many times, Katie flirted with the idea of marrying right after she graduated just like Todd and Christy had. She knew she and Rick weren't ready for that next step. Not that they couldn't be in a few months, but they definitely weren't there yet. Part of her wanted to see a giraffe or feed a kangaroo or ride a rickshaw down a busy street in Bangkok before she walked down the wedding aisle. But first she had to finish this semester and figure out a way to collect all the needed finances for the rest of the school year.

And right now her "job" as social director was where she needed to direct her attention. Things had gotten very quiet in the car.

"What about you, Joseph?"

"Me? I have two more years of studies. God willing, I will pass and become a pastor and a teacher."

"Do you want to work here or in Ghana?" Katie asked.

"Ghana. Of course. Ghana."

They were off the main highway now and heading down a bumpy, narrow road that grew darker the farther they went. The headlights of Eli's car soon became the only light around them. Then he stopped the car, cut the engine, and turned out the headlights. All the world turned inky black and silent.

"Whoa," Katie said, lowering her voice. "It's really dark out here."

Eli leaned over the steering wheel and gazed upward through the windshield.

Katie followed his lead and stretched her neck in an attempt to see the night sky above them. A glorious display of stars took their places on the heavenly stage just beyond the pane of the bug-dotted windshield glass.

Joseph opened the back door and stepped out. They were stopped on a blacktop road that formed a path through the desert sand like a wide strip of dried-up licorice.

A rush of cool air filled the car. Katie reached for her jacket and put it on before getting out. The interior overhead light of the car revealed that Joseph had hopped up onto the hood of the car and positioned himself as comfortably as if the car were a leather recliner.

"Not a bad idea." Katie closed her door and made a less-than-graceful attempt at joining Joseph on the hood. The well-used condition of Eli's car kept Katie from being concerned about denting the hood or damaging it in any way.

"Oh, yeah, this is nice and toasty on the backside, isn't it?"

"Hmm," Joseph replied contentedly. His arms were behind his head, and his eyes were fixed on the sky.

Katie leaned back and took in the view. "Whoa! Where did all those stars come from? There are so many!"

"Umm-hmm," Joseph hummed.

Eli pulled the sleeping bag and thermos from the backseat. He found his way to the front of the car with the assistance of a tiny red penlight attached to his car keys. Handing the thermos and rolled-up sleeping bag to Katie, he jumped up beside her. The hood gave a metallic groan, and Katie was sure their weight was leaving a permanent dent in the hood.

Eli unrolled the sleeping bag and spread it over the three of them, as if they were bugs in a rug and accustomed to tucking themselves in like this every evening.

"This is incredible, you guys. I'm so glad you invited me to come with you."

"Do you want some coffee?" Eli opened the top of his thermos.

"Sure. Thanks." Katie took a sip of the steaming java Eli had poured into the thermos cup.

"You can thank Joseph. He let me fill up at the convenience store."

"I paid for the coffee, though," Joseph said quickly, as if he were concerned Katie would think he had allowed Eli to steal some. Katie was impressed in a tender way to hear a fellow Rancho Corona student make known his integrity in the little things. She was used to hearing from students how they managed to rip off this or that without being caught, or how they had cut a corner here or there without anyone noticing. Katie knew very few students who were trying to make upright and honest choices, even when no one was looking. She admired Joseph.

"It's good coffee," Katie said. "Although I'm more of a tea snob, so I'm not sure I'm qualified to rate convenience-store coffee."

"You like tea?" Eli asked.

"Yes, I like tea," Katie said, understating her affection for the beverage. She summarized the account of how she had spent her first semester at Rancho attempting to create an original herbal tea. Her efforts ended when her humble offerings caused rashes on the guinea pig students who tried her blends.

"However, one of my blends was entered in a food show about a year ago, and no one suffered ill effects. I received an honorable mention."

"Are you still blending tea?"

"No, it turned into one of my many fleeting hobbies. Why? Do you guys like tea?"

"I prefer coffee." Joseph took the cup from Katie and held it while Eli poured more coffee from the thermos.

"We drink a lot of tea in Kenya," Eli said. "I have friends who manage a tea plantation."

"Do you really? Are they Americans?"

"No, they're Kenyans. The land was planted during colonial times by an Austrian family. They sold it to a Kenyan doctor, and now his two oldest sons and their families run the farm."

"That's so cool. I wrote a paper last year about fair trade and how hard it is for indigenous people to make a living in the tea market. Most of my quoted sources were from India. I didn't realize Kenya had a big tea market."

"They do. And it's a growing market because the climate conditions are right. I'm sure most of what you read about India would apply to the fair trade market in Africa. The specialty at my friend's plantation is called 'Nairobi Chai.' I have some at the apartment. Next time you're over, remind me, and I'll make you some."

"Hey, thanks. I'd like to try it."

Joseph had returned to his reclining position, and Eli joined him. Katie followed the unspoken signal to curb the conversation and take in the show. Leaning back, she focused her eyes on the center stage above them. The onslaught of brilliant points of light racing to Earth from the stars had a breath-siphoning effect on Katie. Far to the south, the ivory moon seemed to float like a curl of pale lemon rind. It seemed as if one great cosmic gust could send the waning moon rolling end-over-end off the great velvet tablecloth of heaven.

No such gust came. All was as it should be in this still-life scene. *So many stars. I don't think I've ever seen this many stars.*

The engine beneath them pinged. That was the only noise Katie heard.

The more she stared, the more the still life seemed to be moving. It was as if the universe were exhaling in a great sigh. She felt as if the three of them, the car, and all of planet Earth were shrinking until they were no larger than a speck of sand. Before them was the expansive universe, vast, immeasurable, untamed, and alive with subtle colors and pulsating lights. One star directly overhead appeared bluer than the others. She noticed how other stars were different sizes, and some seemed to flicker.

A shooting star appeared on the eastern horizon, blazing a trail across the sky in a blink. Katie drew in a quick breath through her nearly closed lips. Had she been with anyone else, her response would have been to ooh and ahh, as if this were a display of fireworks. But with Joseph and Eli, the utter silence that now circled the three of them was their offering of awe.

Between her blinks, Katie narrowed her eyes and spotted another, less brilliant speeding meteor, as it hurled itself headlong into Earth's atmosphere and incinerated along with its long tail of light.

During one of Katie's science classes, she had studied a bit about the stars and outer space. A picture from one of her textbooks came to mind. It showed a diagram of the way comets rotated around the sun on a regular course. Whenever the Earth traveled through a comet's stream of icy rock debris, we would see that debris as shooting stars or a meteor shower.

One after the other, a parade of shooting stars collided with Earth's invisible barrier and vanished. Her thoughts about the domed night screen changed from scientific to seeing a dance. Joseph had said earlier they were going to a concert. Perhaps he was hearing music right now. To her, a great ballet was taking place in the heavens. God was orchestrating this performance, as he did every day and every night. She felt as if she were part of a limited, privileged audience that was witnessing Earth being saved moment-by-moment from destruction by vicious, ancient boulders hurled in its direction.

All was calm. Danger was kept outside the invisible barrier of Earth's atmosphere. Life continued as it always had while this spinning blue planet continued on its set course.

The magnitude of such a realization settled on Katie the way the mossy-smelling sleeping bag rested over her, keeping her warm and comforted. She felt safe.

Katie noticed how even and steady her breathing had become. She was barely aware of Joseph and Eli beside her except for the slight sense that their breathing was slow and evenly paced, like hers. That, and the realization that Joseph's jacket carried the scent of gasoline.

Another meteor, this one with the brightest tail so far, appeared in the east and took its time before incinerating into a puff of interplanetary dust. A series of lemming-like dots of brilliant light followed the first one into oblivion.

Does God keep harm from me every day the same way he's keeping Earth from being pulverized by falling stars?

A sense of humble gratitude washed over her.

Without warning, Eli moved his legs and slid off the hood, leaving a cold spot beside Katie. He went to the trunk, opened it, and with only the dull red light on his key chain to illuminate the way, he padded back to the front of the car.

Katie whispered to Joseph, "What's he doing?"

"I don't know. With Eli, I never know."

Just then, in the distance the faint howl of a coyote sounded. At least Katie thought it was a coyote. She and Joseph exchanged startled glances in the dark, not sure what might happen next.

Eli opened the car's front door, and the internal light illuminated the cold darkness with a blue-tinted sheen.

Katie turned and looked in through the windshield from her position next to Joseph on the hood of Eli's car. He was sliding a CD into the stereo and turning up the volume. Rolling down the driver's window, he shut the door. As soon as he did, the night engulfed them once more.

Eli hopped back up next to Katie and pulled part of the sleeping bag over his legs. Behind them the music began. The intro started with the slow, steady rhythm of drums.

"Is that from Africa?" Katie asked.

"Yes. Shhh."

The drums were followed by a clear, singular voice that probably belonged to a young child. The soloist sang with perfect pitch and clarity. Even though Katie couldn't understand the words, the song felt worshipful to her.

Gazing back into the heavens, she let the music wash over her in invisible waves. The singular voice was joined on the refrain by a multilayered chorus with soulful bass voices that caused the windshield to vibrate against her back.

The lyrics changed to English. Katie listened more carefully and soon recognized the first part of the song as words from Psalm 8. She knew this because Todd and their friend Doug also had written a song to these words. The African version was very different in tune and tone, but the Scripture was the same:

> *When I consider your heavens,*
> *the work of your fingers,*
> *the moon and the stars,*
> *which you have set in place,*
> *what is man that you are mindful of him,*
> *the son of man that you care for him?*
> *You made him a little lower than the heavenly beings*
> *and crowned him with glory and honor.*

The song concluded, and the next one rolled over them as beautifully and peacefully as the first. This one also was sung in the deep, earthy tones of the language Katie didn't recognize and then was repeated in English.

> *What does the LORD require of you?*
> *But to do justly,*
> *To love mercy,*
> *And to walk humbly with your God.*

Katie turned to Joseph as he kept time with the song by subtly bobbing his head and shoulders. "Great concert," she said softly.

"Umm-hmm."

Overhead the stars danced.

On TV and in movies, Katie had watched plenty of dances. She had see tribal dancers jumping with long spears. She had watched Tahitian men in island garb pound the sand with toughened feet. Comedies portrayed masked fellows waving their arms around the tribal campfires and crying "ooga-booga" to frighten their enemies away.

But this, Katie hadn't seen before. Or if she had seen it, she had never entered in the way her spirit was being caught up now. Everything around her seemed to be dancing in response to the music and the perfect beauty of the night, and she was part of this immense dance of praise. Yet she wasn't moving.

Katie had pulled the sleeping bag up to her chin, almost covering the smile on her lips. Her nose felt cold, but her heart felt warm and hushed, as if she were kneeling inside in an attitude of prayer. She couldn't remember ever feeling so wrapped up in the immensity and yet minute personal beauty of God and his cosmos.

It was a night like no other night.

When the music ended, Eli and Joseph quietly slid off the car's hood, and Katie followed. Once Eli had turned the car around and had the heater going, she warmed up to a conversation about the music and about Africa.

Eli and Joseph told her that each of them had, at one time during his childhood, lived in a mud hut with a thatched roof. Before coming to California, both had lived in large cities. Eli said he lived in an apartment building. Joseph said he lived in one room of a house with someone named Shiloh.

"And who is Shiloh?" Katie asked.

"Shiloh is my beautiful wife."

"Your wife? I didn't know you were married. She's still in Africa?"

"Of course." He pulled a photograph from his wallet and handed it to Katie. She had difficulty seeing in the dim light, but she could make out that the photo was of a lovely, smiling young woman.

"When was the last time you saw her?"

"Twenty-three months ago."

"Joseph!"

"Yes?"

"That's awful."

"We will only be apart for another seventeen months."

"*Only* seventeen months? Joseph, I'm amazed." Katie handed back the photo.

"Why are you amazed? Is it because a beautiful woman would have me for her husband?"

"No, of course not. I'm amazed that you could bring yourself to leave your wife for so long just to go to school."

"Going to school is a great privilege."

Katie agreed, but she never had considered the sacrifices some students made to attend Rancho. For her it had been a lot of work without support from her family, but her obstacles seemed minor compared to Joseph's.

As Katie quietly processed all this, Eli's steady white car climbed the hill to the top of the mesa where Rancho Corona University was located. The campus appeared to be sleeping in the dewy hours of this new day.

"Thanks for letting me come with you," Katie said. "I'm almost glad my poor car died. Almost."

"Do you have a mechanic who can make the repairs for you?" Joseph asked.

"I'm thinking about seeing if my brother can come have a look at it."

"If he cannot, please let me know," Joseph said. "I am familiar with a few mechanics."

"That's good to know." Katie pulled out her cell phone, and the face lit up as she touched the buttons to open a new contact file. "What's your number?"

"I do not have a cell phone."

Katie didn't know anyone who didn't have a cell phone. "Is there a phone number I could call at the gas station?"

"There is, but I do not know it. If you have the car towed to the station, I can make the arrangements for you."

"Okay."

Eli pulled up in front of Crown Hall, and his car idled as Katie said her good-byes. "I'll see you guys around. Thanks again for letting me go with you. If you ever plan to attend another rock star concert, tell me, okay?"

"Agreed," Eli said. "I'm glad you came."

Katie let herself into the dorm and trekked to the end of her hall, still floating on the euphoria of the night. With only three hours before she needed to go on duty at the front desk, she slipped into her

PJs and set her phone's alarm. She felt beautifully and strangely rested from the inside out.

Instinctively tapping out a quick text message to Rick before going to bed, she told him she hoped he and Josh had a safe trip.

A minute after she sent the text, her cell phone rang. "I can't believe you're still up. Are you at Christy's?" Rick said, sounding wide awake.

"No. I left her place before midnight. I'm in my dorm room, but you'll never guess where I went after I left Christy's."

"Casa de Pedro?"

"No. I went out to the desert with Eli."

The other end of the line went silent.

"Rick, are you still there?"

"Yes, I'm here. Did you say you went to the desert with Eli?"

"Yeah. I went with Eli and Joseph. Do you know Joseph? He's from Africa."

"Katie, are you trying to make a joke or something? Because I'm not getting it."

Katie stretched out on her bed and began the story with the part in which Baby Hummer wouldn't start. Then she gave Rick the full rundown, including the discussion about tea, the unbelievable host of stars, the overwhelming sense of God's presence, the way they heard a coyote in the distance, and the African concert. Then she paused for a breath before saying, "I wish you could have been there. It was the most amazing night. I don't think I can explain how phenomenal it was."

Again, the phone line seemed to go dead.

"Rick?"

"I don't know what to say, Katie. I'm still trying to understand why you took off in the middle of the night and went to the desert with two guys you don't even know."

"What do you mean, 'don't even know'? Eli is your roommate. You were the one who wanted me to get to know him."

"Yes, get to know him as in, be civil when you're over at the apartment and he's in the same room. I never meant that you should take off with him in the middle of the night for some crazy destination."

"It wasn't as crazy as it sounds. What I didn't tell you is that I was trying to convince Christy to go on a midnight adventure with me. I was suggesting skydiving, so with that in mind, this midnight meteor shower was a much better option."

"Then why didn't Christy go with you?"

"She didn't know I went. I didn't go back and tell her that Baby Hummer wouldn't start. But the thing is, I got to know Eli, and now I don't feel weirded-out around him. As a matter of fact, right about now, I think you should be saying, 'Good job, Katie. Way to go.'"

"Okay, good job, Katie. Way to go. And by the way, I did tell Eli the invitation I had extended to him for the pizza night was my mistake, so I hope you didn't change your mind about his coming."

"No. Thanks. How did he take it?"

"Fine. Why?"

"I just don't want to hurt his feelings."

"Katie, you're killing me. Earlier this evening I tried to invite Eli to the pizza night, and you didn't like that. Now you're concerned I might have upset him. You're all over the place."

"Hey, I didn't know Eli earlier this evening like I know him now. You were right; he is a nice guy. Things are good, Rick. Everything is great between you and me, and everything is just fine now with Eli. There's nothing to be frazzled about."

"You know what, Katie? This is probably the worst possible time for me to have this conversation with you. We're at the motel now. Josh just came back with the keys. I'll call you later today, okay?"

"Okay. Call me after five o'clock tonight."

"After five. Got it."

"I hope all your business dealings go great."

"Thanks, Katie."

She pressed the button on her phone and put it aside. It would be so nice when he was done with that café in Arizona. These trips were wearing him out and putting a huge strain on their relationship.

Without realizing it, she slipped into a whispered prayer. "You already know what I want, Father God. I want Rick and me to have a chance to get closer now that we're boyfriend and girlfriend. We waited a year for this next step in our relationship, and yet everything feels like it takes so much more effort than it did before we became official."

A big yawn overcame her, and she left the rest of her prayer unspoken as she fell asleep.

It seemed like only a moment later she heard a persistent knocking on her door. She squinted at the clock on her desk. It was only 8:25 on a Saturday morning. With a groan she rolled over and called out, "Come back later."

The knocking continued, louder.

Without opening her eyes, Katie called back, "Seriously! Go check with the on-duty RA at the front desk."

As soon as the slurred words tumbled out of her mouth, Katie's eyes popped open. "Wait. Saturday? Oh, no! That's me, isn't it?"

Rolling out of bed, she opened her door, squinting at the light in the hallway. Julia, the RA director, stood there with a perturbed expression. She looked as if she had just gotten up and pulled on a pair of jeans and a sweatshirt. Her sandy brown hair was pulled into a clip, and her fair, freckled skin looked pink.

"Katie?"

"My alarm must have ... I thought I ..."

"I'm going back up to the front desk," Julia said. "Come up and take over for me as soon as you can."

"I'll hurry."

Katie fumbled for her phone and found she inadvertently had turned it off when she hung up from her call with Rick a few hours earlier. She had three calls on voice mail. Two were from Julia. She didn't take time to figure out who the third caller was. Racing into a pair of jeans and a sweatshirt, Katie tucked her toes into a pair of flip-flops and dashed down the hall.

"Julia, I'm really sorry. My phone ..."

"Don't worry about it. It happens. You can grovel later if you want. I'm not feeling well, so I'm going back to bed. If you have any problems, call Greg first, okay?"

"Sure. Thanks. Again, sorry!"

The day quickly became a grumpy Saturday for Katie and everyone she encountered during her five-hour shift. First of all, she was hungry, and none of the desk drawers held any of the usual bags of pretzels or cafeteria-confiscated apples. Second, everyone who came to her with a problem was adamant about having an immediate solution. Third, the number of problems, even for a Saturday, was higher than normal. Katie was used to the "I lost my key" problems or the "I need to schedule maintenance to come fix my closet door" situations. Today two ant infestations were reported and one small fire resulting from a glue gun left on top of a bed while the crafty woman went into town to buy more supplies for her art project.

The smoke from the smoldering bedding prompted a call to Katie's desk from the dorm room next door to the disaster, which meant Katie had to assess on the spot whether to call the fire department.

She called, they came, all was made right quickly and efficiently before the art major even returned from town and found her mattress and singed bedding doused and out in front of Crown Hall.

It then fell to Katie to find another mattress and arrange for the damaged one to be hauled away. All of that happened before noon.

At noon, her floor partner, Nicole, entered Crown Hall with a happy surprise. She had a sub sandwich with extra dill pickles for Katie.

"Are you kidding me?" Katie said, as sweet Nicole presented her with the foot-long, starvation lifesaver wrapped in waxed paper. "How did you know?"

"I had Saturday duty two weeks in a row, remember? It's the worst day."

"Oh, baby, you are my new best friend." Katie took a bite of the sandwich.

"I'd be silly to think you were talking to me," Nicole said with a smile. "I know that your expression of affection is for the sandwich. The sandwich is really your new best friend, isn't it?"

Katie didn't answer. She pointed to her closed lips and her mouth full of sandwich and continued to munch merrily while humming.

Nicole pulled up a chair next to Katie. Nicole's sleek dark hair was pulled back in a Saturday sort of ponytail, and even though she didn't look as if she had on any makeup except for subtle eyeliner and mascara, she looked fresh and put together, as always.

Nicole pulled out her cell phone, checking for messages. Her countenance fell.

"Hmm?" Katie asked, still chewing. She pointed to the phone, making it clear she wanted to know what Nicole was bummed about.

"Oh, I'm waiting for a certain someone to get back to me about a certain pizza night on Friday, and it's driving me nuts. This is so humiliating. I liked it better in junior high, when all we had to do was tell our girlfriends whom we liked and let them go tell the boy for us. They always came back right away with the answer of whether he liked us."

Katie swallowed and glanced out into the lobby area to make sure no one could hear them. "Who did you ask?"

"Ah ... Phillip Sett."

Katie cracked up.

"What? He's not that bad. I think he's good-looking."

Katie waved her hand in front of her face and tried to breathe.

"Why are you laughing? Katie!"

"No, no. It's not him. I don't even know him." She caught her breath.

"Then what's so funny? It's humiliating enough to be down to the last week and trying to get a date; you don't have to mock me."

Katie turned somber. "Nicole, I'm sorry. I'm not mocking you. Honest. It's just the way you said his name. I don't know the guy at all.

But when you said his name, I thought you said, 'I feel upset,' and it just struck me as funny that you were so bummed, and I thought ..."

The logical illogic of Katie's assumption came together for Nicole, and she gave way to a small smile. "I see what you're saying. Phillip Sett. I feel upset. Okay. Yeah, that's pretty funny."

"No, it's not. If it were that funny, you would be laughing too. I'm way whacked-out this morning, Nicole. We had two ant problems and a fire already."

"I saw the mattress. What happened?"

In between bites of the sandwich, Katie gave her the rundown. After Katie had taken only a few more bites of the sub, all the lights in the small office flickered. They went out completely for two seconds and then came back on.

"What is with this day? What's going on?"

"We had a power surge last night too," Nicole said. "Were you here when it happened? We were without power for about five or six minutes around nine o'clock."

"No, I was at Christy's. We were having our own power surge problems with her microwave."

"Oh, hey, how did the facials go? Did you guys like my secret formula?"

"I think it worked a little better on Christy than it did on me."

"You should use it consistently. Every week. It's good stuff."

"The color was great. Excellent shade of green. Good for freaking out the boys."

Nicole grinned. "I don't know if I want to hear the story that goes with that line. Not the way my life is going right now. I think I freaked out Phillip. And now, yes, I feel upset."

"So just call him and tell him you're checking in. Keep it light and breezy, and then you'll know if he's going to go with you or if you need to ask someone else."

"That's the problem," Nicole said. "Who else could I ask? I've run out of options. If Phillip doesn't want to go with me, I'm thinking I might not go."

"You have to go. It's your job."

"Well, then my job should have come with an automatic date for all social events because I really don't want to be the only one who goes without a date. I'm not being a brat about this. Honest. It's my senior year, and I have gone to almost all of these events by myself. It's awful. Especially last year when I was an RA for the first time. I kept telling myself it was okay to go solo because next year I would be a senior, and surely by then I would have someone I could do things with at least on a casual basis. But look at me, Katie!" Tears welled in her eyes. "I'm a college senior, and I'm the most undated woman on campus!"

"That's not true. Are you kidding me? Nicole, you're gorgeous and you know it. I mean, you know it in a good way. You have a great shape, perfect skin, and beautiful hair, and you're really gorgeous. Inside and out. You just haven't met the right guy yet."

As much as Katie intended for that last line to sound hopeful, it still came out sounding like something a mother would say and follow with a pat on the knee. Especially because of the way Katie had done a rundown of all Nicole's best features, as if Nicole needed to be told how gorgeous she was.

Sadly, Katie's admonition to Nicole produced the same sort of stifled tears that would have come if a mother were delivering the same fateful line.

Nicole blinked bravely. "I know. I really shouldn't make such a big deal of this. I'm overly emotional right now. Do you have any chocolate stashed away in your room?"

"Cocoa Puffs?" Katie offered, holding out the key to her dorm room.

"I'll check with Em. She usually has the dark stuff lying around. If she doesn't, I'm going to raid your Cocoa Puff supply."

"Be my guest. And Nicole? I meant what I said even though it came out all wrong and sounding horribly sappy. You are amazing and gorgeous, and any guy would be insane not to go out with you. I really do believe you're going to meet some guy. I don't know when, but you will, and it's going to click for both of you. Fairy dust, twinkle-sparkle starbursts in the corner of your eye and everything."

"Fairy dust, twinkle-sparkle starbursts, huh?"

"Christy and I were talking about that last night. Basically, it's the cartoon-princess syndrome." Then Katie remembered that the conversation she and Christy had was actually about dispelling the starburst in the corner of the eye as a myth. Now here she was, coaxing Nicole to believe her handsome prince was just one wishing well away.

"You know what, Nicole? I realize it's not twinkles and sparkles. I probably shouldn't have brought up the fairy-dust stuff. I know it's not that way for everyone. But, the thing is, with you, I just have this cream-puff feeling that's how it's going to be."

"Why, because I'm a cream puff?"

"You're not a cream puff."

"Katie, you can stop trying to cheer me up. I know God has a plan for my life. I really do. I told you during the hike on Catalina how I was raised with the premise that I'm God's little princess, and one day my prince will come. I think a big part of me still believes that."

"Good. That's how it should be."

"Yes, but this year, because of you and our Peculiar Treasures theme for our floor, I'm developing a bigger picture of my life and what matters to God. I don't know if I've ever thanked you for that. I honestly am seeing that I'm God's peculiar treasure, and his value of me is what matters more and more."

"There's no rule that says you can't be a peculiar treasure and a princess at the same time."

"I think I'm in one of those half-and-half places where I want to let go and say that all the dating stuff isn't going to define me or my last year of college. God is doing whatever honors him the most, and that's what I want. But then, the other half of me says, 'Hellooo! Remember me, God? Where's my Mr. Wonderful?'"

Katie gave Nicole a spontaneous hug. "I love you, Nicole. You are so honest."

"That too is one of your finer traits that's rubbing off on me, Katie."

Nicole's phone rang, and both of them sat up straight, with expectant and slightly giddy expressions.

"*Feel Upset?*" Katie asked, stressing the mispronunciation of the name of Nicole's potential date.

Nicole grabbed her phone and flipped it open. Her expression went flat when she saw the caller ID. Putting the phone to her ear and lightening her voice, she said, "Hi, Mom."

Katie hid her bittersweet smile by taking a bite of the sandwich. Nicole tapped Katie on the shoulder and waved good-bye as she walked out of the office saying, "Uh-huh. Really? Oh, that's good."

As Katie munched away in the continuing front-desk lull time, she remembered her phone had a voice message she hadn't checked. Pulling out her phone, she waved to two students who entered the building and called out a hello to her.

She listened to the two voice mails from Julia asking where Katie was and if she remembered she was on duty that morning. Then the third message came on.

"Oh. Well. I don't know what ... Hello? Can you hear this? It's your mother. Katie? You must not be home. Are you there? I don't know if I'm supposed to tell you my phone number or push a button or what. You should leave instructions that tell people what to do instead of ... Well, good-bye. Do I just hang up? I don't know how these things work."

A click and silence followed.

Katie swallowed the bite of sandwich. She drew in a deep breath and dialed her parents' home phone number. Clearing her throat, she waited while the phone rang. Her heart was racing, as if she were about to swim across a very wide, very cold ocean.

Katie's parents were well into their forties when she was born. Even though they had been protective of her early on, once she graduated from high school, she pretty much was on her own, which left her feeling adrift in her relationship with them.

While she waited for her mom to answer, a florist delivery truck pulled up in front of Crown Hall.

"Hi, Mom. It's me, Katie." She hated that she had to identify herself, but it was better to make herself known at the beginning of the call than to wait for her mother to sound confused and then to say, "Who is this?"

"I tried to call you this morning, Katie."

"I know. This is the first chance I've had to call you back."

"You should leave instructions on your phone if you're not going to answer. I didn't know if I was supposed to push a button or what."

"You don't need to push any buttons. All you have to do is talk, Mom. The phone records it for you. Then you hang up. Just like you did."

A short man stepped up to the front desk, his face hidden by the massive bouquet of daisies, lilies, and roses. He placed the flowers on the counter, blocking Katie's view of him.

"I need you to sign here." He slid a clipboard sideways past the bouquet. "Next to the X."

"Katie, is someone else on this line?"

"No, Mom. Just a second." She put down the phone, scribbled her signature on line eleven, and thanked the deliveryman before returning to her conversation with her mom. "I'm back. I had to sign for some flowers."

"Flowers?"

"It's a bouquet. A huge bouquet."

"Are they for you?"

"No. I'm on duty at the front desk. I don't know who they're for." Katie turned the vase and found the card taped to the side of the glass instead of perched in one of the usual plastic-pronged insert sticks. Her heart stopped when she saw that the name on the card was "Katie."

"If you're too busy now to talk, you can call me back," her mom said.

"No, it's okay. What's up?" She tried to sound nonchalant, but her mind spun with the possibilities of why Rick would have sent her flowers. Was he just trying to be nice? They hadn't marked or celebrated any of their "anniversaries" the way some dating couples did. Rick wasn't starting now, was he?

"I need your address," her mom said.

"My address?"

"Yes. There at school. A letter came for you, and I need to forward it."

"Okay." Katie recited her dorm address while picking at the tape that held the card to the side of the vase so she could read the gift enclosure card.

"Your Great Aunt Mabel died. I told you that, right?"

"Yes, Mom. You told me a few months ago. Unless you're now talking about a different Great Aunt Mabel."

"No, it's the same one."

"Okay, well, I probably should get back to work." Katie's fingernails were short, which made it challenging to tear all the tape off the card.

"Your father had a mole removed from his arm, but it wasn't cancerous."

"Well, that's good. Oh, I should tell you. My car died last night."

"The car that Larry bought for you?"

"Yes, that car. I was thinking I should call him, but I don't have his phone number." Katie stopped fiddling with the card on the vase and looked for a pen. She also found a piece of paper on the desk notepad that wasn't completely doodled on. "Can you give me Larry's number?"

"Why don't you have your brother's phone number?"

Katie felt like saying, "You just asked for my address. How's that different from my not having Larry's phone number?"

Instead she said, "I might have it somewhere, but it's not in my cell phone. Could you just give it to me, Mom?"

"Just a minute. Oh, wait. Here it is." Katie's mom read the number and then said, "You know he moved to Bakersfield, don't you?"

"Bakersfield? When did Larry move there?"

"Last summer. You knew he was in rehab there, didn't you?"

"No."

"I thought you knew. He lasted only a week or maybe it was two weeks before he checked himself out. We haven't heard a word from him since August. I'm sure the center won't mind if you call and see if he's there."

"What number did you just give me? His cell phone?"

"I have no way of knowing if he has a cell phone. I gave you the number for the rehabilitation center. It's the only number I have."

Katie pushed the memo pad away. "Mom ..."

"What?"

"This is fairly serious, isn't it? I mean ..."

"Your brother is a grown man. I can't be responsible for his poor decisions. We raised all three of you kids to be independent."

"I know," Katie said quietly. "How is Clint doing, by the way? Have you heard from him lately?"

"Not lately. Do you want his phone number too?"

"Yes, if you have it." Katie wrote her oldest brother's phone number on the notepad. She felt a gentle nudging inside.

"Mom, what are you and Dad doing for Thanksgiving next week?"

"What do you mean, 'What are we doing'?"

"Well, I was just thinking I could come home. I don't have to stay here. I mean, I'm only an hour or so away. I didn't come home all summer because I was working so much, but I don't have to work over Thanksgiving weekend."

A lopsided silence tilted all the conversation responsibility onto Katie's mom, and she apparently didn't know what to do with it.

"We don't make a big deal of the holidays, Katie. We never have."

"I know. I'm not saying that it would have to be a big deal if I came home. I'm just offering. Maybe Rick could come with me, and he and I could make turkey dinner for you and Dad. You guys would like that, wouldn't you?"

"I don't know."

The painfully telling silence stretched between them once again.

"Did Rick's family not invite you to join them? Is that it?"

"Rick and I haven't talked about Thanksgiving yet. I just thought I would throw out the possibility to you. It's not that big of a deal, Mom."

"We're not set up here for company. You're asking quite a bit of me to have the house ready for you on such short notice. We have a lot going on here, your father and I. Just yesterday he had a mole removed and—"

"I know, Mom. You already told me. We can drop the idea about Thanksgiving. I have plenty going on here too."

"If you had given me more notice, I might have been able to work out something, but, Katie, Thanksgiving is only a week and a half away."

"I know."

"You should be more organized, especially when your plans involve other people. I had hoped college would have cured that impulsive nature of yours, but obviously you still think it's okay to do everything last minute."

Katie felt herself sinking into a very old and very disliked mud puddle of shame.

"Now, if you want to talk about doing something here for Christmas, I can talk to your father about that."

"I'll think about it, Mom."

"What's to think about? Do you want to come or not?"

"I don't know. I need to talk to Rick about it."

"Call us when you decide. The sooner the better. We'll be here, you know."

Katie hung up and looked at the piece of paper with her brother's rehab phone number. Without pausing to think what she might say, Katie dialed the number. An official-sounding receptionist answered.

"My name is Katie Weldon, and I'm wondering if by any chance my brother is there at your center. His name is Larry Weldon. He's thirty-five, no, thirty-six years old, and he has red hair and—"

"One moment, please."

While Katie was on hold she glanced at the fragrant flowers and used her thumbnail to once more pick at the tape. She managed to lift off a corner of the card from the vase.

"Hello?" A different female voice came on the phone. "I understand you are calling to check on one of our residents."

Katie went through the same information she had given the first woman.

"One moment, please."

Back on hold, Katie pried the card from the vase. She opened the sealed envelope and pulled out the small card, expecting to see the name "Rick" as the signature under something sweet. Instead, all the card said was:

I'm so glad you said yes.
Our future starts now.

No name appeared on the card. Only those two lines. Katie turned over the card and checked the front of the envelope. The name on the front was definitely "Katie."

"This is bizarre," she mumbled. "What did I say yes to?"

"Hello, Ms. Weldon?"

Katie picked up her cell phone. "Yes. I'm still here."

"Thank you for holding. We've checked our records, and we don't show anyone by the name of 'Larry Weldon' currently enrolled in our program."

"He was there in the summer, though, right? Did he leave any forwarding information?"

"Unfortunately, we are not at liberty to release any of that sort of information over the phone."

"Even to family members?"

"Yes. I'm sorry. We can take your contact information, and if your brother reenters the program, we can pass on your information to him."

"Okay. I appreciate that." Katie recited her phone number and address. Giving it one last try she said, "Are you sure you can't tell me anything at all? I mean, I don't know if he's homeless or ..."

"We have no way of tracking a former resident unless that person chooses to keep us updated."

"I understand. Okay. Well, if he does check in, please tell him I really want to talk to him." Katie's stomach had curled up into a fist at the prospect of her brother being in a dire situation. True, she never had been close to either of her brothers and they hadn't kept in contact after she moved out of the house, but still, they were her brothers. She felt bad that she hadn't taken it on herself to do a better job of keeping in contact with them.

As soon as she hung up with the rehab center, she dialed the phone number for her oldest brother. His voice mail picked up her call.

"Hey, Clint. Hi. It's me, Katie. Your little sister. I know. Odd of me to call. I just wanted to see how you're doing. Mom gave me your number. So ... I guess all I wanted to say was hi and call me sometime. I'm fine. Mom and Dad are fine. I don't know what's going on with Larry. If you do, could you call me and just tell me how he's doing and how you're doing? Okay. Well ... I hope to talk to you later. Bye."

Talitha, one of the other RAs, stepped into the small area behind the front desk. She had her laptop in the bend of her arm, and in her right hand she carried an insulated coffee cup.

"It can't be two o'clock already." Katie looked at the wall clock. "Wow. That was the fastest shift ever."

"How was the morning?" Talitha asked.

"Insane. The last hour or so has been normal, though."

"That's good. I hope it stays that way. I have a paper to finish." She set her laptop on the desk, and Katie pointed to the remains of the unfinished sub sandwich.

"Are you hungry?" Katie's stomach was in too many knots to send any more deli fare in its direction.

"No. Thanks anyway."

Reaching for the flowers, Katie balanced them on her hip and put her cell phone in her pocket so she could carry the sandwich bag back to her dorm and store it in her tiny fridge for a future snack.

"Those are beautiful," Talitha said. "Are they for you?"

"Yeah."

"From Rick?"

Katie dodged her uncertainty by saying, "Who else would they be from?"

"I love the fragrance of stargazer lilies, don't you?"

"Is that what these are? Stargazer lilies?" Katie felt a strange rumbling inside as she pushed away the thought that was trying to break into her consciousness.

"Yes, stargazer. You have to be careful because the yellow pollen really stains, but these have been trimmed. I love 'em. I'm going to have them at my wedding."

Katie did a double take. "Your wedding? Do you have plans I haven't heard about?"

"No!" Talitha said quickly, lowering her voice. "Are you kidding? I have zero love life and just about zero social life. I'm only saying that someday, if and when I do get married, I'd like to have these flowers in my wedding bouquet."

"Here." Katie extracted one of the vibrant flowers from the center of the bouquet and handed it to Talitha. "A flower to make a wish on."

Then, to give a twist to her impulsive gift, she made up instructions for extracting the wish from the flower. "You see, with a wishing flower, you're supposed to give it a twirl and a sniff and say, 'With this lily, I thee wish.' Then the next guy you see after you make your wish will be 'him.'"

Talitha laughed. "I think I'll wait on the twirl-and-sniff until my chances of spotting 'Mr. Him' are a little better than they are at the moment."

Katie followed Talitha's line of sight to the lobby where only two guys were visible. One of them was cuddling with his girlfriend on the couch and the other one, a proverbial ninety-eight-pound weakling, was typing on his laptop at lightning speed.

"I see what you mean. When you're ready, though, just follow those simple instructions and see what happens with your wishing flower."

"If you say so."

Katie could tell that Talitha was laughing at her behind her smile, but Katie didn't care. "You know what I think? I think that if a young woman doesn't engage in the act of occasionally wishing on a star or a flower or a birthday cake full of candles, then we're forfeiting one of the sweetest whimsies of our youth."

Talitha raised her eyebrows at Katie's declaration. "Where did that come from?"

Katie raised her chin. She knew her uncharacteristically fanciful statement had sprung out of the combined experiences of the past twenty-four hours—being with her married friend, Christy; gazing at the stars with Eli and Joseph; talking with her unimaginative mother; thinking of her brothers; and now holding a beautiful bouquet of flowers with her name on it. Since that was too much to try to summarize, her response to Talitha was, "Life goes fast, and lots of things can depress us. But if we don't have hope, then, well ... what is the point of our future, if we can't dream a little?"

Talitha gave Katie a spontaneous hug. "I needed that. Thank you, Katie. I needed this flower too."

"Good. And don't forget the wish-upon-your-lily."

"I won't."

"The wish is only good while the flower is still fresh, so don't wait until it goes brown or starts to droop."

"Got it."

Gathering everything in her arms, Katie tried to carry the flowers as inconspicuously as possible back to her room. She wasn't very successful. Three women on her floor stopped to sniff and admire her bouquet. Since the wish-upon-a-flower fun was fresh on her mind, Katie repeated the made-up exercise with the three women. To each of them she gave a rosebud along with wishing instructions.

"Are you sure you want to dissect your bouquet like this?" one of the girls said.

Katie quickly stated that the bouquet was too big and needed to be trimmed down. "Rick tends to overdo things like this," she added with a fleeting thought about the last time he gave her a bouquet. It was just as enormous as this one, and Katie hadn't exactly appreciated his generous efforts. They quarreled that night, and she had left the bouquet in the backseat of his car. This one she would keep. She might trim it down some, but she would keep it and make sure to thank him sincerely, even if she didn't understand the message on the card.

Christy's observation on the previous large bouquet was that Rick was finding creative ways to express his affection and passion for Katie without doing it in a physical way. If that was true, this bouquet was equivalent to at least a dozen kisses. A dozen kisses she and Rick hadn't yet shared lip-to-lip in this new season of being together.

Most of the time Katie managed not to think about their lack of kisses. Rick's admirable yet maddening restraint frustrated her way too much for her to think the topic through to a conclusion that settled well with her. The only peace she had at the moment was that when the time was right, they would add kissing as a wonderful part of their expressions of affection for each other. She knew after all the months and all the discussions they had had about kissing—or the lack thereof—it would only come to her with that essential magic touch if she waited and let Rick make the first move.

Entering the dorm hall, Katie stopped in front of The Peculiar Treasures Wall. At the beginning of the semester, Katie and Nicole had covered one section of the wall with photos of all the women on the floor. Next to each photo they added a verse as a sort of blessing for the girl.

Pausing to glance at her picture on the wall, Katie repeated her verse like a promise or a blessing. " 'The Lord will guard your going out and your coming in from this time forth and forever,' Psalm 121:8."

Once again, the verse that had been selected for Katie by Em, one of the new students, was applicable to what she was going through at the moment. She was "going out" with Rick, but she was also "coming in" to a new place in her relationship with her mom and possibly with her brothers. That was a good thing.

Since Katie's mom was so emotionally aloof, Katie never had experienced the motherly, caring commitment that many of her friends had with their moms.

I wonder if that's part of the reason Rick has become such an important person to me? I've wanted to be accepted by my mom for so long, but it's never happened at the depth I've needed. I've had a crush on Rick since middle school. Now that he's genuinely interested in me, have I seen him as filling that closeness gap for me?

She looked again at her verse on the wall and thought of how, in some ways, God already had "guarded" her going out with Rick. To her it didn't matter what the deep psychological reasons were for her relationship with Rick. So far their relationship was working.

Why overanalyze the fun out of it? She reminded herself that if the opulent floral arrangement was his way of expressing his passion for her, then she should take it and be thankful.

And if her relationships with those near strangers in her immediate family were the relationships she was supposed to pay attention to now, then she would take that and be thankful, as well.

Nicole's door across from The Peculiar Treasures Wall was open. Katie saw Nicole sitting on her bed with her laptop in front of her. As soon as Katie entered, Nicole turned down the music on her laptop and said, "Wow!"

Katie hoped her tromping right in and flaunting her bouquet when Nicole was still waiting to hear if she even had a date for Friday night wouldn't make Nicole uncomfortable. She still had Katie's room key so Katie had to stop by for it.

"Here." Katie pulled out a pink gerbera daisy. "These are your favorite, right? The pink ones?"

Nicole smiled and nodded. "Thanks, but you shouldn't be taking your bouquet apart."

"Consider it my thank you for the sandwich and just a little something to brighten up your day and your room."

"Thanks." Nicole pulled a small vase from a box in her closet. Of course Nicole would be prepared for any situation.

"Did you go for the Cocoa Puffs?" Katie asked.

"No, I got sidetracked by the call from my mom. She cheered me up, and I forgot about my quest for black gold. Here's your key back. Thanks anyway."

"I have a favor to ask." Katie placed the vase of flowers on the end of Nicole's desk.

"Do you want me to flower-sit your bouquet?"

"Cute. No, I need a ride this afternoon. My car is over at Christy's apartment where it decided to die last night, so I have to have it towed to a repair place. I'll need a ride back to school as well."

"Sure, I'm available. Sorry to hear that Baby Hummer is under the weather. What happened?"

"She wouldn't start last night."

"I can go with you whenever you want. I'm ready now." Nicole always looked fresh and ready to go. So did her room. Everything was in place—dusted, straightened, and put away.

Katie realized while standing in Nicole's fresh and tidy room that she still was carrying a mixed blend of fragrances that the flowers were probably helping to mask at the moment. The scents started with the mutant, garlic-buttered microwave popcorn and green tea mask, followed up with the lingering aroma of engine whiff from the outing to the desert. A shower seemed like a good idea.

"How about if we leave here in about half an hour?"

"I'll be here."

Katie scooted off to her room. She called a towing service and arranged to meet them at Christy's apartment in an hour.

Since the shower was often her favorite place to pray, Katie went down the internal list as soon as the warm water washed over her. She started with her car problems, her financial needs, her family, and especially her brother, wherever he was. Then she prayed about her relationship with Rick and . . .

"Eli!" Katie suddenly spouted into the stream of water. She stood still in the stall as a mini-revelation washed over her.

Eli sent me those flowers! They're not from Rick. They're from Eli. He wrote those two lines because he was glad I said "yes" to going out to the desert with him, and he's glad things are cool between us now, and our friendship is what's "just beginning."

Katie leaned her head back and rinsed the shampoo out of her hair.

So why didn't he sign the card? Did he think I would know he was the one sending the flowers? And why would he send such a huge bouquet? Wouldn't he think it might communicate the wrong sort of message? I mean, he knows I'm Rick's girlfriend.

Katie's shower turned into a steaming think tank, as she tried to figure out why Eli would send her such a note. She remembered that he had made a comment to Rick a few weeks ago about Katie being "unforgettable," whatever that meant.

If Eli thinks this is a good time or a clever way for him to try to flirt with me while Rick is gone, well then, I have a few choice words for that brazen Goatee Guy.

Katie put aside thoughts of Eli as soon as she was back in her room. On the way to Rick's apartment, she tried to call Christy while Nicole was driving. Katie realized she hadn't yet told Christy about her car breaking down. Or about her trek to the desert. But that would be a tale better delivered in person. Katie could wait until their lunch on Tuesday. With Christy, it was always better to get into the more layered sorts of conversations face-to-face.

When Christy didn't answer her cell, Katie left a message. "Hey, it's me. Call me later."

Her phone rang at five o'clock that evening, just as Katie and Nicole were driving into the gas station where Joseph worked. They were right behind the tow truck, and Katie could see that Joseph was at the station, which was a good thing.

But Christy wasn't the one calling Katie; it was punctual Rick. She had told him to call after five, and it was a minute after five.

"Rick, I'll have to call you back. My car died, and Nicole and I are at the gas station now."

"Your car died? What happened to it?"

"I don't know. I'll tell you when I find out. Just tell me really quick, how are you doing?"

"I'm good. Everything is moving along here. Call me when you can."

"I will."

She hung up and Nicole said, "You forgot to thank him for the flowers."

"Oh, yeah," Katie said. "The flowers."

The next few days, every time Katie answered her phone she was surprised.

The first unexpected call was from her brother Clint. He left a message while Katie was in church Sunday morning. He said he was doing pretty well. He hadn't heard from Larry in a couple of months, but Clint wasn't worried because the only time he did hear from Larry was when he was in trouble. Then Clint told Katie to "call me anytime you want."

It had been so long since Katie had regular communication with her brothers, it felt more as if she were listening to a phone message from a well-meaning middle school teacher who was checking in on her. She knew she wouldn't call Clint back just to chat, but it was good to have his phone number and to realize she could call him if she wanted to.

The next surprise call came on Monday from the mechanic friend of Joseph's to whom Katie had entrusted Baby Hummer. The words *restoration* and *vintage parts* were her first clue that she was headed for a financial disaster. The mechanic said he would get back to her with an estimate in a few days. In the meantime he would search for the rare parts.

The nicest surprise call was the one that came from Rick on Monday evening. Katie was leaving the cafeteria when her phone rang. She decided to stroll to upper campus while she talked to him. Rick was in a good mood and said he had some news. Katie assumed it was the same sort of Arizona café business news that had been a consistent part of their weekly and sometimes daily conversations since August.

"Before you tell me your news," Katie said, "I have a few updates for you."

"Good news, I hope," Rick said.

"My news is mixed. Like a bouquet. Like a big, beautiful, unexpected bouquet. So thanks."

Katie waited for Rick to say something along the lines of, "Oh, you got the flowers, did you? Good. Did you like them?"

Instead, Rick said, "What exactly are you thanking me for?"

"You know." She waited.

"No ..." Rick waited.

Katie carefully baited the next hook for him. "Thanks for asking about my news and for always doing such nice things for me. Unexpected things."

"Oh-kay. And what did I do that was so nice?"

Katie knew then that the flowers weren't from Rick.

She bit her lower lip and kept walking through the upper campus parking lot and onto the path that led to the prayer chapel. Beyond the chapel, on the mesa's edge, she saw an open bench that looked out all the way to the blue Pacific Ocean on a clear day.

"What did you do that was so nice? Well, for starters, you called me. Thank you. And also you are basically kind and nice to me all the time. Like when you took out the stinky burnt popcorn for Christy and me last Friday. That was nice. Thank you. I don't know if I said thank you that night, when you did that for me, for us, but I wanted to say thanks."

Rick was laughing on the other end. To Katie it sounded like the way Ricky Ricardo would laugh at Lucy on the old black-and-white episodes when Lucy was trying to cover up one of her many fumbles. This time the shoe fit, so to speak, and her "Ricky's" laughter was warranted. Katie was just glad he was laughing and not pressing her for details. She knew if he was irritated instead of humored, she would have spilled about the flowers to explain herself, and that could have been messy.

Especially since the bouquet was currently about one-third its original opulence. Katie had found great delight all weekend in blessing many women on the floor with a flower and had gone to the bouquet half a dozen times, as if it were her private garden and all the flowers were just waiting to be picked and delivered to someone else.

"So?" Rick asked. "Was that your update?"

"No, there's more." She summarized her call with her mom and subsequent partial connection with her brother Clint.

"That's great, Katie. You were saying a few weeks ago that you really hoped things with your mom would improve. Looks like this might be a first step."

"It's a wobbly first step."

"That's okay. It's a step. Are you sure she's not going to change her mind and ask us to come cook Thanksgiving dinner?"

"She won't want us to come last minute. She doesn't change her mind. She's not like me. Not at all."

As soon as Katie said the last few lines, an odd stretch followed for a few seconds before she was sure what to do with that self-disclosure. "Not that I change my mind all the time. I mean, once I make up my mind, I follow through with whatever I decide to do."

"I know," Rick said.

"However, weren't you the one who told me flexibility is a sign of good mental health?"

"I don't think so. Maybe."

"Well, I'm flexible with schedules and Thanksgiving and whatever else." She waited a moment for Rick to issue an invitation to his family's Thanksgiving celebration as the natural next line in the conversation.

He hesitated another moment. "I don't know what my parents are planning to do this year. So much has been happening I haven't thought to ask them."

"I figured with the new house and the way your mom loves to decorate and do everything up so nice, she might not be ready to host Thanksgiving. I mean, at least not the way she hosted Easter with the china and silver and all that food. How many people were there? Like twelve or fourteen? I couldn't believe they all fit around the table."

"That's my mom. She loves to celebrate in a big way. I'll ask her what the plans are for this year. I'm sure you're invited. You're my girlfriend, you know."

Katie smiled. "It's always good to be reminded of that."

"Are you ready to hear my news?"

"Wait. I have one more."

"Busy weekend for you."

"It was. And this news is sad news. You know how I told you Baby Hummer wouldn't start? Well, it doesn't look good for the old girl. The mechanic hasn't called me back with a final estimate, but Baby Hummer might be terminal."

"Bummer."

"I know. My Baby Hummer is now a Baby Bummer."

"What are you going to do?" Rick asked.

"I don't know yet."

"Well, if it's any help, I can offer you rides where you need to go starting on Tuesday night around six o'clock."

Katie let his statement sink in. "Does that mean you're coming home early?"

"I am. We have one more appointment at the bank tomorrow morning, and then Josh and I are driving straight home for good."

"For good?"

"Yes, for good. We backed out of the deal today. That was my big news flash."

"You're kidding! What happened?"

"We hit some more major roadblocks, so we brought in a business advisor. He looked over all our papers, and after we talked with him for three hours, we decided to withdraw from the project. It's just not going to fly."

"Rick, this is huge news! See what I mean about how patient and kind you are? You let me babble about all my stuff first, even though your news is going to radically alter your life and schedule."

"It is, but I have to tell you, it feels right. Both Josh and I are relieved. On our drive out here, we prayed, and then we asked each other if maybe we were pushing something that wasn't going to work no matter how hard we tried to make it."

"I know what that feels like," Katie said.

"I know you do. You're a hard worker too, Katie. I think I sometimes settle into a mind-set that if I push harder or work longer, then all the broken stuff will get fixed. This time, it wasn't happening. The first two hours of our meeting with the consultant I kept arguing that we could still make it happen. Finally, I just saw it. I saw that the best decision, the right decision, was to walk away, even though I was so committed to the project."

"Wow."

"I know. Wow, huh? This isn't like me at all."

Katie was at the benches now on the mesa and sat with her gaze directed toward the sunset. The horizon was so fogged in she couldn't see the ocean. All that was visible were gray clouds. Inland, on the elevated mesa where she sat, the sky overhead was a pale shade of blue with long strips of silver-gray clouds streaking across Earth's domed ceiling.

"So what are you going to do?" she asked Rick.

"We'll be refunded most of our initial investment because the contractor pushed the project out another five months last week. Since he was the one who moved the date, we had the opportunity to pull out. It was about as smooth of a dissolution as we could have hoped for."

"Sounds like it could be a God thing," Katie said.

"I think it is. The timing was right. I'm going to be able to focus on things back at the Dove's Nest, and Josh is going to scout out other opportunities. We'll start over."

"Would I sound terribly selfish if I said I'm glad you're not going to Arizona anymore?"

Rick laughed again. "I will not miss the heat here, I'll tell you that!"

It had been so long since he had been in such a good mood. From where she was sitting, the future for the two of them was looking a whole lot better than it had the past several months while he was coming and going all the time.

"Nothing about you is selfish, Katie. You were thanking me earlier for being generous and taking out the trash, but you know what? You're the one who should receive all the thanks. You've been extremely patient with me through all this. I should be thanking you for putting up with me for these months. I put so much focus and attention into this business deal that I feel like I've slighted you."

"You didn't slight me, Rick. For the past four months, I've been just as wrapped up in school and the RA position as you've been in your business stuff. We've both been busy."

"I think it's time for a fresh start for us—for you and me," Rick said.

"Agreed."

"What are you doing tomorrow night after six?"

"Seeing you, I hope."

"I'll make reservations at the Thai Palace."

"Perfect." Katie smiled. The Thai Palace was the restaurant where Rick and she had decided to take the next step in their relationship and commit to being boyfriend and girlfriend. Since that happy dinner almost a month ago, not much had changed in their relationship to make it seem as if they were now more committed to each other. They both knew their crazy schedules were to blame, so it had been easy to extend lots of grace and understanding in both directions. Now that Rick no longer had the Arizona café project at the forefront of his life, Katie knew things were about to change for them. This was news she couldn't wait to tell Christy.

As soon as Katie hung up from talking with Rick, she called Christy. Katie still was sitting on the bench on upper campus, looking out on the horizon. The evening fog was rolling in, making it even more difficult to see anything below in the expansive valley that curved out to the ocean.

"Christy? Hey, what are you doing? Are you guys right in the middle of dinner or anything?"

"No. Todd and Eli have confiscated the kitchen table. They're trying to fix Todd's laptop. What are you doing?"

"I'm sitting very close to the spot where you tossed your wedding bouquet and I caught it."

"Ohh. I haven't been up there since our wedding. Can you believe that? How is the meadow this evening?"

"Cloudy and chilly with a chance of Thai food tomorrow night."

"A chance of what?"

"I just talked to Rick. He's coming home from Arizona tomorrow, and we're going out to the Thai Palace." Katie walked back to her dorm as she updated Christy on the conversation with Rick.

Like any best friend would, Christy responded to Katie's update with enthusiasm. Katie moved on to the news of Baby Bummer's imminent demise.

"Do we need to cancel our lunch plans for tomorrow?" Christy asked.

"No, I'm sure I can borrow a car. I'll be at the bookstore at 1:30." Katie held back on her two most interesting pieces of news, the flowers and the side trip out to the desert Friday night. She still felt those two subjects would best be presented in person, as she and Christy lingered over lunchtime conversation.

That was partly the reason the next day Katie suggested they stay at the Dove's Nest for lunch instead of driving somewhere. Katie wanted to secure as much talking time as possible. On other lunch dates with Christy, they had opted to go someplace else so that employees wouldn't be within listening range of their private conversation. That wasn't a problem today.

What was a problem was the way Christy reacted when Katie told her the next bit of news. "So guess what I did last Friday night when I left your apartment? You'll never guess."

"You went skydiving after all." Christy was leading the way to the table in the farthest corner. They had ordered simple salads and water and were carrying their own food to the table in an effort to make it clear they didn't want to be interrupted.

"Not skydiving. Better than that. I went out to the desert and watched a meteor shower with two guys from Africa, and we were practically surrounded by wild coyotes."

Christy dipped her chin and examined Katie's expression, as if she was sure Katie was kidding.

"I'm serious. When I left your place, Baby Hummer wouldn't start. Eli came by and offered me a ride back to campus, but then he picked up Joseph Oboki, and the three of us ended up driving out to where we could see the stars. It was incredible, Christy. I've never seen so many stars. And when the music started with the African children ..."

"Katie, wait. I'm so confused. Which part of this is true, aside from Baby Hummer not starting?"

Katie gave Christy a mock wounded look. "What do you mean, 'Which part is true'? All of it's true."

Christy put down her fork and looked perturbed. "When your car wouldn't start last Friday, why didn't you come back to my apartment? We could have waited for Todd, and he would have given you a ride to campus."

"I know. But Eli was right there."

"So why didn't you get a ride from Eli?"

"I did. Eli was going to take me back to campus after he picked up Joseph at the gas station, but then they invited me to go with them, and I was still in the mood to do something, so I said yes. And it was amazing. We watched the stars from the hood of Eli's car under a sleeping bag. One of those old, green, flannel-lined sleeping bags."

"All three of you? Under one sleeping bag?"

"It was opened up like a big blanket. It was the only way to stay warm."

"Katie!"

"What?"

"You're telling me on Friday night, after you left my apartment, on a whim, you just went out to the desert with two guys you don't even know and cuddled up under a sleeping bag with them?"

"Why do you make it sound like that? We didn't cuddle. You're making this sound risqué. It wasn't at all. It was beautiful. It was a holy night."

"Then what was all the stuff about two guys from Africa and singing children?"

"Eli grew up in Africa. So did Joseph. We listened to a CD with children singing in some African language. I'm not making this up. Everything I'm saying is the truth, and it was wonderful. I can't understand why everyone keeps trying to ruin it for me."

"You honestly can't see how crazy it sounds when you say you went out to the desert in the middle of the night with two guys you don't even know?"

"It didn't seem crazy at the time. Not half as crazy as the camel rides and skydiving I had been promoting at your place. And what's with the 'two guys I don't even know' line? Rick said that too. Are you guys in on this together?"

"In on what together?"

"Trying to make me feel bad about what was actually an amazing, worshipful experience. Not to mention that I was making an effort to get to know Eli and to be nice to him. Have you guys forgotten how that has been your goal for me for the past few months?"

"No one is trying to make you feel bad. We just care about what happens to you." Christy narrowed her eyes and gave Katie an intense look. "What if something awful would have happened?"

"What are you doing?"

"I'm asking you a question."

Katie leaned back and crossed her arms. "No, you're not. That's not a question. You're making it sound like an accusation. You're trying to act like my mother."

"Your mother!"

"Yeah, my mother. You're treating me as if I'm twelve years old and not smart enough to make my own decisions."

"No, I'm not."

"Yes, you are!"

"Katie, why are you so upset? I'm the one who feels caught off balance by all this. Here we were having a great time at my apartment on Friday night, and then you run off with these two guys. What were you thinking?"

"I was thinking it sounded like fun."

"Katie, there's more to life than trying to come up with new ways to have fun."

"Oh, that's good!" Katie could feel her face turning red. "You sit there and act like you have it all figured out now that you're married."

"No, I'm not."

"Yes, you are. And you're trying to make me feel bad because I'm not serious and responsible all the time like you. You think I'm a big loser."

"I did not say that!" Now Christy's face was turning red as well. "I said nothing remotely like that."

"Then why are you treating me as if my decisions are immature and irresponsible?"

Christy paused. Then she blurted out, "Well, because maybe sometimes, Katie, they are."

Katie felt as if she just had been slapped in the face. She pushed herself away from the table. "Oh! So you do think I'm immature and irresponsible. I can't believe this. First you sound just like Rick, and now you're repeating my mother word for word. What did you guys do? Call each other up and say, 'Hey, how can we mess with Katie this week?' Is that it?"

"Of course not." Christy jutted out her chin. "Maybe all three are saying the same thing because we care about you."

"That's not it. No, you're saying all this because you think I'm too irresponsible to make my own decisions. Especially if those decisions have anything to do with relaxing and having fun and not working or studying 24/7. You think I'm making such bad decisions that one day I'm going to end up in a rehab center in Bakersfield!"

Christy's face had gone from red to white. "What are you talking about?"

Katie didn't answer. She felt her jaw trembling.

"You know what?" Christy said, her face still red. "I don't know what's going on, but I do know that I can't have this conversation with you. Not now. Not here."

She got up from the table and walked away.

Katie couldn't remember a time Christy had walked away from her like that. Katie was in shock. Then she became aware that several people in the café were looking at them and had been listening in. Their conversation obviously had been loud enough for the curious onlookers to get a pretty clear idea of what was going on.

The room felt as if it were getting smaller and closing in. Katie dared to look around the café. Two tables over she saw the last person she wanted to see.

8

Julia, Katie's resident director from Crown Hall, met her gaze across the café.

Katie looked away. As if it weren't bad enough that Katie had missed her shift on Saturday and Julia had to come get her, now, in this public place, Julia had undoubtedly witnessed the entire argument.

The odd thing was that part of Katie wanted to run to Julia and receive the same sort of compassion and understanding she had experienced with Julia before. As Katie's mentor, Julia had given great advice and encouragement on several occasions. At the moment, though, Katie didn't think she could face Julia. Not the way she was feeling.

Without stopping to consider any other options, Katie stood, grabbed her shoulder bag, and bolted for the door. Jamming the keys into the ignition of Nicole's car, she backed out of the parking space quickly, before any tears could race down her cheeks.

I can't believe that just happened! Christy and I don't fight like that.

Another thought took over as Katie rehearsed what Julia had just witnessed. Not only was Julia her mentor and friend, but she was also Katie's overseer. She was the one who evaluated Katie's job as an RA. *If she gives me a bad report on my performance review, I might not be hired on for the second semester, and then what would I do? My job pays for my room and board. I already don't have enough money to repair my car. If I have to pay for room and board next semester . . .*

Katie felt her hands shake as she flipped on the turn signal and exited the parking lot. Part of her wanted to peel out and leave an angry tire burn on the pavement. If she had been in Baby Hummer, she would have left a huge streak of rubber. But this was Nicole's car, and Katie was aware of how careful she needed to be, especially since she didn't know who might be watching in this small community.

Driving under the speed limit, Katie cautiously steered her way back to campus. Along the way, she muttered aloud, as if finishing the quarrel by herself. "I'll show you guys how responsible I am. I can be trusted. I'm not doing anything wrong. See? I'm a competent driver. And for your information, I'm also a competent midnight stargazer. You guys weren't there. You don't know how great it was."

As Katie arrived on campus, her cell phone rang. Checking it, she saw that Julia was calling. Katie's stomach twisted. She knew she should answer the call now rather than put off the inevitable conversation.

"Hi," Katie said quietly. She pulled Nicole's car into a parking spot next to the softball field and turned off the engine, prepared for a reprimand.

"How are you doing, Katie?"

"Horrible."

"I can imagine."

"Yes, I'm sure you can." Katie didn't feel the sense of shame she had expected. Julia had every reason to pour on the judgmental attitude after what had just happened. Instead, she was calm and strong-hearted in her words to Katie.

"Where are you now?"

"Rancho. By the softball field."

"Do you want your salad? I had it wrapped to go. I can bring it with me."

"I'm not hungry."

"I'll bring it in case you get hungry later. Why don't you meet me in my room in about twenty minutes?"

"Okay."

Julia paused. "Wait, did you say you're at the softball field?"

"Yes."

"I'll meet you there instead. While you're waiting for me, could you check out a bat and a bag of softballs from the rec office?"

Katie knew she should agree to whatever Julia asked. So Katie marched to the athletic office, where she checked out a baseball bat and a canvas bag of softballs. With long strides she returned to the bleachers and sat in the cool afternoon breeze waiting for Julia.

She didn't have to wait long. Julia came across the parking area wearing sunglasses and dressed in casual clothes the way someone on her day off and running errands would be. Julia had a youthful appearance with her sun-kissed brown hair and scattering of freckles. Whenever Katie saw her, she thought Julia looked as if she had just gotten off a sailboat.

"Come on." Julia reached for the canvas bag. She headed for the pitcher's mound, leaving Katie with the baseball bat.

Katie followed, taking a comfortable stance over home base. She hadn't played softball in months, but the way she was feeling, she could hit that ball all the way to Cincinnati. As a matter of fact, she really liked the idea of hitting something with a baseball bat at the moment.

Opening the cinched neck of the canvas bag, Julia reached for a softball. She stretched right and left and then pitched the ball at Katie.

Katie swung and missed.

Julia smiled broadly. She had come to play.

"Hey," Katie called out, tapping the end of the bat on the dirt and putting on her game face. "Try getting this one over the base."

Julia let loose with an underhand slow pitch. Katie swung the bat, giving it all she had. The ball flew far past third base and landed in the outfield with a tiny hop.

"Okay, I see what it's like with you," Julia said. "No more pampering, Miss Katie. Let me see what you've got."

For the next five minutes, Katie took out all her aggression on the steady stream of softballs, making contact and sending about 80 percent of them sailing to the outfield with a series of precision hits. As soon as the bag was empty, Julia grinned. "You have hidden talents, Katie."

"So do you." Katie headed toward the pitcher's mound. "Did you play on a team?"

"Ages ago. I've missed it."

"Me too."

"You feeling a little better?" Julia asked.

"Yeah, a little."

They walked to the outfield together with Julia carrying the canvas bag. Like two wearied toddlers at the end of an Easter egg hunt, they scouted out the softballs and returned them to the bag.

"So, I have to ask about the reference to the rehab center in Bakersfield." Julia's conversational tone was as calm as if they had been hashing out all of Katie's problems for the past hour and were settling some of the final points. "Where did that one come from?"

"My brother." Katie stopped collecting softballs and stood with her hands on both hips, giving Julia the rundown of her conversation with her mom and subsequent attempt to call the center in Bakersfield.

"Now you know where my craziness comes from," Katie concluded.

"I'm going to stop you right there, Katie. Smash that thought. Knock it right out of your heart. First of all, you are not your brother, and second, you are not your mother. And for that matter, Christy is not your mother."

Katie looked down at the softball in her hand and gave it a spin before returning it to the bag. "You're right. I need to apologize to Christy. She and I have had some tiffs in the past, but nothing like this. I don't know why I got so upset. Well, maybe I do. It was a combination of everything, starting with how she made it sound as if I had done something lewd just because we shared a sleeping bag.

It was like a blanket. Nothing inappropriate happened. It really was amazing and worshipful."

Katie took a breath and kept going. "I mean, I know now it would have been wise to tell someone where I was going and with whom. That part I get. Even though both the guys are students at Rancho, nobody else knew where I was going or whom I was with. And I know RAs are expected to manage their social lives within the same parameters as the other students. So, if you want to write that part up on my review, that I was out until 4 a.m. or whatever it was, I won't contest it. That wasn't good judgment or good example-setting on my part. None of the women on my floor knows that I was out that late. But that doesn't matter. Even if they don't know, you know and I know, so if you have to write me up, I understand."

"Who said I was going to write you up about anything?"

"That's how it goes, isn't it? We have a lot of rules at Rancho Corona. I'm the one who is being paid to assist in enforcing those rules with the women on my floor. If I'm pressing against the rules, then you're the one who is paid to enforce the rules with me."

Julia didn't answer. Katie expected her to give a speech about how the resident assistants and resident directors were there to foster relationships first and enforce rules second. Katie had memorized that line in the training sessions. Julia, however, seemed more inclined to demonstrate that directive to Katie rather than repeat the words to her.

"I want you to know, Katie, that you could have called me when your car wouldn't start. I would have come to pick you up no matter where you were or what time of day it was."

"Thanks." Katie hadn't thought to call Julia, but she knew she could have.

Julia bent over and picked up another softball. Turning to catch Katie's eye, she said with a tender tone, "Don't worry. You're not heading for Bakersfield anytime soon. Not on my watch."

Katie couldn't explain why Julia's simple affirmation went so deep into her heart, but it did. She blinked away a fresh splash of tears that came rushing forward. Then she turned her back to Julia and collected the last few softballs.

This was a rare and piercing moment for Katie, as she absorbed being affirmed and loved by another woman. The well in her heart that stored up such words of womanly kindness was so shallow that on those unsolicited and life-giving occasions when words were dropped into that well, the echo resonated all the way to her soul.

The two women walked to the rec office and turned in the sports equipment. "I have your salad in my car," Julia said. "It might be a little on the wilted side."

"That's okay. Thanks for bringing it."

Julia grinned. "Thank *you* for 'bringing it' on the diamond. Let's get a game together sometime."

"Good idea."

"I think another good idea would be if you and I set up a time to meet again in the next few days," Julia said.

"With or without a baseball bat?"

"Without. Although I might have one on hand just in case."

"Okay." Katie smiled and gave Julia a hug. "Thanks. Really. Thanks."

Katie drove Nicole's car back to the Crown Hall parking area and hurried to her room. She shoved the salad into her tiny refrigerator and grabbed her laptop. Her next class started in four minutes, and she knew it wasn't possible to run across campus fast enough to make it on time. She would be late. Seemed fitting for this day.

Katie slipped into a chair in the back of the classroom. Her mind wasn't on the lecture. She tried to take notes for the first twenty minutes before admitting it was pointless. She had to talk to Christy. Rick was coming to pick her up in an hour and a half, but Katie wouldn't be able to enjoy her time with Rick if she felt her relationship with her best friend was in such a tangle.

After asking the guy next to her if he would email her his notes, Katie slipped out of class and made a beeline for her dorm. She checked her phone for messages and saw that Christy had called twice.

Rehearsing her apology as she strode across campus, Katie planned to make the call as soon as she reached her room and could close the door for this important conversation.

She hurried down the hall to her room. It was open dorm afternoon and evening, so lots of students were socializing in their rooms, with a variety of music playing. Katie had just stepped into her room when her cell phone rang. It was Christy.

"Hey." Katie sat on her bed and caught her breath. "I was just going to call you. I left my class early because I want to apologize."

"So do I. I'm really sorry, Katie."

"I am too. That was awful. I don't want to fight like that with you again."

"I don't either."

Both of them drew in a deep breath over the phone at the same time without planning it. Katie felt a hundred pounds lighter.

"That was really awful. I don't think the let's-influence-each-other plan worked out very well," Christy said.

"What are you talking about?"

"You know how last Friday you said I was too polite? Well, I thought about that a lot. And when you were getting all heated up, I felt so frustrated I decided to try being a little ... no, a lot more aggressive. It really didn't work. It wasn't right. Not for me. I don't enjoy conflict at all."

"But were you saying things at lunch that you honestly felt? I mean, do you think I'm irresponsible?"

"No. I wasn't saying you were irresponsible. Not at all."

"You're sure."

"Katie, you're an RA. They don't give those jobs to irresponsible people. You're putting yourself through college. How many women do you know who have managed to do that? You and Rick have been in an amazing, mature relationship for almost a year. Katie, you are responsible. You know you are. Take what I said within the whole picture of my trying to understand why you took off with Eli and

Joseph. Give me a little grace considering that I didn't know what was going on."

"Understood. Grace on you."

"And shame off you."

"I like that. Shame off me. Grace on me. Grace on both of us."

"Yes, grace on both of us."

Katie drew in a stabilizing breath. "Do you want to try to have lunch again later this week? I think we should talk more about this without things escalating. I need your input. You see things I can't see in myself. I need to listen to what you have to tell me instead of going ballistic."

"Why don't you email me when you know what days work for you. We'll start fresh."

"You aren't going to believe this, but you're quoting Rick again. When he and I talked yesterday, he said that since he isn't going to travel to Arizona anymore, this is our chance to give our relationship a fresh start."

"I hope you guys have a really good time tonight."

"I do too. I'll email you later."

Katie paused a moment, staring at the bouquet that filled the center of her desk. She wondered if she should tell Christy about the flowers. No, better to go right to the source. Katie placed a call to campus security and asked for Eli Lorenzo.

However, she had no idea what she would say when he answered.

9

As soon as Katie heard Eli's voice on the other end of her phone, her throat tightened up, and she gave in to a fit of coughing.

"Katie?" Eli said. "You okay?"

"Yeah. Sorry. Tickle in my throat all of a sudden. Hey, umm ..."

"Is your car fixed yet?"

"No, I'm waiting for the estimate. It could be deadly. Parts for my car apparently fall into the collectors' category."

"Not good."

"I know."

A pause followed.

Katie wanted to cough again but refrained and fumbled around for some inroad to move the conversation in the direction it needed to go. "So, Rick is coming back tonight. Did he tell you?"

"Yeah, he called."

"Good. So ..." She looked at the flowers and decided to revert to the kinds of clues she had used when trying to figure out if Rick had sent the arrangement to her.

"I just wanted to call and say thanks for the flower ..." She stalled, hoping he would insert a telltale response.

He didn't.

Katie made the best of it. "... the flowery way you brightened up my day the other night at the meteor shower-concert thing." She pinched her eyes closed and made a face.

97

That was pathetic!

"You're welcome," Eli said slowly. Another pause followed before he added, "Are you sure you're okay?"

"Yeah, I'm good. Hey, listen. I have to go. I just wanted to make sure you heard that Rick was coming home earlier than he first thought, since he's coming home tonight."

"Right. I've got it. Rick is coming home."

"Okay. Well. That's all. See ya." Katie pressed End on her phone and flopped on her bed. Slapping her hand across her eyes she muttered, "I can't believe what a—"

Before she could finish her sentence, a knock sounded on her door.

With her hand still over her eyes, she called out, "Enter only if you dare to be associated with dweebs!"

Her door opened, and Katie parted her fingers to see if Nicole or one of the other women from the floor was the person who had knocked.

The oh-so-handsome face that peered around the corner didn't belong to Nicole.

"Rick!" Katie tumbled out of her bed in a less-than-dainty fashion and ran to give him a big hug. "You're here! I've missed you so much!"

"I missed you too." Rick pulled back and grinned at her. His warm brown eyes seemed to be taking in her post-batting-practice appearance.

"You're early!" Katie protested, pushing him out the door. "And I'm not ready. You have to come back in half an hour. No, twenty minutes. I can be all cute-i-fied in twenty minutes."

"I can wait here, can't I? It's open dorm. You'll be down the hall in the bathroom. I'll check my emails while you're gone." Rick pressed back into the room and apparently noticed the bouquet for the first time. "Who sent you the flowers?"

Katie double-checked his expression just to make sure he wasn't playing it cool and trying to hide that he had sent them. She knew

Rick well enough to read in his slightly jealous look that he definitely wasn't the bouquet bestower.

With a shrug she tried to make her expression as cute as she could. If she could have sprouted more freckles in that moment, she would have done so in an attempt to charm Rick out of asking any more questions about the flowers.

"It's a mystery," she said.

"What did the card say?"

"It wasn't signed."

Rick moved over to her desk. He picked up the card, looked at it, and then looked at Katie. "It's not signed."

"I know. That's what I just said. Hence the 'mystery.'" She used two fingers on each hand to pantomime the quotation marks around "mystery."

Rick turned the vase around. "Does it seem kind of unbalanced to you?"

"What, that some phantom admirer would send me flowers? I wouldn't call it unbalanced. A little out of the ordinary or unexpected, maybe, but I happen to be rather popular in certain circles."

"No, I meant the bouquet. Doesn't it seem like it's not finished or something? I mean, I'm not saying I'm an expert on flower arrangements, but for a huge bouquet, this looks odd, like it's been picked over."

"Oh, that's because I've been using it as my personal garden for the last few days. Whenever one of the girls on the floor has needed some cheering up, I've given her a flower to wish on. We must be entering one of the depressing dips of the school year because I've been busy giving out flowers. That's why it looks weeded."

"Makes sense." Rick looked down at the card again and then at the front of the envelope. "This card doesn't make much sense, though."

Another tap sounded on Katie's half-opened door. This time she knew it was Nicole by the way she knocked.

"Come on in, Nicole. You're just in time for the meeting of the Junior Sleuths Club."

Nicole entered gracefully and cast a shy smile at Rick before looking at Katie. "Hi."

"Have you guys met yet? I mean officially?" Katie pointed back and forth. "Rick, Nicole. Nicole, Rick."

"Nicole Sanders." She extended her hand to Rick with a lot more class than Katie's attempted introduction. "I'm Katie's floor partner."

Rick did his impressive-manners thing. "I'm Rick Doyle. Katie's boyfriend. It's good to meet you after all I've heard about you from Katie. It sounds like the two of you are having a good time so far this year."

"I guess I could say the same thing about the two of you." Nicole's eyes looked fresh and sparkly as she smiled at Rick. Katie loved that Nicole and Rick were hitting it off. It mattered very much to Katie that all her friends were friends with each other. In this new season of life, now that Christy and Todd were married, and Doug and Tracy were busy with their new baby, Katie wanted her friends from earlier years to blend with her current friends.

She realized that was the same reason Rick had wanted her to be friendlier with Eli since he was living with Rick and already was part of Todd and Christy's circle of friends.

Note to self: Don't be so stubborn and reactionary. If Rick wants you to be nice to his roommate, remember that you also want him to be nice to your floormate. It's the same thing.

Nicole turned to Katie. "I think I missed the part about the sleuth club when I came in."

Nodding toward the bouquet in an effort to come off sounding nonchalant, Katie said, "They aren't from Rick. The enclosed card is pretty cryptic. We were just trying to figure out who sent them."

Rick still had the card in his hand. He looked at the envelope again. "Are you sure they were for you? There's no last name. Maybe they were for a different Katie."

Katie froze. Her hand slowly covered her mouth as her eyes grew wide. Nicole had the same reaction with equally open eyes.

"I take it there is another Katie on this floor?" Rick asked, looking at both of them.

"She's not in this dorm, but yeah, there is another Katie. She's an RA too."

"She's in Sophie Hall," Nicole added. "And you're not going to believe this, but yesterday I heard she got engaged."

Katie felt her stomach drop.

Rick read the card. " 'I'm so glad you said yes.' "

The three of them exchanged glances.

" 'Our future starts now,' " Katie repeated, having memorized what seemed like a strange message on the card. "Oh man, oh man, oh man! This is not good. This is not good at all. How could I have been such a doof? I need to fix this. I have to take this over to Sophie Hall right now."

"First thing you'll need is some more flowers to fix the bouquet," Rick said. "I know what a bouquet this size costs, and I'm thinking her boyfriend, or actually, her fiancée, must be pretty upset that she hasn't said anything about receiving it."

"You're right. We need more flowers. Let's go right now." Katie grabbed her bag. "Come on! You have a flower shop you've been to, right?" She reached for Rick's hand. "The one where you bought the bouquet for me a few months ago."

"You should take the flowers with you," Nicole said. "That way you'll know what to add."

"Right! Good thinking." Katie scooped up the bouquet and paused, looking at Nicole. "Come with us."

"Me?"

"Please? You have a much better eye for stuff like this than I do. I'll probably order all the wrong flowers and make an even bigger mess of this."

"Okay, sure, I'll come."

The three of them hurried down the hall and climbed into Rick's cherry red Mustang.

"My dad used to have a Mustang," Nicole said from the backseat, as Rick's car rumbled out of the parking lot and he headed into town.

"What year was his? Do you know?"

"I don't know. It was blue, and it was a convertible. He sold it when I was in junior high so I don't remember a lot about it except how fun it was to pile in the backseat on a summer's evening and go for ice cream cones."

"Did you grow up around here?" Rick asked.

"No, I grew up in Santa Barbara."

"Really? That's where my mom grew up," Rick said. "Did your family live there long?"

"My dad has lived in Santa Barbara his whole life. He might know your mom. Wouldn't that be strange?"

Rick told Nicole his mom's first name and maiden name, and Nicole kept the conversation going with details of where she grew up and how much things had changed in what was once a sleepy coastal town.

Katie appreciated the way Nicole was keeping the conversation going. She was too flustered at the moment to think of things to talk about. All she cared about was restoring this bouquet to its original vivaciousness and handing it over to Katie in Sophie Hall. As Rick pulled into the shopping center, Katie mentally rehearsed her apology speech for the other Katie.

Rick held the door open for Katie and Nicole as they entered the flower shop. Fortunately, they were the only ones in the shop, which made Katie's condensed confession to the clerk less painful than if a larger audience had listened in.

The woman looked at Katie with a mixture of sympathy and humor. "Not a problem," she said with a sweep of her hand. "I actually think I remember this bouquet. We used lilies, didn't we? Stargazer, I think."

"That's right," Katie said.

"Let me take that from you." The woman reached for the bouquet. "We'll work on this right away. It will take about half an hour. Maybe a little less. Would you like to wait or come back?"

Katie looked at Rick.

"It's up to you," he said.

"We'll come back."

The three of them exited, and Katie said, "How about ice cream for everyone? It's on me. Not exactly a summer evening, but we could roll down the windows on Rick's car and crank up the heater, drive around the block, and pretend it's a convertible."

"Or we could just go sit inside that coffee shop over there," Rick suggested.

"I'm for that." Nicole wrapped her arms around herself as a chilling breeze cropped up. Nicole was in a short-sleeved top. They had run out of the dorm so quickly she hadn't had time to stop for a sweater.

"Fine, but I'm still paying. You guys are both being really great about this. I feel awful. I can't believe I didn't consider that maybe the flowers weren't for me."

Rick put his arm around her shoulders, as they walked toward the Bella Barista coffee shop. "Why didn't you ask me if I had sent the flowers? That would have cleared up the mystery, or at least started you on the track to solving the problem."

"I kind of did ask you."

"When?"

"On the phone. On Sunday. Or maybe it was Monday. I don't remember when, but I know I brought it up. Sort of."

"Do you remember how you brought it up?"

"First, you need to know that right away, when they were delivered to me on Saturday, I assumed they were from you. But then the note didn't make any sense. Do you remember when I said during a phone call that my news was *mixed* like a big *bouquet*? And then I tried to thank you for being so great."

"I thought you were paying me a compliment."

"I was."

"Weren't you thanking me for taking out the trash the other night at Christy's?"

"Yes, but it was more than just your taking out the toxic popcorn trash. I was offering a sort of universal thank you for everything you do for me, including the flowers." Katie looked up at him and offered one of her cutest grins.

Rick smiled back.

She slipped her arm around his middle. "You're my hero. You know that, don't you?"

Rick pressed his lips against the side of her head and kissed her hair. She wished she had taken a shower and freshened up before he arrived. She also felt a little awkward walking next to Nicole while Rick was snuggling with her. Not that she minded the snuggling.

Rick let go of Katie and went ahead of both of them to hold open the door as if he still were auditioning for the role of Katie's hero.

"Thanks." Nicole stepped into the warm shop first. She drew in a deep breath. "I love the smell of coffee, don't you?"

"I always think it smells better than it tastes," Katie said.

"Not me. I love coffee. Have you had any of their espresso drinks here? They make great decaf double Americanos," Nicole said.

"Americanos? That's what Rick usually orders. Isn't that what you like, Rick?" Katie asked.

He nodded, looking up at the menu on the wall behind the barista station. "I haven't been here before. Nice menu. Easy to read. Great lighting."

Katie turned aside to Nicole. "I should warn you. He always 'takes notes' whenever we go to cafés."

"Do you know what you would like?" The guy at the cash register was looking at Katie.

She pointed at Nicole to go first. Nicole went with her recommended decaf double Americano. Rick ordered the same. Katie was considering the fall pumpkin harvest latte but caved to peer pressure and said, "Make that three of those."

She pulled out her wallet, but Rick stopped her. "Let me get this."

"But I told you guys this was my treat. I want to do something to thank you for coming with me and helping me fix my gigantic flub."

Rick smiled at her and gave her a wink. "And I want to pay so that you'll have a reason to keep thanking me for being so great."

Katie smiled back. She felt so happy. Not just because Rick was home, even though that was great. And not because he was paying for the coffee like a gallant gentleman, although she had to admit, that was pretty nice.

She was happy because Rick seemed different. He seemed like he was back to his old self—his charming, suave self that she had been so crazy about in high school. He seemed to have lightened up on his role of responsible businessman, and the less serious, more flirty side of his personality was coming on strong.

Katie liked Rick more than ever.

Without giving her response to him a second thought, Katie tilted her chin up, and right there, in front of Nicole and the employee at the cash register, she flippantly said, "Fine. I'll agree to let you pay on one condition."

"Okay, what's that?" Rick's chocolate brown eyes were melting her happy little heart.

"First you have to kiss me."

I'm going to invent a time travel machine. That's what I'm going to do." Katie pulled her comforter up to her chin. She was lying on a futon mattress on Nicole's dorm room floor. It was well after midnight, and the two of them were going over the details of the past six and a half hours.

"Yeah, that's what I'm going to do. I'm going to figure out a way to go back in time and warn myself before I do all the outrageous, unthought-through things that I do. Did you see the look on Rick's face? Of course you did. You were standing right there. I've never seen him look like that. It was like I had wounded him."

"He handled it great, Katie. When he kissed you on the cheek and handed his credit card to the guy at the register, he made it all look clever and smooth. No one knew it was an impulsive comment on your part." Nicole turned over on her back in bed and adjusted the covers.

"I knew it was impulsive; Rick knew it was impulsive," Katie said. "Which is why he brought it up while we were having coffee. And what you said was great, by the way. I think he needed to hear your thoughts on how 'some couples' make too big of an issue of one aspect of the relationship and how the whole relationship needs to be in balance."

"Katie, the only reason I said all that was because I thought we were just having a conversation about relationships. I had no idea what

I said had special significance for you and Rick because you haven't kissed yet. I mean, I just assumed once you announced that you two were officially a couple that your expressions of affection had extended to kissing. Does that make sense?"

"Yeah." It made perfect sense. Only she and Rick apparently weren't like other couples. That reality had been clear from the beginning of their back-and-forth relationship.

"You know," Katie added, "Rick's point was true too. In many ways, the reason our relationship is in balance, or at least more in balance than any of his previous relationships, is because our physical expression is at a very low level."

"And that is so commendable," Nicole said.

"Yeah, if I were looking for a badge of commendation for handling a budding relationship, I guess I'd be happy that we're so 'commendable.' But I don't want commendable. I want romance. I'm ready for romance, Nicole. I'm ready to be cherished."

"Rick does cherish you. That was very clear tonight, not just by the conversation but also by the way he treated you. He's trying to do what's best for your relationship."

"I know, I know, I know. Rick is the embodiment of all Christian virtue. And I'm trying to respect his preferences, you know? I mean, I didn't come into this relationship, especially the dating part of our relationship, with the same super-high abstinence sort of objectives that he had."

Nicole gave Katie a surprised looked.

"I'm just telling you the truth. At the risk of sounding like a hussy, I don't see anything wrong with couples kissing, particularly once they're at the boyfriend–girlfriend stage. But he does. At least, kissing on the lips. He's harbored some sort of idea in his head that it's better for our relationship this way. That may be all fine and good in theory, but in reality, when I feel really close to him like I did tonight, I want to kiss the boy!"

"I know what you mean," Nicole said quietly.

"I shouldn't say kiss the 'boy.' What I want is to kiss Rick Doyle, the man. I already kissed Rick, the boy. Twice."

Nicole sat up and leaned over the edge of her bed, giving Katie a wide-eyed, do-tell-all look.

"It was a long time ago. In high school. Well, I was in high school, but he was in college. We went to the Rose Parade in Pasadena, which, by the way, was a much cooler thing to do then than apparently it is now."

"How long ago was this?" Nicole was on her side, her arm propping her up.

"I don't know. Four years ago. Maybe it will be five this January."

"And he kissed you?"

Katie nodded. "At midnight. I mean, it's mandatory, right? Happy New Year! Kiss the girl you're closest to, then ignore her for a long time, keep her wondering, and then kiss her again when you're in a cast and all vulnerable, and she's really insecure."

"That was the second kiss?" Nicole seemed to be keeping up with Katie's sporadic hop down memory lane.

"Yeah. That one was at the apartment he used to share with Todd and Doug in San Diego. He was doing handsprings into the pool that afternoon before Christy and I got there, showing off like a big college boy, and he twisted his wrist and tore something or sprained something. The guys took him to the hospital."

"And he had a cast?"

"It was actually more like a big wrap bandage. But the point is, I felt sorry for him. He was acting more humble than usual. Or maybe the painkillers they gave him at the hospital made him seem more vulnerable. Anyway, that night, out in the dark in front of his apartment, when he smashed his face against mine, I let him kiss me. Then, when he started to pull away, I kissed him back. It was pretty unromantic. I felt stupid. He ignored me the whole next day, and that was that."

"Katie, you make it sound so unpleasant. I can't imagine that kissing Rick could be *that* bad."

Katie sighed. "It wasn't horrible, but it wasn't exactly romantic. I just really wanted him to kiss me tonight."

"Do you think if he kissed you at the cash register at Bella Barista, it would have been romantic?"

Katie twisted her mouth back and forth. She hated it when her close friends nailed her illogical statements so accurately. If Nicole would be somehow combative, Katie could at least start up a good argument, but she knew she couldn't disagree.

"Okay, so not in front of the barista boy. But really, Nicole, enough with the patience and planning and waiting and all that stuff Rick was talking about."

"I thought what he said was mature and noble."

"Yeah, but the way I'm feeling, I want to throw caution to the wind. He just needs to kiss me and get it over with."

Nicole laughed softly. "I hate to say this, Katie, but now you're the one who isn't sounding very romantic."

Katie stretched to retrieve the bag of M&Ms that ten minutes ago they had put out of reach to end impulsive eating. She popped three candies in her mouth and gave Nicole a comical snarl.

Nicole laughed lightly and threw a pillow at Katie.

"Okay, so I'm not romantic. Neither is Rick. Therein lies the secret of what makes us such a great couple. We're the ultimate 'friends forever.'" Katie crossed her eyes and stuck out her tongue in a gagging expression.

"Stop it!" Nicole threw another pillow at her. "You two are a great couple. Rick is a great guy. I mean, the way he sat there over coffee and openly talked through the whole topic of kissing and relationships and the value of planning ahead ... what woman wouldn't want a guy who has so thoroughly thought through every step?"

Katie laughed.

"What?"

"'Thoroughly thought through.' Did you hear yourself say that? Now there's a tongue twister."

"I think you're going into sugar overload," Nicole said.

"I think you're right." Katie closed up the bag and pushed it farther away. "I just can't handle my sugar the way I used to when I was a kid."

"Katie, I want to say something to you, and I want you to hear this as coming from only the best of intentions because that's how I mean it."

"Okay, give it to me straight, sister. I can take it."

"I think if you don't press Rick about demonstrating his affection for you physically, it will just happen naturally and in balance, and it will be very romantic."

"I know."

"Even if he does have some sort of hidden plan, like you accused him of at the Bella Barista ..."

"I didn't accuse him. That wasn't an accusation. That was a friendly challenge. Rick understands my sense of humor. He can take it."

"Are you sure?"

"Yeah. Why?"

"Well," Nicole said slowly, reaching over and retrieving her pillow. "The first part was cute, when you said that the downside of dating a superhero was that you had to go by his code of conduct. It was the next part that came across pretty strong."

"All I said was that he had been giving his lips a rest for a long time."

"Actually, Katie, your exact words were, 'You might as well go shave your head and become a monk since your lips have forgotten how to find their way to mine.'"

Katie grimaced. "Did I actually say that?"

Nicole nodded.

"Did you have a recorder on or something?"

"No, I just remembered it because, well ... it was a fairly memorable statement."

"You're right. That was pretty severe. I think I was a little too amped up by that point." She snapped her fingers. "You know what I think? I think that Belly Barista Boy gave us regular coffee and not decaf and more than a double. I think he gave me super-uber caffeine, and it made me go a little crazy during that part of the conversation. So, see, it really was the java speaking, not me."

Nicole settled under her covers but didn't say anything, which let Katie know that Nicole wasn't buying any of it.

"Okay." Katie reached over to her jeans on the floor beside her and pulled her phone out of the pocket. "I better call Rick and apologize again."

"I think he accepted your apology on the way back to the flower shop. And by the way, I think when we went to Sophie Hall, the other Katie accepted your apology really well when we gave her the flowers. I don't think you have any outstanding apologies you need to make."

Katie snapped her phone shut. "I thought she took it extremely well too."

"It helped that the lady at the flower shop called her before we arrived and explained it was their oversight for not putting the name on the enclosure card. I'm glad she checked the computer and saw that Katie's fiancé put his name on the note when he placed the order online. The flower shop should have put his name on the card and her full name on the envelope."

"I just appreciate that the lady at the flower shop started all over with a fresh bouquet. I think the second one was even more gorgeous than the first one."

"I agree."

"You also have to agree that the lady at the flower shop was pretty nice to us."

"She was wonderful. Rick was pretty wonderful too. I think the lady liked that he bought the flowers for you and me. I know pink gerbera daisies aren't your favorite."

Katie looked over at the vase on Nicole's dresser with the perky pink bouquet. "No, but they're your favorite."

"I know, but you were nice to say that you liked them too, to make Rick happy about giving us the gift."

"Yeah, well, I'm all in favor of making Rick happy about giving gifts." Katie lay back on the air mattress, staring at the ceiling. Nicole had draped sheer fabric across her ceiling, making her room look like a cozy fairyland cloud. "How did you do that?"

"Do what?"

"The fabric across the ceiling."

"Never underestimate the power of a woman with a staple gun, a glue gun, and an insatiable passion for decorating everything she can get her hands on."

Katie laughed. "It's your art. I love it. You know, you would like Rick's mom. She's the same way. She loves to decorate. She also loves to celebrate by making her home and birthdays and holidays beautiful. Which reminds me, I might be staying here over Thanksgiving. So, if you need me to check on anything while you're gone, I can cover whatever floor responsibilities we have."

"You're staying here? Really?"

"Yeah." Katie hated the yes-I'm-practically-an-orphan-but-please-don't-stare feeling that washed over her at that moment.

"Well, guess what? I think I'm staying here too."

"You are? Why?"

"I feel like Little Orphan Annie."

"Tell me about it."

Nicole said, "Well, my parents are leaving for Singapore on Wednesday for an international pastors' conference, and my sister is going to be with her boyfriend's family in Idaho. I could go home to Santa Barbara and have Thanksgiving dinner at my aunt and uncle's, but I think I would rather stay here."

"Why don't you and me do something together? We could go on a road trip."

"I thought you were spending Thanksgiving with Rick's family."

"I might. His parents just moved to their new house, and they probably aren't ready to entertain yet. Like I said, his mom loves to go all out. Last Easter she had a huge Sunday afternoon dinner. We all sat at a big table with china plates and crystal. Very posh. I'm thinking that if she can't make Thanksgiving a Norman Rockwell reenactment, she probably is going to wait and do Christmas in full gala mode."

"That's the way my mom has always done the holidays," Nicole said. "I could go home, but I would be in the house, all alone. It would be too depressing."

"We definitely should do something."

Nicole nodded and covered her mouth as a yawn snuck in. "Oh, excuse me. I'm fading fast, Katie. Would you mind if I turned out the light? We can keep talking, if you want, but I have to warn you that I might fall asleep."

"That's fine with me. I'm ready to let this very long and very exasperating day be over. I have a class at eight in the morning, and I know I'm going to be dead when my alarm goes off at seven. At least I took my shower tonight. I was really wishing I had taken one before I saw Rick because, next to you, I was definitely not the freshest pumpkin in the patch."

Katie could see Nicole smiling at her punch line right before she turned out the light.

"By the way, Katie, thanks for letting me go to dinner with you and Rick. I felt like I was crashing your date."

"No, it was fun having you there. Besides, what were you going to do? I snatched you off to the flower shop and dragged you with us to Sophie Hall. By the time you finished being my moral support in repairing my big blunder, the cafeteria was closed. You pretty much didn't have any choice but to come with us, and I'm glad you did. It makes me happy the way you and Rick get along so well. He wanted me to be nicer to his roommate, but it took me far too long. I appreciate what he was trying to say now because I can see how great it feels when everybody in your different life circles gets along with each other. Do you know what I mean?"

The steady ticking of Nicole's antique desk clock was the only reply Katie received.

"Wow. You weren't kidding when you said you were going to fall asleep on me. I thought I was fast, but that's impressively fast. Remind me to tell you in the morning how quickly you fell asleep on me."

Katie pulled her comforter up to her chin and snuggled in. "I'm still liking my idea of a time machine," she muttered to herself since Nicole was already asleep. "I definitely would do this day over. Except not this part. I'd keep this sleepover time. I feel at home with you, my new friend."

11

What do you mean you're not going to Pizza Doubles Night tomorrow?" Katie was standing next to Rick in line for the movies, but she was on her cell phone with Nicole.

"Phillip just now emailed me. He didn't even give a reason. He just said, 'Maybe another time.' I know he didn't mean that. I hate it when guys say things they don't mean."

"What a jerk," Katie said.

Rick calmly pressed his hand on Katie's shoulder. She assumed it was his way of letting her know her voice was elevating and she was talking too loud in such a crowded public place.

"He's not a jerk, Katie. He's a nice guy. I know you would think that too, if you met him."

"Yeah, well, if I ever do meet him, I'm going to have a few choice words for him."

"He probably has a good reason he doesn't want to go with me tomorrow night. I'm not holding it against him. But now it's too late to ask anyone else."

"It's not too late. There has to be someone, Nicole."

Rick pressed Katie's shoulder again. She looked up at him and asked, "What? Am I still too loud?"

Rick smiled. "What about Eli?"

"What about Eli?" Katie asked.

"Who is Eli?" Nicole asked.

Katie looked at Rick and remembered how less than a week ago they had argued at his apartment when he was trying to match up Eli with Katie's floor partner. Katie offered Rick a half grin. "You know what, Nicole? Not only do I have the most understanding and patient and handsome boyfriend in the world, I also have the best matchmaking boyfriend in the world. Would you mind if Rick and I fixed you up with his roommate, Eli? I'm sure he's available."

"Is he the guy on campus security who drives around in the little golf cart?"

"Yeah. That's him. The one with the crazy, light brown hair that always looks like he just got out of the spin cycle on a dryer. The one with the goatee."

"Right. That's who I thought you meant." Nicole didn't sound enthusiastic.

"He's not like you think," Katie said quickly. "He's nothing like he looks. I mean, he looks pretty good in my opinion. He has those pensive eyes that sort of peer into your soul while you're looking the other way. And he grew up in Africa and went to Spain with Todd, and he seems to have a tender heart, you know? Like it's been broken and now he knows how other people feel when they're hurting. I think you'll really hit it off great with Eli. He's an artistic sort of person, and oh, Nicole, he has a great laugh. I mean, a great laugh. He's definitely a catch. Much better than ol' 'feel upset' guy."

Nicole stopped Katie before she could go into a longer pitch on Eli's behalf. "Okay. You had me at 'available.'"

Katie turned to Rick and nodded feverishly with a big grin. She pointed at his cell phone and indicated with her free hand that Rick should call Eli to set it up.

"No way," Rick said.

Katie blinked at him and made a face. "Just a minute, Nicole." She pressed her cell phone against her stomach. "What do you mean, 'no way'?"

"I already invited Eli. I also uninvited him. If you think he's such a perfect match for Nicole, I think you should ask him this time."

"Okay. Fine." Katie put the phone back to her ear. "Nicole? Here's the plan. I'm going to call Eli to see if he's still available tomorrow night, and then I'll give him your number and have him call you back because we're about to go into the movie."

"Thanks, Katie."

"Don't thank me yet. Wait until after you spend some time with him tomorrow night. Then you'll thank me, and I'll know you really mean it because he's great."

She hung up and looked at Rick. "Are you sure you don't want to call him?"

"I'm sure." Rick scrolled through his phone list and handed her his cell phone as the line moved into the theater.

Katie squinted at the screen on Rick's much-more-elaborate phone than hers.

"All you have to do is push the button."

Katie pressed it and said, "Yeah, that's what Christy said the night I tried to make the popcorn at her house."

"Hey, about that popcorn," Rick said. "I heard from Todd last night that you bought it at a garage sale."

Now Katie was pressing her hand on Rick's shoulder. He was definitely talking too loud in a crowded public place. Blessedly, Eli answered his phone on the first ring.

"Eli. Hey. It's Katie. Hi. How are you?"

Why is it I still go monosyllabic whenever I try to talk to this guy? I am such a social doof.

"What's going on, Katie?"

"I wondered, well, actually, Rick and I wondered, Rick is right here with me at the movies, we're walking into the movies right now, and I'm calling you on his phone."

She thought she heard Eli muffling a chuckle.

"Anyway, we were wondering if you weren't doing anything tomorrow night, Friday night, if you wanted to go to the Pizza Doubles Night at Crown Hall."

"I thought you guys already uninvited me to that event."

"Well, now I'm un-uninviting you, and that's the same as re-inviting you. All you have to do is say, 'Sure, I'd be happy to call your floormate, beautiful Nicole, and tell her I'd be honored to accompany her to the cafeteria to make a pizza with her tomorrow night.' What do you say? Seven o'clock? Meet us in the lobby at Crown Hall?"

A long pause followed on the other end. Katie glanced at Rick. He was repressing a grin. She used her free arm to loop circles in the air as an indication for Eli to hurry up with his decision. "Well?"

"Did he hang up?" Rick asked. "If he did, you can't exactly blame the guy."

"Eli?" Katie pressed the phone closer to her ear. "I can hear you breathing, Eli."

He laughed that fantastic, from-the-gut laugh of his. "That was just way too much fun watching you sweat like that."

"What do you mean, 'watch me sweat'? Did I press the camera button on Rick's phone?"

"No. Look over at the popcorn machine."

Katie turned toward the concessions stand. Eli stood leaning against a pillar and holding a large-sized popcorn. He had a bandana tied around his head, and his hair danced in every direction under it.

Katie turned and slugged Rick in the arm but not very hard. "You knew all along that he was here."

"Yes, I did." Rick's grin was wide and full of mischief. "Did I forget to mention that Eli was coming to the movie with Carley?"

"Carley?" Katie spewed the name way too loud, and she knew it. Lowering her voice, she said, "When did Eli start going out with Carley?"

"Tonight when she asked him."

Katie had never quite found a way to settle into a peaceful, easy, ebb-and-flow sort of relationship with Carley, a girl on her floor. Last summer Carley was hired to work at the Dove's Nest with Katie, but it always seemed to Katie that Carley was vying for Rick's romantic attention. When Carley and some other girls pulled a practical joke on Katie a little over a month ago, the two of them had a face-to-face talk that seemed to settle things between them and put them into a better place relationally. Still, Carley wasn't at the top of Katie's list of favorite people.

This surprise, though, hit Katie harder than she would have expected. Carley definitely wasn't the right girl for Eli. Nicole was a much better choice, and Katie knew it.

She and Rick handed their tickets to the attendant and crossed the lobby to where Eli stood by the popcorn machine.

"So?" Katie gave Eli a bright-eyed, expectant expression. "Is an answer forthcoming, oh-great-rebel-without-a-soda-to-go-with-all-that-popcorn?"

"Yes. The answer is yes. I'll go with you tomorrow night," Eli said.

"Not with me. With Nicole."

"Right. That's what I meant. I got the impression it's a double date."

"It is. Okay. Good. Here. Hang on just a second, okay?" Katie pulled out her phone, pushed Nicole's name, and waited for her to answer. She felt a funny sort of panic, as if Carley would appear at any moment and make things more awkward than they already were.

"Hey, Nicole, Eli is right here, and I'm going to let him talk to you." She handed the phone over before hearing Nicole say anything.

Eli did a commendable job of sounding warm and interested in Nicole, as he confirmed the plans. He told her, "See you then," and handed the phone back to Katie.

She snapped it shut. "Great! All set then. Thanks, Eli. Ready, Rick? Or did you want to get some popcorn?"

"Not me. Do you want some?"

"No. I've lost my appetite for popcorn lately."

"Funny," Eli said. "Christy said the same thing."

"You're just making that up."

"No, I'm not."

"When did you see Christy?"

"She and Todd were in line behind us for the last showing, but it sold out, so they were going to eat something and come back."

"That means they're coming to the same showing we are. Cool!" Katie looked at Rick. "We should go in and save seats for all four of us."

"Would you mind saving another seat?" Eli asked.

"Are you going to see it again?" Rick said.

"No. I was part of the cutoff group that didn't make it to the sold-out matinee. I got some studying done in the interim, believe it or not."

"What about Carley?" Katie asked.

"She went to the earlier show. She and her roommate got their tickets online so they had no trouble getting in."

"And they left you?" Katie said.

Eli shrugged. "What can I say?"

"Come on." Rick took Katie's hand. "We'll save some seats, Eli. Tell Todd and Christy we went on in."

"This is getting stranger and stranger by the minute," Katie mumbled. She and Rick had been talking about going to this sequel to a movie they had enjoyed last February on one of their early dates. As is the case with many long-anticipated sequels, opening night was the best time to go in spite of the crowds, just to be among the first to see it. Katie hated being in a group of people when they talked about a sequel she hadn't yet seen. College students at Rancho Corona avidly kept up on films and talked about them at meals.

"We should have gotten organized," Katie said, as she and Rick hurried into the theater to snatch five seats together. "If we had known Todd and Christy were coming, we could have eaten with them."

"Maybe they'll want to go out to dessert afterwards." The theater was filling quickly, and the noise made it difficult for Katie to hear what Rick had said as they made their way up the steps.

"Did you say they might want to go out to the *desert* afterwards?"

"No, not out to the desert. Out to get some dessert. Coffee? Cheesecake? Pie?"

"Christy will probably want cheesecake. She had a craving for it the other night. I asked her if the craving meant she might be pregnant, but she said no."

"How about here?" Rick slid into an aisle about halfway back, and Katie followed. The seats were near the end of the aisle, but the way the auditorium was filling up it was going to be impossible to find five seats together in the center.

Spreading their jackets on the three seats in between them, Katie and Rick sat on either end and watched the entrance for their friends.

Of all people, Carley came around the corner, spotted them, waved, and came up to their row.

"I thought she went to the last showing," Katie muttered low enough so Rick wouldn't hear her.

"Hi, you two." Carley scooted down the aisle and stood in the space in front of the empty seats they were trying to save. "I just came to say hi. I saw Eli, and he told me you were here. You are going to love this film. The end is a big surprise. It's not what you expect."

"Carley, don't you dare tell us what happens!" Katie felt her face turning red.

"Don't worry. I wasn't going to tell you. I'm only saying it's not what you expect. You know the guy in the first film who had the tooth that came out? Well — "

Katie cut her off. "Carley, don't! Don't say anything. Nothing! Not a word! Oh, look. There's Todd and Christy. They're going to want to sit right where you're standing."

"No problem. I'm leaving. I just wanted to say hi and also to say thanks, Rick, for the flowers. That was really nice of you."

Rick nodded politely and stood so that Todd and Christy could slide past him while Carley waved and inched her way out of the aisle the other direction.

"You guys having a fight?" Todd asked Katie.

"No. Why?"

"You're sitting so far apart." Cool surfer-guy Todd gave Katie a half grin that showed his dimple and even more clearly showed that he was messing with her.

"Don't start with me tonight, Todd. Not a good idea. We were sitting apart so we could save seats for you two." Katie stood up and slid past Christy so Katie could sit in her rightful place, next to Rick. Christy sat on the other side of Katie and gave her arm a squeeze.

"How fun! I can't believe this worked out," Christy said. "You know how so often we've tried to get together with both of you, but we couldn't coordinate our schedules? Well, this is perfect, and none of us planned it."

"I know. This is great." Katie's response wasn't entirely enthusiastic. She turned to Rick and in a low voice said, "So, flowers, huh? Anything I should know?"

Rick leaned close and whispered in Katie's ear. His breath tickled her hair. "I wanted to do something nice to thank all my employees for doing such a great job the past few months while I was going back and forth to Arizona. I went back to the flower shop since the lady there was so helpful to us the other night. She put together some small arrangements for all the women employees."

"Just for the women?"

"Yes, just for the women. For the men, I got pocketknives."

"That was nice of you."

"You know what else is nice of me?" Rick asked, stretching his arm around Katie's shoulder and drawing her close. "It's also nice that I'm here, and we get to spend time together like this."

Katie felt herself settling back in his partial embrace. Leaning her head on his shoulder, she said, "Yeah, this is nice. For the record, if I still worked at the Dove's Nest, I would have wanted the pocketknife instead of the flowers."

"I know," Rick said. He kissed the top of her head.

"Especially if it was one of those tiny pocketknives that have the little collapsible scissors. Eli has one. Did you know they make those in colors? I saw a red one that matched your car. You know what?" Katie pulled back and looked at Rick. "You should get a little red one and keep it in your glove compartment."

"Hey, what did you hear back about your car?"

Katie made an exaggerated pout. "I'm afraid Baby Bummer is heading for the glue factory."

"What does that mean?"

"I don't know. My dad used to say it. I think it has to do with old horses that they used to make glue out of or something."

"Are you saying your car isn't repairable?"

Katie nodded. "The mechanic left me a message today and said he found one of the parts online in Hawaii, but it was too rusted to use. I have to call him back tomorrow and basically agree with him on the inevitable. She's done. She was a good friend while I had her, but sadly, our great relationship has come to an end."

Christy, who apparently overheard Katie, asked, "Are you talking about Baby Hummer?"

Katie turned to her and nodded.

"Katie, how sad."

"I know. It's like the end of an era."

Todd reached across Christy's middle and gave Katie's arm a squeeze. He could be a big goof-off, but when he wanted, Todd could be sympathetic. "Sorry to hear that, Katie. I felt like it was the end of an era when Gus the Bus bit the dust."

"What are you going to do for a car?" Christy asked.

"I have no idea. It hasn't been as bad as I thought it would be this week not having a car, but that's because Nicole has let me borrow hers. I'll have to see if I can sell Baby Hummer off in parts or something."

"Do you think you might keep some of the parts?" Todd asked.

"What, like you saved the backseat out of Gus the Bus when you got in that accident?"

Todd's half grin returned. "I could make some furniture for you."

"I'll get back to you on that," Katie said, her sarcasm riding high. She looked past Todd and saw Eli headed their way. Todd saw him too and motioned for him to take the saved seat next to him.

Eli sat down and held out his bucket of popcorn. "You guys want some?"

Todd was the only one who took a handful.

The lights dimmed, and the previews began. Katie turned back to Rick, and he cuddled her up close to him. Todd and Christy were snuggled up too. It was one of the double-date scenarios Katie had imagined ever since she and Rick had started dating. They had managed to coordinate far too few of these kinds of times together.

As happy as Katie was, she felt bad for Eli. Talk about a fifth wheel! Katie knew all too well what it was like to be that extra person, as over the years, she had hung out with Christy and Todd and the rest of their gang. In a small—very small—way, Katie wished Carley had changed her ticket so that Eli would at least have someone with him.

Katie leaned closer to Rick and made one of her ongoing notes to herself: *Stop worrying about Eli. This is what you've dreamed about for a long time. Relax! Enjoy the moment!*

The big surprise of the evening wasn't the end of the movie, although it was a brilliant way to tie the story together and leave viewers hungry for a third episode. The surprise was how great the movie turned out to be.

"The second film is never as good as the first," Rick said, as their group exited the theater.

"This one sure was," Todd said.

Christy chimed in, "That part at the end where the guy ..."

Katie grabbed her arm and stopped Christy from finishing her sentence. They were walking past the line of viewers waiting to get into the late-night showing. "I happen to be very sensitive to the proper care of plotlines and punch lines. I just didn't want you to spoil it for any of those guys standing in line."

"Oh. Right." Christy pressed her lips together.

"I'm glad we got in to see it tonight," Katie said. "I would hate to be sitting in the cafeteria tomorrow and overhear a bunch of amateur critics tearing the film apart and giving away all the good parts."

"What if we form our own amateur critics group?" Rick asked. "Katie and I found a new place for coffee. The Bella Barista. Have you guys been there?"

"No," Christy said, as Todd shook his head beside her.

"What about you, Eli?" Katie asked.

"I'm more of a convenience store coffee drinker, as you know."

Everyone turned to look at Katie for an explanation as to why she would know that. She did *not* want to get Christy, Rick, or Todd going on a discussion of her trek to the desert last week with Eli and Joseph.

Diverting the inquisition, Katie said, "How 'bout it? Do you guys want to go for coffee?"

Todd and Christy looked at each other and exchanged a series of shrugs and head bobs that reminded Katie of two birds conversing on a telephone wire.

"We better not," Christy said.

Katie suspected they had used their entertainment funds for the month on the movie and dinner.

Todd and Christy's decision seemed to determine Eli's. He said he was going to head back to the apartment. Looking at Katie in one of his direct ways, he said, "I'll see you tomorrow night."

"Right. Pizza Doubles Night. Crown Hall. 7:00. In the lobby." Katie hoped no one else noticed how choppy her sentences always got around Eli. Her flusteredness bugged her.

The group said their good-byes in the parking lot, and Rick and Katie walked hand-in-hand to his car.

"I didn't tell you yet," Rick said. "My mom is planning on having Thanksgiving dinner at their new house. She said she was going to call you. She wanted you to know you were invited, and I told her I'd make sure you were there."

"That was nice of her. And nice of you. I'd love to have Thanksgiving at your house. Tell your mom I'd be happy to help out if she needs me to do anything."

As they walked, Katie swung their clasped hands between them. "Do you know if she has invited a lot of people?"

"I'm not sure. Why?"

"I was thinking if there was room, it would be nice to include one more person who doesn't have plans for Thanksgiving. But that's only if your mom doesn't mind hosting another orphaned college student."

"You know my mom. I'm sure she wouldn't mind." Rick gave Katie's hand a squeeze. "I'm glad you thought of Eli. I'll tell him he's invited too."

"Eli? I was talking about Nicole. She's not going home for Thanksgiving. In fact, she and I were talking about taking a road trip next weekend if we didn't have any dinner invitations."

"Like I said, you know my mom. I'm sure she wouldn't mind. I'll invite Eli, and you can invite Nicole."

"They're going to think we're trying a little too hard to match them up."

"That's okay. If it works, they'll thank us."

They arrived at Rick's car, and he unlocked the passenger door and opened it for Katie. She was about to slide in when she noticed on the seat a small box with a silver ribbon around it.

"What's this?"

Rick didn't answer. He just gave her a smug grin, as if his surprise was working the way he had planned.

"Is this for me?"

"Why don't you open it and find out?"

Katie pulled the ribbon and opened the small box. Inside was a pocketknife, just like the one she had described to Rick in the theater. Instead of red like Rick's car, this one was yellow, like Baby Hummer.

"Rick! How did you know?"

"I know you, Katie. I knew you would like one. I also knew if I gave you flowers, it wouldn't mean as much to you as one of these. I saw the yellow and thought of your car. That was before I knew it was irreparable."

"This will always remind me of my sunny yellow Baby Hummer," Katie said tenderly.

"Have you opened this kind before? This is where the scissors are, and when you pull this one out, it's a nail file."

"Rick, thank you!" Katie wrapped her arms around him in a warm hug.

As she pulled back, they heard a horn tap and both looked over to see Eli driving past, giving them a hand-held-up-straight-in-the-air sort of wave. Katie could see her wedding wreath was still hanging from his mirror.

"I don't know why he kept that," she muttered. "He said it reminds him to pray. But pray for what?"

"Katie?" Rick put his hand under her chin and drew her face back so that she was looking up at him.

Katie dropped the muttering thoughts she had about Eli and warmed up a smile for Rick. "Sorry. What was I saying?"

"You were saying that you like the knife."

"Yes, I do. I like the knife. And I like you. Very much."

"Good. Because I like you very much." Rick grinned. "Do you want to get some gelato?"

"Gelato? Sure. Do you have two plane tickets to Venice hidden there in the pocket of your jacket?"

"We can get gelato right here in town."

"Where?"

"The place we went with Nicole. The Bella Barista. I saw gelato on the menu and thought you and I needed to go back there and call a truce."

"A truce on what?"

"The ice cream date fiasco from last summer with the taste test. Square box versus round box?"

Katie tilted her head back and groaned. "Please. I'm trying to forget that mess. All of that happened a long time ago when I was outspoken and impulsive and demanding. As you and I both know, I've changed dramatically since then."

Rick laughed.

"Okay. Maybe not dramatically. But I do know that I wish I hadn't made such a big deal of the ice cream, and, well ... everything else that night." Katie left unspoken how, the same night she had pressed him into an ice cream tasting challenge, she also had pressed him about his determination not to invite kissing into their relationship. The challenge hadn't ended well.

Part of Rick's later attempt to smooth over the evening was his own awkward taste test, which Katie found to be very irritating. Rick used only one carton of ice cream and thereby rigged the test in what he said was an effort to be clever.

"That whole ice cream event was a fun idea gone wrong. Very wrong," Katie said. "Can we not revisit any of that?"

"Agreed," Rick said. "That's why I think the gelato is the answer. It's a fresh start. We can eat ice cream without any of the conflict over container shape or taste. What do you say?"

"Okay. New beginnings. Bring on the gelato." Katie got into the car and smiled to herself. *Rick Doyle, you have to be the most determined man on the planet. Once you get going on something, you never want to let go until you have the pieces in place just the way you like them.*

Katie reminded herself that was a good quality and a complement to her sporadic way of accomplishing goals.

"You know, if we hadn't finally agreed a few weeks ago to stop trying to come up with nicknames for each other, I think I'd call you 'Bulldog' right about now."

"Bulldog?" Rick's response made it clear he wasn't excited about that one.

With a wave of her hand she said, "Never mind." Pulling out the nail file on her new pocketknife, Katie worked on smoothing the edges of her thumbnail. She wished she hadn't brought up the nickname topic. For months Rick had been trying to come up with just the right nickname for her, but every option made her wince. Except "Katie-girl." She liked that one, but Rick decided he didn't.

About three weeks ago, as they were leaving church together and Rick suddenly announced that he didn't like the tag "Katie-girl," she had stopped and said, "End game. That's it." She told Rick from now on she only wanted him to call her Katie, and she would stick with Rick, except for those occasional moments when his last name fit the occasion and "Doyle" just tumbled off her lips.

They had settled with a truce on the quest for a nickname that Sunday morning. Katie hoped this jaunt to Bella Barista would provide a truce on the quest for a pleasant ice cream experience for both of them.

Half an hour later, Katie was telling herself, *So far, so good! As a matter of fact, everything about tonight has been good. Very good. Maybe the best date ever for us.*

When they ordered their gelato, just to be cute, Rick reinacted the kiss on Katie's cheek as he handed over his credit card at the register.

"What was that for?" she asked.

"I thought I'd start a new tradition. You said last time we were here that if I was going to pay I had to kiss you. I like that. From now on, every time we come here, if I pay, I get to kiss you."

"And what if I pay?"

"Then you get to kiss me."

"Promise?" Katie raised an eyebrow.

Rick grinned at her and kissed her again, this time on the forehead. It was sweet, like a blessing or a brotherly gesture of affection. She let the warmth of his kiss on her forehead settle on her and soothe her inside. For perhaps the first time Katie felt content with Rick's gestures of affection. She didn't have to try to hide an expression of disappointment that he wasn't sweeping her up in his strong arms, dipping her like a ballroom dancer, and planting a big one on her lips.

He was showing her she was cherished. Adored. Why hadn't she seen his intentions this way before?

Affectionate Rick and enamored Katie sat across from each other at one of the small corner tables. They comfortably jostled their feet against each other and shared tastes of their gelato flavors. The soft amber lighting of the low hanging lights and the stirring Italian music in the background made their moment as romantic to Katie as if they were side by side in a gondola floating down a canal in Venice.

Rick reached over and smoothed back her hair, touching her cheek and telling her how much he liked her hair, her freckles, her green eyes. "Sometimes your eyes look deep, like jade," he said. "Those are the times when I know you're thinking hard. It's like the light dims on the outside and turns to the inside. Then other times your eyes are the color of grass or leaves in the spring. I can always tell when you're happy. Your eyes look like springtime."

"What color are they now?" Katie laced her fingers in his.

"Springtime. Definitely, springtime."

"Your eyes are like hot chocolate right now. Real hot chocolate. Not the milk chocolate powder that comes in a packet. They're like dark chocolate. Like my chocolate mint gelato." Katie playfully held up a small spoonful of her gelato next to Rick's eyes. He posed, widening his eyes as she made the comparison.

"No, your eyes are darker. Much more mysterious."

Rick gave her a dashing-man-of-mystery look, posing like an author of suspense novels, with his hand on his chin.

Katie laughed. "There you go. That's the look you want on your next business card." She moved from her seat. "Hey, I'm going to get some water. Do you want anything to drink?"

"Yes, I'd like an Americano to take with us."

"Take with us? Are we going somewhere?"

Rick checked his watch. "Sure. Why not? How much time do you have before you lose your glass slipper and get locked out of your dorm?"

Katie held out her foot. "No glass slippers, as you can see, and you forget that I have a master key. Hey, that rhymed!"

"Clever. Now get me an Americano and let's go."

"Okay, Mr. Bossy. I take it I'm paying?" Katie asked.

"I don't see why you shouldn't." Rick was making it clear that he was enjoying the banter as well as everything else about this date as much as Katie was.

"Okay. Fine then." She reached for his arm, pulled him up, and marched him to the cash register. "One double Americano and one medium Darjeeling tea. To go. Got that?"

The woman at the register said yes and Katie pulled some cash out of her pocket. As she handed the money over, she went up on her tiptoes and placed a dainty kiss on Rick's cheek. Grinning at him she said, "I think this new tradition might work out nicely."

They left with their steaming beverages and their arms wrapped around each other. "It's not as cold as it was the other night when we were here," Katie said.

Looking up, she noticed a handful of stars. The gauzy cloud cover that usually blocked the skies from them this time of year had cleared enough to reveal sprinklings of the twinkling beauties here and there. "It's a nice night."

"It's going to be even nicer where we're going." Rick opened the car door for her in his Prince Charming mode.

"Oh, a little clue as to where we're going. Aren't you Mr. Suave tonight?"

Rick looked as if he enjoyed being Mr. Suave. He kept that look all the way back to the Rancho Corona campus. Katie felt a wistful sweep of disappointment. She thought he meant they were going somewhere adventurous like the beach, or the mountains, or even the desert.

Maybe Eli was right about this part of southern California being a great place to live. Within an hour we could be in any of those places—beach, mountains, desert. So why did Rick decide to come here?

He kept driving past the turn for Katie's dorm and headed to upper campus.

We're going to the bench. The bench where he tried that lame-o ice cream taste test. It's the bench where I sat and talked to him a few days ago when he said he wasn't moving forward on the café in Arizona.

Katie was right. Rick was taking her to "their" bench. What she didn't know was that the palm trees along the trail were wrapped in white twinkle lights.

"Look! The trees are all lit up! I love it!" She climbed out of the car with her cup of tea still in her hand. "When did they do this?"

"Eli told me about it. He worked on the wiring yesterday. Apparently they have canopies going up tomorrow because they have this area rented for a number of events over the holidays. Christy and Todd started something when they figured out how to hold their wedding up here."

"Good ol' Aunt Marti. She's the one who figured it out."

"It's nice, isn't it?" Rick put his arm around Katie's shoulder.

"It's like a fairy tale." She sipped her tea as they walked. The fragrant beverage was just the right temperature and just the right strength. Rick's arm around her felt just right. Being the only ones strolling on this enchanting trail also felt right.

They were a few feet down the trail when Rick stopped. He turned so that he and Katie were face-to-face in the magical radiance of the hundreds of tiny white lights glowing their little hearts out in the calm night air. The wind in the tops of the palm trees was stilled. The sounds of the school and the city below were silent.

All Katie could hear was the sound of her heart pounding in her ears as Rick leaned closer. His chocolate eyes fixed on hers, and she knew. She knew. This was it. Rick was going to kiss her. He was really, truly, finally going to kiss her!

13

Katie closed her eyes. Her tea-warmed lips turned toward Rick as she felt him lean closer. The moment was as perfect as it could be.

She held her breath.

Rick kissed Katie.

His kiss was not just any kiss. His kiss was the perfect kiss she had waited a very long time for.

They lingered just long enough before drawing apart. Their noses touched, and in an affectionate gesture, they paused for a moment with their noses side by side.

As Rick drew back, Katie opened her eyes all the way. She opened her mouth and drew in a breath, ready to say something warm, witty, and wonderful to mark this moment for all time in her heart and mind.

Before a word could escape, Rick placed his finger on her lips and issued her a gentle, "Shhh."

Katie closed her lips and kept all her spontaneous thoughts and feelings inside. Nothing needed to be said. No statements needed to be delivered to clarify what had just happened. They both knew. She knew. She knew this was the affirmation of Rick's growing commitment to her.

Everything about their "first" kiss was perfect. Rick *gave* her this kiss. He didn't take it. And at the exact same moment, Katie gave him her kiss in return. She knew everything for them had just changed.

Reaching for Katie's hand, Rick led her down the twinkle-lit trail. They didn't stop and sit on the bench, which looked like it was covered with chilly drops of condensation. Instead they kept walking, hand in hand, through the silence of the twinkling lighted path. Katie pressed her lips together, reliving the warm, tingling sensation of Rick's kiss. She thought she tasted a hint of chocolate mint. A trace of her gelato must have clung to her lips. Or maybe it was a trace of gelato that had clung to Rick's lips when he was trying Katie's gelato. Katie smiled to herself, thinking of the chocolate-laced kiss she had just shared with her chocolate-eyed boyfriend.

On they went until the path of lit palm trees ended. They had their arms around each other now, and Katie rested her head against his shoulder. He was wearing a long-sleeved, collared polo shirt made of a cashmere blend. She knew because the last time he wore it she had cuddled up to him and asked why his shirt was so warm and cozy. Then she made him stand still, with his chin bent so she could pull up the label and see what it was made of.

None of those frenetic, normal, Katie actions seemed like a part of her now. She felt elegant and calm and—dare she say it? Like a princess.

As Rick drove Katie to her dorm, they held hands and stole glances at each other. Both of them were still smiling but neither spoke. Even that seemed right and fitting. When he walked her to the door of her dorm, Rick wrapped Katie in his arms and held her close for a few moments.

"I'll see you tomorrow," he whispered into her hair.

"Tomorrow," she echoed.

He let go of her slowly and turned to go, glancing back and waving before getting into his car. Katie stood by the front of Crown Hall, watching his car disappear, still dreamy-eyed and dazed. When the taillights were no longer visible, she finally turned and used her master key to open the door. A few students were hanging out in the lobby area. Even more students were still up on her floor, as she floated down the long passageway to her hideaway at the very end.

Katie unlocked the door to her room, turned on the light, and stepped inside. The first thing she saw on her desk was a bouquet. It was a stunning bouquet of a dozen white roses.

This time Katie knew the flowers were from Rick. *Rick Doyle, you planned this night down to the last twinkle light and white rosebud, didn't you?*

On top of the enclosure card was a pink sticky note from Nicole that said, "I snuck the flowers into your room so they wouldn't be waiting at the front desk all night. Knew you wouldn't mind. So happy for you! N."

Opening the gift card, Katie turned on the light over her desk. She paused to breathe in the faint fragrance of the delicate roses before reading the card, written in Rick's handwriting.

> *"Blessed are the pure in heart: for they shall see God."*
> *White roses stand for purity of heart.*
> *Katie, I see God at work in our relationship and feel very*
>   *blessed.*
> *You're beautiful.*
> *Your boyfriend, Rick*

She read the card three times before putting it back into the envelope. It was not what she expected the card to say, yet the sentiment was sweet and seemed like something Rick had spent time thinking about before he wrote it.

Plucking one of the white rosebuds from the bouquet, Katie tucked it under her pillow. She knew she wouldn't need assistance to prompt her dreams to be of Rick that night, but a little flower under one's pillow never hurt.

Keeping afloat in her dream world wasn't difficult that night or even the next morning when she hurried off to class. In a crazy yet happy sort of way, the innocence of it all was giving her a buzz that lasted far longer than she thought it would. The funny part was that she didn't want to tell anyone. She didn't want to rush to Nicole's room or call Christy. For now, this was Rick and Katie's special, shared experience and not something Katie was ready to pull out for discussion.

One thing she was sure about for that evening's pizza event: she wanted to look good. And smell good.

With two full hours to prepare, Katie rummaged through a box in the floor of her closet looking to see if she had any unused shower gels or lotions that would be an added nicety to her shower. She found some peach-scented spray foam for shaving, more of Nicole's green facial mask, and a box of hair lightener. She had bought the box earlier in the summer when she was feeling depressed about working every day as well as going to summer school. Since she couldn't spend time out in the sunshine or go to the beach, she figured she might as well try to look as if she had.

Her summer hours had proved too full for a little pampering time, and Katie never had applied the highlighter to her hair. She had time today. Checking the expiration date on the box, she read the instructions and decided, "Why not?"

Pulling out all the contents, Katie went step-by-step, squeezing the highlighter solution into the small plastic tray and mixing it with the smelly concoction from the other small bottle. With the funny little plastic rake, she applied the pasty stuff to her hair starting at her part, as the directions indicated.

Once her hair was thoroughly immersed in the pungent solution, Katie put on the provided plastic cap and checked her clock. She had to wait twelve to seventeen minutes before showering. Kicking into multitasking mode, she applied the facial mask and promptly opened the window and turned on her small fan. The combination of all the fragrances was too much. She decided to wait on the peach shaving foam until her shower.

With her remaining energy, Katie changed the sheets on her bed, smoothed back her comforter, and laid out the clothes she wanted to wear. That took exactly twelve minutes. Off she went down the hall to the bathroom, managing to avoid anyone seeing her. Once in the shower, she watched as the color from her hair and green from her face pooled in the shower, making a weird shade of brown on the tile.

The peach shaving foam freshened the air nicely, and Katie exited the shower just as three other women entered in a hurry to get ready for the night. All three of them were talking about pizza night.

Katie felt a twinge of disappointment, or maybe it was jealousy, that none of the women on their floor had seemed as excited about the All Hall Get Acquainted Night that she had been in charge of at the beginning of school. That event wasn't set up to be a date night, and a lot of people didn't know each other yet. Now they were far enough into the year that the organized social events were sparking excitement. She knew she should just be grateful that enthusiasm was high for tonight's event.

As soon as she was in her room, Katie stood before her mirror with the towel still wrapped around her head. A gush of risk-taker's remorse came over her. *What if this is one of the most foolhardy things you have done? What if it isn't? What if you end up liking it? Only one way to find out.*

But not yet.

She turned her back to the mirror, reached around to the side for her blow-dryer, and leaned at the waist, drying the underside of her hair first. Standing up and giving her head a shake, she quickly dried the rest of her hair by flipping it every which way. She wanted it to look carefree when she turned around.

Shutting off the blow-dryer and taking a deep breath, Katie let out an optimistic "ta-da!" and turned around.

What she saw in the mirror shocked her.

Her hair looked amazing.

She loved it. Her signature red was definitely still dominant, but the raked-in highlights gave a sun-kissed, strawberry blond touch that brightened her countenance and accentuated her glowing skin, thanks to the green mask.

"I don't believe it," she muttered. "I did something that turned out right. I love my hair!"

Such a moment, no matter how small the victory, was not to be wasted. Katie quickly dressed, had a little fun with her makeup, and then stood back and took a picture of herself with her cell phone.

She sent the photo to Christy with a text message saying, "I lightened my hair. I love it!!!!!"

Katie checked her clock and realized the small victories were continuing. She was ready, and she was early. Suddenly she was a woman with options. She could go to the lobby and help out if her fellow RAs in charge of organizing the event needed her. She could take a power nap. She could check her email. She could stroll down the hall and see how many accolades she received for her new look.

This was great. Life was sweet. Katie couldn't remember the last time she had felt like this.

With a grin at herself in the mirror she thought, *Maybe Rick's kiss last night really did turn me into a princess.*

The thought charmed her, as did the memory of his kiss. It was only about the eight hundredth time she had thought about it. And every time she pondered the way he had so romantically kissed her, Katie smiled. The smile turned up just the corners of her closed lips. A Mona Lisa smile.

Like Mona, Katie had a secret. A delicious secret. A secret she eventually would reveal to Christy. But for the moment, her secret wasn't diluted. It was just hers. Hers and Rick's.

I wonder if Rick has told anyone yet. Do guys do that? Who would he tell? Eli? Todd? What if he told his brother or his parents? Will they look at me differently when they see me at Thanksgiving?

Katie decided she definitely would tell Nicole. And Julia. This would be a good life moment to share with Julia and celebrate in some way. Oh, and Tracy. Tracy would find out eventually since Rick, Todd, and Tracy's husband, Doug, were so close. Tracy should hear this news from Katie before she heard it from Doug.

And Sierra! I should email her in Brazil and tell her. How much time do I have now?

Checking the clock on her desk again, Katie decided to wait on emailing Sierra. She reached for one of the white rosebuds and pulled it from the vase. It would be fun to somehow wear the rose tonight, even though it was only a pizza night and not a prom night.

Katie tried to figure out a way she could affix the flower in her hair. That didn't work. She tried it behind her ear, Hawaiian style. No good. Between her teeth, Latin flamenco dancer style? She raised her hands to the side and clapped twice, stomping her heel for emphasis. No.

The rose went back into the vase, and Katie went out the door. Strolling down the hall, she tapped on Nicole's door and found her floormate in the middle of trying on what Nicole called, "Outfit possibility number four. No, make that number five."

Viewing the stacked-up options on Nicole's bed, Katie said, "Now, this is why I'm suddenly glad I have a minimalistic wardrobe. It would take me six hours to comb through all the combinations you have there."

Nicole pulled a white shirt over her head, and as she did, she noticed Katie's hair. "Katie, your hair! I love it! When did you have time to get your hair done?"

"I did it an hour ago."

"You did it yourself? I'm impressed. It looks gorgeous."

"Thanks." Katie turned to glance at herself in Nicole's mirror. In the reflection, she saw Nicole smoothing the sides of the white shirt and looking pensive.

"Do you think this shirt is too plain?"

"Not if you wear some of your fun jewelry with it. What about one of your bead necklaces?"

"Great idea." Nicole flitted to the wall next to her desk where all her accessories hung in an orderly fashion, looking more like a three-dimensional art piece than a utilitarian storage space.

"Try the red one. Or the turquoise one with the silver," Katie suggested. She stepped over and lifted one of the necklaces off the hook. "This is cute. Would you mind if I borrowed this one?"

"Of course not. It'll look nice with your blue top. What do you think of this one?"

"Fantabulous. Not that you need to worry. You always look great. And besides, Eli is a low-key kind of guy, so you don't need to feel like you're trying to impress him."

Nicole gave Katie an appreciative smile. "Thanks for setting me up with him. It still feels humiliating, but at least I have a date. Being with you and Rick will make it fun."

"It will definitely be fun. Are you about ready?"

"I'm almost ready. Let me figure out my shoes and brush my teeth. It won't take me long. You can go ahead. I don't want to make you late."

"You won't. I'm early."

Nicole checked her watch. "You are!"

"I know. It's like alternate-Katie-universe night. My hair turned out great, I like what I'm wearing, and I'm early. This never happens." With a flip of the ends of her happy hair, Katie said, "I think I'll skip all the way to the lobby and maybe even sing a little song. Fairy-tale Land suits me, don't you think?"

"Definitely. If my mom were here right now, she would say that the Lord is blessing you, and she would quote James 1:17."

"Why James 1:17?"

"It says, 'Every good and perfect gift is from above, coming down from the Father of the heavenly lights.'"

"And why would your mom quote that verse right now?" Katie knew Nicole's dad was a pastor, so it didn't seem unusual that Nicole had grown up with Bible verses as a part of her everyday life. Katie wasn't sure what this one meant, though.

"My mom always quotes that verse when things go well. She says we should appreciate all the gifts God gives us, including fun times with friends and even good hair nights."

Katie wanted to tell Nicole about a certain other "good and perfect" gift she had received last night in the form of a certain kiss from a certain Prince Charming. She held back, though. They didn't have much time. This was a topic better delivered when plenty of discussion time was available.

"I'm going to go ahead," Katie said. "I'll see you there in a few minutes."

Feeling radiant as she entered the lobby, the first person Katie saw was Eli. He smiled when he saw her. His hair wasn't as tussled as usual. He looked cleaned up, the way he had at Todd and Christy's wedding when Katie had first encountered him.

"Rick should be here in a few minutes," Eli said.

"Nicole too. Here, I mean. She's coming. Also."

Eli nodded as Katie took a breath and tried to tell her brain that she really needed to remember to use full sentences when she was around this guy.

"I have a question for you," Eli said.

"Okay."

Rats! That was still only one word.

"Rick told me about the mix-up with the bouquet that was delivered here."

"Yeah, that was a pretty big mess. It turned out okay in the end, thanks to Rick."

There. Now you sound normal. Stay normal.

"When you called me the other day, were you trying to see if I was the one who sent the flowers?"

"Sort of. I was fishing for clues."

Eli leaned forward and looked at her more intently. "Why would you think I was the one who sent them to you?"

"Because of the card. Did Rick tell you what it said?"

"No."

"It said, 'Thanks for saying yes.' I thought maybe it meant yes to going out to the desert, which was so amazing, by the way. I keep thinking about all those stars, like even a few minutes ago when Nicole was quoting me a verse about how good gifts come down from the Father of heavenly lights. I immediately saw an image in my mind of all those stars. I told Rick we need to go out there. I mean, he and I are going out, obviously, but I meant go out to the desert sometime."

Eli nodded, taking in Katie's rapid sentences.

Okay, now you're using too many words. Take it down a notch.

The lobby was quickly filling with people, and the conversation volume was rising. Katie watched the door for Rick and then turned the other direction to see if Nicole was coming. When she turned back toward Eli, he seemed to be studying her with his piercing gaze.

In an effort to act like her "normal" self, Katie formed a rectangle with the thumb and forefinger on both hands. "Take a picture, buddy. It lasts longer."

"Longer than what?"

"Longer than a stare. You're staring."

"Sorry. Old habit. From a tree. When I was a kid." Now Eli was the one with the partial sentences.

Katie tilted her head, inviting an explanation. "In Zambia?"

He nodded. "We lived on a compound. There was one big tree that was perfect for climbing. It was right next to the clinic. I used to hide out up there, watching all the people going into the clinic. I could hide there a long time before anyone noticed and told me to come down."

"Well, here's a friendly little tip, if you don't mind me giving it to you. Most girls don't enjoy being studied. So tonight, while you're with Nicole, try to remember that you're not up a tree. You're with my friend, and she's wonderful, and we're all going to have a good time, so you can just relax."

"Got it," Eli said.

Katie looked through the crowd for Nicole and then to the front door for Rick.

"What if we had a signal?" Eli asked.

"A signal for what?"

"Tonight, if you see me acting like some strange kid out of Africa, you could give me a signal to lighten up."

When Katie looked at Eli, she realized for the first time that he might be nervous about this date. She knew that if she were in his position, about to go on a blind date, she would be nervous too. Katie never enjoyed being the leftover who was fixed up with other people's friends. Especially at the last minute. Her empathy for Eli grew.

"Okay," she said. "Here's my favorite one. You ready?" Katie scratched her right eyebrow and brushed her hair back.

"Go ahead," Eli said. "What's the signal?"

"That was it." She did it again.

"That looked like something natural."

"Well, Einstein, that's the point. You don't want a signal like this." She slapped her left shoulder twice and tapped three fingers on her forearm.

Eli laughed, and in the deep rumbling, he seemed to relax all at once. "You play baseball, don't you?"

"Softball, usually. You?"

"I grew up with what you guys call soccer. We call it football. Baseball is on my list of sports to try while I'm here. I haven't had a chance yet."

"We'll have to see what we can do to change that. I'm long over-due for a good game down on the baseball diamond. There is nothing better than a great softball game on a Saturday afternoon. Except in the summer. That's when the night games are the best. The air is just right, and the way the dust rises up from the bases in the floodlights, it's like ..."

Before Katie finished her sentence she saw Nicole shyly standing behind Eli waiting for Katie to finish.

"Oh, hey. Nicole is here. Good. Nicole, this is Eli. Eli, meet Nicole."

Nicole looked great. Her manners were flawless. She came across casual and breezy, and Eli took in every word she said, tilting his head and listening carefully. When it seemed he was drifting toward being a little too focused, Katie slid around and stood directly behind Nicole. She scratched her eyebrow and flipped back her hair.

Eli caught Katie's clue and responded with an on-the-spot reply signal. He smoothed his thumb and forefinger over his goatee. At least Katie thought it was a return signal. It was kind of cute. If it was his "okay" signal, Eli delivered it effortlessly without taking his eyes off Nicole. But his posture relaxed, and he seemed less intense, which was good.

Katie looked around and saw Rick standing about six feet away and looking her direction with a great smile on his handsome face.

Katie winked at him, as if that were her special hello signal for him. Her "Mona Lisa wink," she decided to call it.

Rick didn't wink back.

She raised her hand in a little wave, and Rick seemed to move his gaze from Nicole to Katie. He raised his hand and motioned for her to come over where he stood.

My prince beckons.

Y ou look great," Rick said.

"So do you." Katie slipped her hand into Rick's.

With a chin-up gesture, he asked, "How's it going with the two of them?"

"Pretty good, actually. I think Eli was nervous. It was cute."

"He was nervous, all right. Apparently he hasn't done much dating since moving to the States. What about Nicole? Is she nervous too?"

"Not too bad. She did change several times before deciding what to wear. But that's normal. Especially when you have a lot of options to choose from like she does."

Rick seemed to be studying Nicole as Katie spoke. "She made a good choice. She looks fantastic."

Katie pulled back and gave Rick a curious look.

"What?" he asked, catching her expression.

"If I didn't know better, I'd say you were checking her out a little too thoroughly."

"I'm just saying she made a good choice. You said she changed several times."

"I know. Okay, come on." Katie pulled Rick into the crowded lobby, eager to drop the subject before she and Rick settled into one of their pointless arguments over nothing. "I have to make an announcement."

Katie made her way to the center of the lobby and had Rick help her stand on top of the coffee table. "Okay, everybody, listen up!"

When the conversations didn't die down, Katie put her thumb and forefinger to her lips and gave a shrill whistle. That got their attention.

"Thank you! Hey, welcome! If you're here for the Pizza Doubles Night, you're in the right place. If you're here for Biology 101 study group, you're not in the right place."

Her attempted joke fell flat so Katie decided to get right to the point. "Okay, so this is how it's going to go this evening. Talitha and her crew are over at the cafeteria preparing everything for us to team up and make our pizzas. Everyone needs to be on a team of four people. If you don't have four in your group yet, you'll have a chance to find another couple but ... wait! Listen! Don't try to pair up yet. Let me finish the instructions first."

The voices in the crowd were still rising so Katie reverted to her shrill whistle once again. She caught Rick's expression; he seemed not to like her whistle. She made note of his disapproving expression.

"So everyone will hike on over to the cafeteria and get together in groups of four. Each team will have a lump of pizza dough, sauce, and cheese at the tables. Then you can select up to five toppings and go for making your pizza the most creative one of the evening. Your group will eat your own pizza, so don't add any of your own foreign objects."

"Like a shoe!" The comment came from Vicki and was intended as a private joke between Katie and Vicki. It referred to an incident the previous year when Katie had hid Vicki's shoes in one of the ovens. The way everyone laughed it seemed that more than one person knew about the shoe-in-the-oven incident.

"Keep going, Katie." Julia was on the other side of Katie and was motioning that she should complete the instructions before she lost the crowd.

"Prizes will be awarded for a variety of categories so have fun, pick your team of four people, and that's it. You can head on over to the cafeteria now."

The rumbling of voices immediately grew as Katie stepped down from the coffee table. "Why did I agree to do that?" she asked Rick. "Talitha should have been the one giving out the instructions."

"Yes, but can Talitha whistle like you?" Rick asked.

"Probably not."

"Then I think you have your answer. Let's try to find Nicole and Eli before they're trampled."

Rick led the way through the moving crowd over to where Eli and Nicole were standing where Katie had left them. Nicole looked a little flustered, but she brightened up when she saw Rick and Katie.

The four of them walked across campus with Rick keeping the conversation going. They entered the cafeteria and found an open area with the beginning basics for their pizza. Some of the groups already were at work collecting pepperoni, olives, and a dozen other potential toppings.

The foursome took their places around the table and looked at each other.

"I was thinking we could do a big happy face," Katie said. "You know, pepperoni eyes and ..."

"Or," Rick said, "we could focus on making the best-tasting pizza since we are the ones who are going to eat it."

"But it's a competition for the design," Katie said.

"And we have to eat it," Rick repeated. "Two pepperoni eyes between four people isn't exactly gourmet."

"What if we tried for cute *and* delicious?" Nicole asked. "We could go for a unique shape as well. It doesn't have to be round, does it? We could make it a different shape, like a house."

"A house?" Katie repeated.

"Nicole has a point," Rick said. "Maybe not a house but something other than round. I like where you're headed, Nicole."

Katie had a feeling this was going to turn into a much bigger production than she had anticipated. She had a café owner/chef along with a creative designer on her team. Turning to Eli she said, "What do you think?"

"I'm not an expert in this area, so I'll leave it to you guys to tell me what you need me to do."

Rick pushed up his sleeves. "Let me go wash my hands, and I'll work with the dough. You guys see what kind of toppings we can use. Go for the mushrooms, sausage, and shallots, if they have any. We want this to taste good."

Rick took off for the restroom, and Katie turned to Nicole. "Shallots?"

"Those are the little chopped up onions. Do you want me to pick out the toppings?"

"Good idea," Katie said. To her surprise, Eli didn't follow Nicole, and Nicole didn't seem to notice that he wasn't sticking with her.

"So," Katie said, "how's it going with Nicole?"

Eli looked much more relaxed than he had earlier. He didn't offer an answer. Instead he said, "Your hair is nice."

Katie had almost forgotten that she had colored it. "Oh, thanks."

She realized Rick hadn't said anything. He was usually pretty attentive, but apparently he hadn't noticed. When he returned and sank his hands into the dough, Katie said, "Did you notice my hair?"

"I noticed it looks good," he said, his gaze intent on the dough. "Did we come up with an agreed-on shape yet?"

Nicole stepped up with a tray full of toppings. "I had an idea, you guys. What if we did a rectangle and turned it into a frame? You know, lots of olives around the edges for a black frame. Then we could do a picture inside the frame with all these different toppings."

"Do you mean a picture like the Mona Lisa?" Katie asked.

Nicole laughed. "I'm not quite that ambitious! I was thinking something simple like a landscape."

Katie wasn't catching the vision, but Rick seemed to be right on track with Nicole. He expertly shaped the dough into a rectangle and fluted the edges while Nicole filled in the sides with neatly lined-up olives. Eli and Katie watched.

"Too bad we can't use pesto instead of marinara sauce," Rick said. "We could do a more realistic landscape with the green base. This spinach is going to work well, though, for the top of the tree. Good choice on the spinach."

Katie wanted to laugh but kept her astonishment to herself. Never in a million years would she expect Rick to get into the artwork of pizza landscapes, yet here he was, stepping up the pace, shaping a tree trunk with sausage and telling Katie to "work with the mushrooms" to make them look like a field of flowers.

"Why can't they just be what they are? A field of mushrooms?"

Rick reassigned the design to Nicole, who had a knife ready just in case they needed to cut the pepperoni into specific shapes.

"I'm going to find something for us to drink," Katie said. "This highly creative work is making me thirsty."

"I'll go with you," Eli said.

The two of them strolled past all the other groups and peered over shoulders to see what was going on. Most of them were just smearing the sauce on a not-so-round circle of pizza dough and arranging pep- peronis in non-creative patterns or writing out initials with olives.

"Over there." Eli motioned to Vicki's group at the end of one of the tables. "Second happy face I've seen."

"Okay, so I'm not original."

Eli stopped Katie and looked at her with his intense gaze. "Yes, you are. You are definitely original."

"O-kay," she said slowly. "I'm original. But my pizza-decorating skills are sadly lacking."

They were at the soft drink machine by then, and Eli was filling glasses with ice. "We could go around and take drinks to everyone. What do you think?"

"Sure. Might be a nice thing to do." She reached for a cafeteria tray, and they each loaded up a tray with a dozen plastic orange cups filled with ice and an assortment of soft drinks. They walked around, talking with people and offering beverages. Katie liked to do this sort of thing. It gave her a chance to interact with everyone and mingle.

Eli seemed to like the serving role as well. He didn't have much to say to anyone, but he knew a lot more people than Katie did, and he greeted all of them by name.

The two of them did a second round of drinks. By the time they arrived back at their table, Rick and Nicole were ready for cups of soda.

"Is it in the oven?" Katie asked, since the pizza was no longer on the table.

"Yep." Rick looped his arm around Katie's shoulder. "Wait till you see our prize-winning masterpiece."

"Better yet," Nicole added, "wait till Julia and Greg and the other judges see it. I think we blew the competition out of the kitchen."

Rick laughed and held up his plastic cup as if to toast Nicole for her statement as well as her creative contributions. The two of them clinked cups. Katie turned to Eli, to include him in the toast.

As Katie took a sip of her drink, she noticed Rick was smiling in his old Rick-the-flirt way at Nicole. He still had his arm around Katie and was making it clear that the two of them were together, but his gaze at Nicole was a little too suave-boy in Katie's opinion. Earlier that week Katie had been warmly basking in the fact that Rick was more his high school self than ever. At this moment, she wished he were back to his all-business self like he was at the Dove's Nest.

"Just about time to check on ours," Rick said, pulling out his buzzing cell phone.

"Did you set a timer?" Katie asked.

"Yes, I didn't want it to burn. Come on."

The four of them went over to the ovens where six Crown Hall students in aprons and cafeteria hairnets were wielding large paddles as they pulled the pizzas in and out of the oven.

"Take your time with that one," Rick said, standing a little taller and stretching his neck to see what was going on over at the ovens. "Yeah, that's looking like it needs another three minutes or so. Just to brown the edges more."

None of the other students was giving directions on the cooking specifics for their pizzas. By the looks of some of the first contenders, they should have been more demanding. One of the pizzas didn't even have all the cheese melted. The judges were marking down their comments, and thankfully Julia asked that the less-done pizzas be returned to the oven.

All in all, Katie thought the event was going pretty well. Everyone was having fun and mingling, and that was the objective. Everyone except Nicole and Eli. Not that Nicole had to pay undivided attention to him, but he was her date, after all.

The four of them watched as their rectangular pizza came out of the oven looking nicely browned. When it was placed on the counter for the judges to have a look, all the judges pointed and smiled. Rick murmured, "We've got it bagged, you guys."

He turned to Nicole and held out one of his hands like a basketball player inviting a "low five" from another team player. Nicole nonchalantly responded with a smooth *fwap* of her hand across Rick's, as if the two of them had practiced this little victory signal before the event.

What's going on here?

Katie tried to give herself some perspective. She reminded herself of how amped up she had gotten over the summer when Carley showed extra attention to Rick. Carley later said she was doing it as a game to see if she could get Rick to notice her and therefore bug Katie. Carley's deal was unusual and borne of what Katie considered to be deep insecurities and jealousy.

Nicole's efforts to get Rick's attention wouldn't come from the same place. She was nothing like Carley.

Am I being overly sensitive? Is Nicole just trying to fit in and have a good time, and I'm misreading her interactions with Rick? So what if they have a cute little victory hand slap?

Katie reminded herself that she and Eli also had a secret signal they had come up with before the event, and there was nothing out of whack about that. Still, Rick and Nicole's confident gesture didn't sit well with her. Nicole should be clinking glasses with Eli and slapping hands with him.

Shaking off her uncomfortable twinges, Katie made her way right next to Rick as he was given the tray with the finished pizza and waved off by the judges. The four of them were free to return to their table and dive into their creation. With Katie by his side, Rick took his time walking the long way back to their table. It was fun watching everyone peek at their pizza and simultaneously drop their jaws.

Oh, my competitive boyfriend! You crack me up!

The baking process had deepened the colors of their modern art landscape. The mushroom slices had curled up nicely, and some of them did look like flowers. The tree trunk, composed of ground sausage, browned up well, and the spinach leaves dotted with chopped tomato pieces surprisingly gave the effect of an apple tree. It was a surrealistic landscape, but it worked.

"I hate to cut it," Nicole said once the four of them were seated with the pizza in front of them. A steady stream of lookie-lous were passing by, making comments, including the accusation to Nicole that she had brought in a "ringer" to sway the competition.

"He's not with me," Nicole said, looking around as if she just remembered she had come with Eli that evening. "Rick is Katie's boyfriend."

Just so long as all of us keep remembering that significant fact, I'll be able to put my apprehensions aside and not let any crazy jealousies take root.

Nicole smiled at Eli, who was sitting across the table from her, and said, "Thanks for getting the drinks for us, Eli."

"It was the least I could do for such a focused artist," he said.

Nicole got up from her seat on the other side of Rick and went around to the side of the table where Eli was sitting by himself. He looked pleased that she had at last acknowledged him as her date, and Katie calmed down, finally feeling ready to enjoy their double date.

"Who wants to do the honor of cutting the first slice?" Rick asked.

"Wait!" Katie said. "We should take a picture first. Where's your fancy phone camera?"

Rick pulled out his phone and snapped a variety of shots. He took one of Eli and Nicole leaning shoulder to shoulder and both smiling. Katie thought they made a cute couple. She was hopeful that Nicole would think the same thing once she saw the photo.

Nicole, however, didn't seem to have any feelings about Eli one way or the other, even after Rick emailed the photos to her Saturday morning. She and Katie were driving into town to get some "good" coffee at the Bella Barista when Katie started to evaluate the Pizza Doubles Night with Nicole.

"So what are your thoughts about Eli?" Katie asked.

Nicole rocked her head back and forth in a so-so fashion and kept her eyes on the road.

"He's a deep and caring guy," Katie said. "You should have seen how people reacted to him when we were taking drinks around to everyone. He knows everybody on campus, and everyone seems to respect him."

"He is a nice guy," Nicole said.

"But ..."

"But he's not really my type."

"What is your type? More like Rick, right?"

Nicole glanced over at Katie with a hint of hurt or panic or something less than tranquil in her expression. "I think Rick's great," Nicole said quickly. "He's crazy about you. Does he happen to have a brother?"

Katie felt her shoulders relax. "Yeah, as a matter of fact, Rick does have a brother."

"He does?"

"His name is Josh, and you know what? This isn't a bad idea at all! I can see you with Josh. I was supposed to ask if you wanted to come to Thanksgiving at the Doyles'. This will be great! Would you like to come?"

"Are you certain that it's okay with Rick's parents?"

"Yes. He already asked his mom. He's inviting Eli, and I'm inviting you."

Nicole glanced at Katie again. "Eli is coming?"

"Yes, only because Rick is inviting him. I don't even know if he's coming, but he's invited, just as you are. Are you that uncomfortable being around him? I mean, would you not come to Thanksgiving dinner just because Eli might be there?"

"No, no, not at all. I'm really not trying to make a big deal out of this, Katie. I'm sorry if it's coming across that way. I just feel like Eli is too earthy for me, you know? He comes across fairly intense, yet when you talk to him, he seems uncomplicated. I like guys who are more layered and complex, you know? More of a mystery."

Katie thought about Nicole's assessment of Eli. He was earthy. Katie appreciated that about him. She liked that Rick wore ironed shirts, but she also liked the way Eli wore crumpled hemp shirts that looked as if they had been on a long journey all by themselves before ending up in his closet. She liked the way Rick always looked good and kept regular haircut appointments, but at the same time there was something about Eli's unstyled mane that made her feel as if she didn't have to check her own appearance before starting a conversation with him. Eli's relaxed and earthy ways gave Katie freedom to be equally relaxed and earthy.

"Mysterious men are overrated," Katie said. "Rick is a continuous enigma, and I can tell you that the unsolved puzzle of his mind is exhausting. Well, not exhausting. *Challenging* would be a better word. Rick keeps me on my toes. He keeps me wondering."

"I love that in a relationship," Nicole said. "Not that I've had dozens to draw my experiences from, but I like surprises."

"Josh might be a lot like Rick in that department. I don't know him that well. I'll tell Rick you're able to come for Thanksgiving, and he'll have a chance to prep Josh."

"No! Don't say anything about trying to match me up with his brother! Please! I honestly think that might have been the biggest hindrance to my feeling at ease with Eli. From the beginning it was a setup, and we both knew it. I think just knowing that I was desperate for a date and that he was available on such short notice took all the charisma out of the connection, you know?"

Katie nodded. She was feeling much more at ease with Nicole and how things had gone the night before. Katie had been in those same blind-date matchups, and she knew exactly what Nicole was saying.

They pulled into the shopping center, and Nicole parked. The two of them sauntered into Bella Barista, which was busy with Saturday morning customers. As they stood at the cash register, Katie remembered how Rick had kissed her on the cheek their first night there and then how she had returned the kiss the next time they went and she paid. This little spot, right in front of the register at the Bella Barista, would always be a magical spot for her. Just as the pathway on upper campus under the twinkle-light, decked-out palm trees would be an enchanted spot for her.

Rick hadn't kissed her on the lips since their memorable stroll, but that was fine with Katie. They had taken the affection part of their relationship so slow for so many months that now it felt like every kiss held a high value and should be spent like a gold coin.

If she had any lingering queasiness about Rick not paying enough attention to her the night before, those thoughts flew away as she stood in this, her special kissing spot, and thought of him.

The only small image that wouldn't leave her mind was the picture of what happened the night before as soon as the winners of the most creative pizza were announced. Everyone seemed to already know it would be Rick, Katie, Nicole, and Eli. So when Greg called out their names, even though Katie was standing right next to Rick, in front of everyone, Rick went to Nicole first and scooped her up in a victory hug. It was a quick hug, and yes, well deserved since Nicole was the one who aced the "design" part of their pizza.

But Katie was left standing alone next to Eli. The two of them gave each other awkward pats on the back, as they smiled and nodded. Katie waited for Rick to turn around and come back to her. When he did, he lifted her up in a victory hug and gave her a half turn while everyone watched and clapped. It was cute, fun, and romantic.

Katie would have preferred, of course, that Rick would have reached for her first. She didn't mind that he hugged Nicole. It was just that Katie wanted to know she was first with Rick even when lots of other people were around.

That, she decided, as she placed her order for a jasmine green tea, would always be the challenge with Rick, her favorite puzzle person. She had a feeling she would never be able to have a complete and firm lock on him and his way of doing things. It was best to let things roll out the way they were and not challenge the motives or complain about how their relationship was working itself out.

The point was, she had the growing, caring relationship she always had wanted with Rick, and in spite of all the potential obstacles, it was working. Why would she mess with it?

Katie had two overdue conversations, and by Tuesday morning, she knew she better try to have both of them before Thanksgiving, which was only two days away.

The first conversation was with Julia, whom Katie had agreed to check in with after their softball exercise, and the second conversation was with Christy. She needed to tell Christy about kissing Rick.

Katie didn't *have* to tell her best friend, but she wanted to. No one knew yet. At one point, she had considered opening up to Nicole; however, after the awkward pizza night, Katie decided she would tell Christy first and then loop Nicole back into the newsflash.

Always the type who appreciated the motto about "killing two birds with one stone," Katie set up a time to meet with Julia at four o'clock on Tuesday afternoon and then arranged to borrow Nicole's car to meet Christy as soon as she finished working at five o'clock. What Katie hadn't counted on was the wildcard of Nicole needing her car to drive someone to the airport.

Katie met Julia at her room at four and began her sales pitch. "How would you like to go to Dove's Nest for something to eat? My treat. I'll even pay for gas because, actually, I planned to meet Christy, but the car I was going to borrow isn't available."

"No problem," Julia said. "Let me tell Greg where I'm going. He is checking a lot of students out early for Thanksgiving break, and I told him I would help if he got swamped."

161

"A lot of them are going home early. I have a feeling class attendance will be slimmed down tomorrow. Makes you wonder why they don't just cancel all Wednesday classes."

"I remember thinking the same thing when I was a student," Julia said. "Are you ready to go?"

"Home?"

"No, I meant, are you ready to go to the Dove's Nest. I'm ready if you are."

Several people stopped them to ask a quick question or chat as they made their way through the Crown Hall lobby and out to the parking lot. Julia had a basic sort of blue, four-door sedan with Hawaiian floral seat covers in blue and white.

"How's it working out for you without a car?" Julia asked.

"It's only been a week and a half, and already I feel destitute," Katie said. "I was planning to go to church Sunday, but it turned into a tangle. I told Rick I would meet him there, and then Nicole didn't go because she had a huge project due on Monday. But she already had loaned her car to someone else. By the time I figured out all this, it was too late for Rick to pick me up and still make it to church on time, so I just stayed on campus and went to breakfast. Nobody goes to breakfast on Sunday mornings, did you know that? I took my Bible with me and had my own sort of quiet time with the Lord. And believe me, it was a quiet, quiet time."

"How are you doing with everything else?" Julia asked as she exited the main entrance to Rancho Corona and began the curving drive down the hill.

"Good. Everything is good. I'm going to Rick's parents' new house for Thanksgiving, and Nicole is coming with me so that should be fun."

"I noticed at the pizza night that Nicole and Rick get along pretty well."

Katie looked over at Julia to see if she should be reading something between the lines of Julia's comment. Julia didn't appear to be doing anything more than making a simple statement.

"Yeah. They get along well. I'm hoping to sort of fix her up with Rick's brother, Josh. Rick and I tried to fix her up with Eli, but that didn't go anywhere."

Julia drove silently for about a mile before Katie said, "Did you have the same sort of drama when you were a student here?"

"Of course. Most of my 'drama' revolved around my boyfriend."

"Your boyfriend?" Katie looked at Julia again, hoping a spilling of details was forthcoming.

"His name was Trent."

"Nice strong name," Katie said. "I don't think I've ever met a 'Trent.'"

"He was one of a kind. An original."

"And ...?" Katie hinted for more details.

"We were in love and—"

"Don't tell me if it's gruesome. I hate hearing about women who get their hearts broken. Why does love have to be so painful?"

Julia drew in a deep breath. "It certainly can be painful, can't it?"

"How did you know you loved him? I mean, really knew it was love?"

"I just knew. I still know. If he were to step into my life today, I'd still have that flip-over feeling in my heart. Love doesn't go away just because people go away."

Katie tried to decide if she agreed with Julia's statement. "You're saying you can genuinely love someone but not end up with them for the rest of your life. Is that what you're saying? You can love them—really, truly love them—and yet not stay with them."

"Yes."

"I don't know if I agree. I don't like the thought of going through life with a true strand of love just dangling there, not connected at both ends."

Julia smiled a small, tender smile. "I don't like it either, but there it is."

"So are you going to tell me he ended up marrying someone else?"

"No."

Katie waited for more details, but Julia ended it there. Her no was firm enough that Katie knew she would do well to leave the topic alone, at least for the time being.

Note to self: When the topic of Trent comes up again, find out where he is these days. If he's not married, why couldn't he and Julia reunite? Now that would be a great love story.

"How is everything with your family?" Julia asked, changing the subject.

"The same, I guess."

"Since you said you're going to Rick's for Thanksgiving, I'm assuming you're not going to be with your parents that day."

"No. I tried to set up something with them, but it didn't work out. Maybe for Christmas. I don't know."

"I hope you do get to spend some time with them at Christmas," Julia said. "It doesn't have to be a lot of time or a big effort. Just connecting with them on whatever level would be a very good thing."

Katie looked down at her hands. She always felt uncomfortable when the topic circled around to her parents, even though she knew Julia was right. The truth was, she would love to have more of a relationship with her parents, but how could that happen? It wasn't realistic.

Katie opened up her thoughts to Julia and told her how hard it was to connect with her parents. She summarized her most recent conversation with her mother and said, "So how am I supposed to change any of this? I mean, what can I do?"

"I'm not sure you can change anything. The only thing you can ever change is yourself."

"Do you think I need changing? I mean, do you think my attitude is wrong?" Katie felt an edge of defensiveness building inside and tried to push it back down. She certainly didn't want to start a challenge-me-on-anything-uncomfortable-and-I'll-bite-your-head-off sort of argument with her resident director. She valued her relationship with Julia too much to do that.

"I think all you have to do is what God commanded all of us to do."

"What's that? 'Love one another'?"

"Yes, true, we are called to love one another. But the command I was thinking of was the fifth commandment."

"Which is ...?"

" 'Honor your father and mother.' That looks different in many parent – child relationships, but the directive is the same. Honor them. Whatever that means to them and to you, you'll have to figure out. But do what makes them feel honored."

Katie bobbed her head in agreement. "Okay, I'm good with that. I'm not sure how I'm going to honor them at Christmas or whatever, but I see what you're saying, and yeah, I do want to honor my parents."

"I know you do. You have such a great heart, Katie. You're so open, willing, and responsive. I really appreciate that about you."

"And I appreciate that you tell me what I need to hear and do it in a way I can swallow."

Julia turned into the parking lot at the Dove's Nest, and at the same moment they both said, "What is going on?" The lot was nearly full.

"You can pull around to the back," Katie said. "The employees park back there by the dumpster, and there's usually room."

They found a spot and entered the café to find a line of elementary school students waiting to order. Interspersed between the students were harried-looking adults trying to keep their individual little pods under control.

"Looks like it's a field trip," Katie said. "We had a few of these last spring. Do you want to go someplace else?"

Julia looked at her watch. "You know, if you want, Katie, I could leave you here. We don't have to go anywhere or eat anything. I just wanted to check in with you before Thanksgiving. I think our conversation in the car was a good update. What do you think?"

"I feel bad, as if I used you for a ride here, and that was all."

"Don't feel bad. I told you I'd be available for rides if you ever needed them. Christy is going to take you back to school, right?"

"That's the plan."

"Then I'll head back to Rancho. I really need to be available to help Greg check students out for the long weekend. I'm leaving tomorrow, but I'll be back Saturday. Come by anytime, if you end up staying in the dorms for the rest of the weekend."

"Okay, I will. Thanks for the ride."

Julia offered a little wave and left. Katie couldn't be sure, but it seemed that when Trent's name came up, a heaviness had settled on Julia. Katie might have imagined it, but Julia's countenance seemed to have clouded over and remained low afterwards. That made Katie only more curious about Trent, but at the same time, more aware that she needed to be cautious and sensitive if and when the topic came up again.

Katie stood to the side, trying to decide what she should do. She knew she could go over to the adjoining bookstore and browse or follow Christy around if she was stocking books. Or she could stay here and watch the field trip carnival.

Without much effort, she moved to where she could see Rick behind the counter, trying to efficiently help the flustered staff person who was taking down all the orders from the line of students. Katie kind of liked being in the background like this and watching Rick. He had such a commanding presence. He was so good-looking.

A smile played across Katie's lips as she thought, *That's my boyfriend. Rick Doyle, you amazing man, you. You kissed me, you know. You kissed me good. And I love you.*

The instant Katie had that concluding thought of "and I love you," Rick looked up and gazed across the long stretch of the café. He made eye contact with Katie, and she felt a shiver go up her back and tickle her neck. It was as if he had heard her.

Rick, I love you. Did you hear me think that? I can't believe it: I know! I really know. I love you!

A thick lump tightened Katie's throat, and she felt as if she were going to cry, except she had no tears. She just had a smile. A big, happy smile for Rick, who now was motioning for her to come up to the counter.

Many of the students turned around to see who the guy at the counter was motioning to. Katie felt like a singled-out Cinderella who was approaching the prince at the ball while all the short, little squires were making a pathway for her. None of the elementary students was bowing, of course, but Katie imagined they were since they were so short.

"You're a welcome sight," Rick said as soon as Katie was close enough to hear him. "Are you meeting someone?"

"Christy, but not until five."

"Any chance you want to come around back, put on an apron, and make a couple of pizzas?"

"That depends." Katie was aware that the students as well as their chaperones could hear every word of their conversation. They were certain to grow impatient and start throwing invisible darts at her if she delayed Rick much longer, so she kept her quip quick. "I'll make as many pizzas as you want as long as I don't have to embellish them with landscapes. I'm a happy-face kinda woman, you know."

"Yes, I know," Rick said. "No landscapes, I promise. Put on a hairnet and help me start this assembly line." His expression turned quizzical and he tilted his head. "Hey, did you do something different to your hair?"

Katie grinned. "Ah, that's the observant Sherlock Holmes we all know and love." She emphasized the "love," in hopes that Rick would catch a hint at what had just happened in Katie's heart. She was in love. She knew it. She loved Rick. She probably always had carried a capsule of love for him in her heart, ever since junior high.

But today, just now, as Katie was standing there, watching Rick, something had changed. It was just the way Christy had said it would be. Katie had taken one step after another, as she and Rick walked down this long and winding relationship road of theirs. Then, without any clue that the next step was going to be different from the rest, Katie stepped over that invisible line, and there she was.

In love!

For Katie, making individual-sized pepperoni pizzas at the Dove's Nest was something she could do in her sleep. She probably had been asleep more than once during a shift when she had turned out dozens of the little delicacies for various groups. Slipping back into the assembly line in her apron and hairnet felt familiar and made her happy.

Of course, the extra burst of happiness could have come from the delight she secretly carried inside, knowing that she was in love. Truly in love. Officially, over the edge, in love.

At one point in the twenty-minute pizza-making frenzy, Katie looked over at Rick, who had joined the marinara sauce brigade. She heard a little sing-song tune in her head: "First comes love, then comes marriage, then comes baby in a baby carriage."

A smile broke out. She had no idea where she first had heard that jingle. It was definitely vintage and barely applicable to her generation, but at that moment, the lines felt familiar and friendly.

The last time those song lyrics had jangled her thoughts was that summer at the beach. Doug and Tracy had brought their baby, Daniel, and had carted loads of baby gear down to the sand. Christy and Todd brought their honeymooning mode with them and spent the evening entangled with each other in cozy embraces. Katie brought Rick, but Rick brought his cell phone and had spent much time cheek-to-cheek with the annoying piece of plastic on lengthy business conversations with Josh about the Arizona café.

That summer day, Katie wasn't sure where she fit in the little jingle when lined up next to her friends with the "marriage" and the "baby carriage" parts all figured out. But today she knew. She was in the first step. Love. First comes love, then comes ...

Her heart did a little flutter when she allowed herself to wonder if marriage was next. Why not? Whenever those thoughts had come in the past, Katie had brushed them away. Today she liked the idea very much. It would certainly answer a lot of her "what's next?" questions.

Humming to herself, Katie stepped up the production line and had those field trip students all served before five o'clock.

Rick slipped his arm around her waist when no one else was looking. "Do you want to do something together tonight? I can be out of here by about eight."

"I can't."

"Why?" He pulled back, looking stunned that she would turn him down.

"I'm having dinner with Christy, and then I have to work on a paper that's due tomorrow, and I haven't even started it."

"You still have classes tomorrow?"

"I only have one class. It's at 10:30. After that, I have RA duty at the front desk from noon to five."

"So what you're telling me is that I'll have to wait a full twenty-four hours before you'll remember that you have a boyfriend who is looking forward to spending time with you."

"Oh, I'll remember every single second of those twenty-four hours. But, yeah, you'll have to wait until tomorrow night at five before I'm officially on Thanksgiving break."

"I can wait."

Katie smiled. "I know you can wait. You're a professional waiter. And a professional chef. And a professional café owner. But you started as a very good waiter. Get it?"

Rick took Katie by the wrist and led her around to the back of the restaurant where his office was located and a table was set up in the corner for employees. No one was back there at the moment. He looked right and left and then scooped up Katie's face with both hands and drew her close. Before Katie knew what was happening, Rick was kissing her. And it was a good kiss. A very good kiss.

"What are you doing?" she whispered as they pulled away.

"If you don't know what that was, I must really be doing something wrong."

"I know what that was, you doof! And that was a very nice one, by the way."

Rick smiled.

In a low voice she said, "But what are you doing kissing me?"

Rick only smiled more, as if her question didn't require a response.

Katie pulled back so that the only part of them that was touching was their intertwined hands. "What I meant, was . . ." She lowered her voice to barely a whisper. "What are you doing kissing me at work? You always had strict rules about us not giving anyone the impression that we were dating or that we were being affectionate at work."

"Do you work here?" he asked with a cocky grin.

"No, not anymore."

"Then what was your question?"

Katie gave him one of her cute-freckle-faced-girl looks that she knew he liked. In a playful voice she said, "No more questions, Your Honor."

He leaned over and kissed her on the side of her head and let go of her hands. "You better go meet Christy. I'll come to Rancho tomorrow night at five, and we'll have dinner somewhere."

"Okay." Katie still was giving him a dreamy-eyed gaze.

"It's a date," Rick said.

"It's a date," Katie repeated. She wrapped her arms around Rick's middle and gave him a big hug. That same sort of spontaneous hug had set off a string of conflicts last summer when she had expressed affection at work. Tonight it was received by her boyfriend and responded to with an equally warm hug.

Katie untangled herself from strong Rick and tossed her hairnet into the trash. She dropped her soiled apron into the laundry bin. Kissing the ends of her fingers, she waved at Rick and smiled her "see you later" grin at him.

He looked smitten, and she couldn't be happier.

Winding her way back into the café and over to the bookstore-side of the building, Katie saw Christy at the front glass doors looking out into the parking lot. She had her purse over her shoulder.

"Looking for me?"

"There you are. I didn't know if you were being dropped off or not."

"Julia dropped me off earlier. I ended up helping out at the café." Standing as straight as she could in front of her best friend, Katie lowered her voice and said, "Do I look any different to you?"

"Your hair!" Christy exclaimed. "It's lighter. I love it!"

Katie had forgotten about her highlights and brushed off Christy's comment saying, "What else do you notice? Anything? Can you see it in my eyes?"

Christy looked more closely. "Did you get contacts or something?"

"No." Katie slumped slightly in defeat. "I guess it's invisible since it really happens all on the inside."

Christy still didn't seem to know what Katie's clues alluded to so Katie went ahead and told her.

"I am in love."

Christy's eyebrows rose inquisitively. "Really?"

"Yes, really."

"Wow, Katie."

"I know. Wow, huh? It was just like you said. I was going along step-by-step and then ..."

"Wait. This is far too important of a conversation to be having here. Come on, I want to hear everything." She checked her watch. "I have to pick up Todd at 6:45."

"That doesn't give us much time," Katie said.

"I know, but it's a good thing you know how to talk fast. I was thinking we could go to Casa de Pedro. What do you think?"

"I'm with you, Chimichanga Mama. Let's go!"

Katie linked her arm with Christy's as they exited and made their way to Christy and Todd's Volvo.

"Start at the Pizza Doubles Night," Christy said. "I want to hear everything."

Katie gave a condensed overview. She left out the parts about her flittering twinges of jealousy that evening over Nicole and Rick pairing up as such a contented team.

"The four of us went out for coffee at the Bella Barista afterwards, and that part was fun because a bunch of other Rancho people were there. We all pulled the tables together and talked. That's becoming our new hangout. I never noticed it until we went to the flower shop to have the bouquet fixed up for the other Katie."

"Wait." Christy parked the car in front of Casa de Pedro and turned off the engine. "What bouquet and what other Katie?"

Katie made a face. "I really am behind on news flashes with you, aren't I? I'm never going to get to the good part."

"Yes, you will. Keep going. Tell me about the bouquet."

Katie summarized as the hostess seated them. Changing the topic only long enough to order, Katie then moved ahead to the part she was eager to talk about. "So then Rick and I went to upper campus, and the palms trees are all roped with lights. It's gorgeous, Christy. You and Todd need to go up there to see what you guys started with having your wedding in the meadow. The walkway has been improved too. It's magical."

"I want to go see it. I'll tell Todd. Maybe we can squeeze in a visit this weekend. But go on. You and Rick went for a walk on upper campus under the twinkle lights of the palm trees and ..."

"He kissed me."

Christy froze for a moment, and then she let out a little squeal and reached for Katie's wrist. "Katie! I can't believe you waited this long to tell me."

"I know. I wanted to tell you face-to-face. It was so perfect, Chris. Perfect in every way, and I know this will sound crazy, but I didn't tell anyone because I didn't want to wake up if it was only a dream. But it wasn't a dream. It was real, and it was wonderful. Perfect. And you're the first person I've told."

Christy's face looked like she was squealing again, but this time it was a very quiet squeal. "I'm so happy for you guys, Katie."

"I'm in love, Christy. I really am. I know I've said that before in a flippant sort of way, but this is so different."

"How?" Christy looked openly and expectantly at Katie.

"It was just like you said. I was standing in the Dove's Nest less than two hours ago, watching Rick at the cash register, and there was a sea of elementary school kids. I just thought, 'That's my boyfriend,' and then I thought, 'I love him.' And something inside me just ... I don't know. My gut just affirmed my thought. It wasn't a flippity 'I love Rick' in a come-and-go sort of feeling. This time it was like a statement. It was like ..."

Katie paused and smiled, more to herself than to Christy.

"I can't believe I'm going to say this," Katie said, "but I knew. I mean, everyone who has ever been truly in love always says, 'When you know, you'll know,' and I've always thought that was the lamest excuse for an explanation. But it's true. I know. I know I love Rick. It's like a stone in my heart. A boulder. A Rock of Gibraltar. It's not going to go away."

Christy's smile was warm and tender. She had tears in the corner of her eyes. "Oh, Katie, I feel like saying, 'Welcome to the other side' or something."

"I'm in, aren't I?"

"You're in," Christy said. "You're in love, and you're in the next stage of your relationship with Rick. You're in at the heart level and at the gut level, and I'm so happy for you."

"Thank you." Now Katie felt as if tears were going to creep up to her eyes as well. Before the droplets made their happy appearance, the food and drinks arrived in all their steaming, spicy glory.

"I want to pray." Christy reached for both of Katie's hands, and they held hands across the table.

As Katie closed her eyes and bowed her head, she felt Christy blessing her with her tender words to their heavenly Father, thanking him for giving the gift of love and for pouring out his love on Katie. Christy thanked God for Rick, for Katie, for their relationship, and for how he had led them to this place. Christy's words were simple, beautiful, and heartfelt. She sounded like Todd when he prayed.

The moment felt so sacred that Katie didn't want to open her eyes even after Christy said, "I pray all this in the name of your Son, Jesus. Amen."

When Katie did look up, all she and Christy did was smile at each other.

"I want to build an altar here," Katie said.

"What?" Christy's expression went from bliss to befuddled. "What are you talking about?"

"When I was on Catalina last summer, during our day of silence, I was looking for the verse about being peculiar treasures and read this verse in Exodus that said, 'Build altars in the places where I remind you who I am, and I will come and bless you there.' I feel like God just blessed me here through you. He reminded me who he is. God is love. I'm in love. I want to mark this moment somehow and always remember this."

Christy seemed as if she was unsure how to respond. Cautiously she said, "I'm not sure we're supposed to be building altars ..."

"I'm not saying I'm going to stack up refried beans here in a little shrine. I'm just saying I want to mark this moment as a God moment."

"I think it's already marked," Christy said. "In your heart. You'll never forget the moment you knew you loved Rick. I'll never forget the moment I knew I loved Todd. When that place is marked in your heart, you can return there anytime, and trust me, you will find the Lord is already there, and he will bless you there."

"It's so strange, isn't it," Katie said, not interested in biting into her chimichanga the way Christy had chomped into hers. "I mean, you're going along and everything is same-o, same-o, and then all of a sudden, God shows up and everything changes."

"Todd has an opinion on that." Christy wiped her mouth with her napkin. "People say, 'God showed up,' and this or that happened. Todd says God doesn't 'show up.' God is the Alpha and the Omega, the beginning and the end. He is all-present, all-knowing, and all-powerful. The way Todd frames those moments is by saying that God is already there. He was, and is, and is to come. We're the ones who show up. We stay on track with what God desires for us, and we seek him, and pay attention to his leading. Then all of a sudden this holy moment happens not because God decided to step into our lives, but because we're in step with God's eternal life plan."

"Hmm."

"Anyway," Christy said, as Katie contemplated Todd's perspective on God moments. "Tell me what happened next at the Dove's Nest. After you knew you were in love with him. Did you say anything to him or just dive in and make pizzas with him, as if nothing was different?"

"I didn't tell him I love him, but I have a feeling he sort of knew."

"How?"

"He took me in the back and kissed me quite romantically."

"He did?"

"Yeah. You know how he always went slightly ballistic about us expressing any sort of affection at work?"

Christy nodded, her mouth full of food.

"Well, this time he was the affectionate one. He said I didn't work there anymore so it wasn't like he was making out with an employee."

"Did he say that? Did he say 'making out'?"

"No, he didn't say making out, and we definitely weren't making out. It was a kiss. A beautiful, memorable, heart-melting kiss."

Katie sighed. "You know, I think Rick might be right about something he said last summer when we had that ridiculous big argument in his kitchen because he wouldn't kiss me when I wanted him to."

"What did he say?"

"He said guys never forget their kisses with a woman, and I said we never forget either. It's just different, you know? I mean, a hug you kind of remember for a while, but when your lips touch, it really does burn a memory in your head, doesn't it?"

Christy leaned closer and lowered her voice. "Wait until you're married and give yourself completely, body and soul. Now *that* is something you will never forget. The memory burns brightly. Trust me."

Katie liked the way Christy was turning a bit glowy and rosy, as if she were the keeper of some fine secrets and she was revealing a bit of the treasure to Katie.

"I don't see how anyone can give themselves at that level of intimacy without the beautiful, protective covenant of marriage, you know?" Christy continued. "Sex is so sacred and so binding. I know I've said it before, Katie, but I just have to say it again. Creating those soul-searing intimate moments with only one man and only in your marriage bed is like nothing else you've ever experienced. When you wait for those moments and know that he has waited to share those moments with you ..."

Christy teared up again. "It's really a gift. An amazing gift."

Katie handed Christy a napkin. She took it and dabbed her eyes. Then, reaching for her glass of iced tea, Christy held up her glass to Katie. "Here's to love and to God, who made it such a beautiful thing."

Katie clinked her glass of soda with Christy's and added, "And here's to you and Todd for waiting to give yourselves to each other and doing such a good job of advertising to me the reward of virtue."

Christy laughed. "I didn't know we were advertising."

"You are advertising but only in the best sort of way. It's a good thing. It's a God thing, actually."

Katie sipped her soft drink. "Sometimes, Christy, I pull way back and I think, 'Who would I be right now if I'd never met Christy?' I know I wouldn't be who I am today. I don't think I would be making such good choices. Especially if I'd only stayed with the same circle of friends I had at Kelley High before you moved to Escondido. Chris, what if you hadn't moved here from Wisconsin? What if we hadn't become such good friends from that very first night when we went and TPed Rick's house? God did this, didn't he?"

This time the tears really did spill over from Christy's blue-green eyes. "I need another napkin." She looked to see if a waiter was headed in their direction. "I am so emotional right now."

Katie hopped up and pulled two napkins off one of the vacant tables, leaving the silverware in a pile on the tabletop. "Here you go. Cry all you want."

Christy dabbed her eyes again and blotted her nose.

Katie stared at her large chimichanga burrito. "This is really strange."

"What's strange? Your chimichanga?"

"No, the chimichanga looks great. What's strange is me. I'm not hungry. Can you believe that? I'm sure this must mean something. I'm sitting at Casa de Pedro with my most favorite chimi in all the world in front of me, and I can't eat."

Christy smiled broadly. "Of course it means something that you can't eat. You're in love."

Katie motioned for Christy to run her fingernail between her front two teeth. "You have a little piece of shredded beef or something right there."

Christy's expression turned to one of embarrassment but only for a moment. She used the second napkin to remove the beef bit. "You and I need each other more than either of us knows. Thanks, Katie."

The waiter stepped up to their table. "I need a to-go box," Katie said. "And the check. We need to get moving."

"I'll take a box too," Christy said. "I can never finish one of these."

"I have a feeling once this stunned-silly-because-I'm-in-love sense of happiness fades, I'll be starving. When that moment hits, Mr. Chimie Baby will be waiting for me in my little fridge, and I will be one happy girl."

Katie's chimichanga took up a whole shelf in her dorm fridge and stayed there untouched through the night. She worked with enlightened speed on her paper for her Wednesday class and slept three hours. Then she dressed and trekked across campus wearing a soft smile on her face.

She still wasn't hungry after class. Returning to the dorm, Katie went to the rooftop-hidden deck and stretched out on one of the lounge chairs. Below in the parking lot, dozens of students were backing up their cars and packing the trunks with luggage for the long weekend.

Overhead the California sky was streaked with mare's tail clouds that were a sure indicator that autumn was packing her bags as well. Winter, with its sweeping winds from off the desert, would soon send the smog and heat out to sea and grace the southern California basin with crisp air and clear skies. A trip back to the desert during the next few months would provide fantastic stargazing opportunities.

Katie thought about the stars as she closed her eyes in the comfort of the lounge chair. She could hear the faint voices of African children singing. She could feel the warmth of the late morning sun resting on her like an old, green sleeping bag. A sense of being caught up in a twirling universe came over Katie.

She knew two things at that moment under the blanket of sunshine. First, she knew she was miniscule in comparison to the spinning cosmos. Second, she knew that the One who designed heaven and earth had handcrafted her heart, and in her custom-made heart, he had planted a seed that was growing into something wonderful, eternal, and ethereal. Something called "love."

A short time after Katie dozed off with all her happy thoughts, she felt something tickling her cheek. She flipped her hand at the annoyance and slowly opened one eye as a shadow blocked the sunshiny warmth.

"Hello." The warm, chocolate brown eyes that met hers could belong to only one person.

"Rick!"

He stroked her cheek with a pink gerbera daisy. "For you," he said.

Katie opened both eyes and received Rick's flower as well as a kiss on the top of her sun-warmed head. "How did you know I was here?"

"Nicole. She's in the lobby checking students out and said you told her you would be up here until your shift started."

"Am I late?" Katie sat up and squinted. "Or are you early? You're not supposed to be here until five. Wait. Am I dreaming all this?"

"I'm early," Rick said. "It was slow at the Dove's Nest because of the Thanksgiving weekend so I took off a couple of hours early. You don't have to worry about your shift downstairs. Nicole said she would cover it for you. I told her you and I had plans."

"That was nice of her. I should give her my flower." Katie twirled the stem between her fingers as if it were a pinwheel.

Note to self: You really need to explain to Rick that you only said you liked this kind of flower to make for a smooth conversation when Nicole said these were her favorite. If you don't say something soon, you're going to be smothered in these obnoxiously perky daisies the rest of your life.

"You don't have to give Nicole your flower. I brought some for her to say thanks."

Katie ran her fingers through her hair, trying to wake up all the way. "Thanks for what? For taking my shift this afternoon?" She yawned and covered her mouth. "Sorry."

"Yes. I called her earlier and asked if she would cover for you. I told her I had planned a little surprise."

"What is it?" Katie was awake now. She held out her hand, and Rick helped her up from the chaise lounge. As soon as she felt his warm hand grasping hers, she knew for sure that she wasn't dreaming all this. Rick really was here, and he had a surprise for her.

"You'll have to wait," he said.

Katie grinned. "I'm good at waiting, just like you. I'm a professional waiter." She couldn't help but think of what had happened the day before when she had said that line. Her cuteness earned her a kiss.

Today her sleepy cuteness got her an opening of the door that led down the hall to the stairwell. "So am I supposed to close my eyes or something?"

"No, don't close your eyes. I have a feeling you'll fall asleep standing up if you close your eyes again."

Katie yawned again involuntarily. "Sorry. I was so dead asleep."

"I should have let you snooze some more."

"No. Are you kidding? You and I finally have time to do something together. This is rare. I don't want to sleep through this. Am I dressed okay for wherever we're going?"

"You look great. Just bring a jacket or sweater and meet me in the lobby."

"I'll be there in three and a half minutes." Katie dashed to her room. Rick had said the night before they were going out to dinner.

Now that he was here so early, she wondered if their date had turned into more of a late lunch.

It didn't matter. Rick, anytime of day, was a treat.

Katie left her room with a sweatshirt in her hand and felt her stomach grumbling. It had been almost twenty-four hours since she had eaten. Maybe the glorious high of her discovery that she was in love was diminishing just enough to bring her back into the realm of normal life, like sleeping and eating.

She found Rick in the lobby talking to Nicole at the office. Displayed on the counter was a substantial bouquet of pink, yellow, white, and orange gerbera daisies.

Rick sure likes giving flowers. I still have the white roses he gave me last week. I just hope he doesn't have more flowers waiting for me in the car.

"I think the black is still the best way to go," Nicole was saying as Katie approached. "I know it may seem overused, but for dramatic effect, you can't go wrong with black. It'll give the room a more defined sense of stability."

"What are you guys talking about?" Katie asked.

"My apartment. Eli and I were thinking of painting the living room, and Nicole was giving me some ideas."

Katie turned to Nicole. "You're telling him to paint his living room black? You can't be serious."

"Not the living room. His picture frames. I was saying he could keep all his pictures but paint the frames black. I think it would make a dramatic statement."

"When did you guys decide to paint your living room?" Katie asked.

"Last week when we moved the bookcase and television. We saw how bad the wall was."

"Why did you move everything?"

"The sun puts a glare on the TV even with the shades down. Eli suggested we move it a few feet over, out of the glare, which was a great idea. I never thought of it. Once we moved the TV and the bookshelf, the wall was exposed, and it looks awful. We moved the furniture around, and now it's a lot easier to walk through to the bedrooms. I just have to decide what color to paint the wall."

"Did Eli have a preference?" Nicole asked.

"No, not at all."

"You should have Nicole do color samples for you," Katie said. "You know, like those paint color strips you put together for that class on Renaissance art."

Nicole explained, "I think you're remembering the project I did a month ago in which I had to create a color palette for Vermeer's painting of *The Milkmaid*. I should have gone with Rembrandt like most of the class did. His colors were much easier."

"Do you like stuff like that?" Rick asked. "Painting and decorating, I mean."

"I guess," Nicole said.

"Don't be so modest. Have you seen her room, Rick? Nicole is an artist when it comes to colors and decorating. She's just like your mom that way."

"I would pay you," Rick said to Nicole. "I mean, if you want to come have a look at the apartment and make color suggestions."

"You don't have to pay me. I'll run by the paint store this weekend and pick up some samples. Then you can decide what you like. What color is your couch?"

"Brown," Rick said.

"Kind of brown," Katie added. "It's kind of black in some places. Actually, Nicole, you should see his apartment first. If you want, we could go over there on Friday or Saturday since you and I are going to be around all weekend anyway."

"I'll cook for you," Rick said.

"Great idea!" Katie said. "If we were really ambitious, we could turn the whole day into a painting party. The room would be done in no time."

"I'm liking where this is going," Rick said. "I can take most of Friday off but not Saturday."

"Sounds like we have a plan," Katie said. "What do you think, Nicole? Friday okay for you?"

Nicole looked slightly hesitant, but she nodded her agreement. Katie wondered if it was because Eli undoubtedly would be there. Nicole seemed to be having the same qualms about Eli that Katie used to have. She decided that when she had a chance, she would assure Nicole that Eli was a really great guy. Once you got to know a little about him, he was intriguing and pensive but not unnerving.

"Looks like we have a date." Rick smiled at Nicole. Turning to Katie, he said, "And it looks like we better leave for our date before the afternoon slips away from us."

"Have fun, you guys," Nicole said.

"We will." Katie held Rick's hand as they turned to go. She looked at Nicole over her shoulder and said, "At least I think we'll have fun. I don't know where we're going!"

Rick playfully tugged her along out the door. "That's because it's a surprise. No fair trying to pry any clues out of me."

"Are you sure I'm okay in jeans? We're not going anyplace fancy, are we?"

"It's not fancy."

"Is it going to be really cold? Because if this sweatshirt isn't going to be warm enough, tell me now, and I'll go back for a jacket."

Rick let go of her hand and put his arm around her shoulder, pulling her close. "You're trying to pry clues out of me."

"Only a few."

"No more clues. You're just right. Jeans, sweatshirt, all of it. You'll be fine."

"And if I do get cold, you'll keep me warm, right?"

"Absolutely." Rick kissed her on the side of her head. "By the way, I'm liking your hair. When did you have it done?"

"Friday. Before the pizza night."

"You'll have to tell my mom where you went. Since they moved here, she said she hasn't found a good dry cleaner or a good hair salon."

Katie laughed.

Rick looked at her, waiting for her to explain what was so funny.

"I'm sorry, but I can't help your mom with either of those. I've never had anything dry cleaned in my life, and I colored my hair."

Rick looked amazed. Not impressed. Amazed. "You really are the most resourceful woman I know."

"I would have made a great pioneer woman," Katie said. "What about you? Do you think you would have made a great pioneer man?"

"Definitely not. I never would have gone west if I was all set up in a city in the east. Arizona was about as rugged a place I ever want to go, and I was in air conditioning every chance possible."

Rick opened the passenger's side door of his Mustang for Katie with his usual gentlemanly manners. On the seat was a box tied with a blue bow.

"Rick, you don't have to always give me things, you know."

"I know. I like to. Wait until I get in to open it."

Once Rick was behind the steering wheel, Katie undid the bow and opened the small box. Inside was a necklace on a silver chain. At the end of the chain was a green, teardrop-shaped stone or piece of polished glass. It was pretty, but Katie didn't understand its significance.

"Do you like it?" he asked.

"Yes." She liked that he had thought of her and had given her something sweet more than she liked the necklace itself. "It's pretty."

"I saw that necklace at a gift shop the last time I was in Arizona. The stone reminded me of your eyes. Look, when you turn it in the light it changes slightly, just like your eyes. Do you want to wear it?"

"Of course."

Katie handed the necklace over to Rick because she knew he saw little gestures like clasping jewelry or tying Katie's shoes as small acts of romance. Rick leaned close as she pulled her hair off her neck, and he clasped the necklace in place. Then he kissed her on the neck.

Katie's response was to turn to Rick, who was only an inch away, and initiate a sweet, tender kiss on his lips.

"Thank you," she whispered.

"You're welcome. I'm glad you like it."

Katie looked down and smoothed her fingers over the green stone. "I wonder what it is," she said. "I mean, what kind of stone is it?"

"I don't know. We can call it the Katie stone, if you like."

"Sweet! I've never had a stone named after me before."

Rick started the car, and the music from the stereo instantly blared. He reached to turn it down, but Katie stopped him with her hand on his.

"I love this song," she shouted. "Keep it cranked."

Rick obliged. With the music loud, their windows down, and the autumn afternoon's sunlight pouring through the windshield, Rick and Katie took off on their date. She touched the smooth green stone around her neck one more time and wondered if the necklace was her surprise or if their destination would also be a surprise. One thing was certain. The sooner they stopped to eat, the better. She was starving. Katie had a feel she was going to scarf down more food than she had ever eaten in front of Rick. It was a good thing he was crazy about her and used to her carnivorous ways.

They drove for more than forty minutes and were approaching Escondido, where both of them had grown up, when Katie started to feel queasy. Her stomach wasn't upset from starvation. She felt nervous about being so close to her parents' home.

"Rick." She reached over to turn the stereo way down. "Please don't tell me we're going to see my parents. I'm not prepared to see them. Mentally, I mean."

"We're not going to your parents."

"Good. Not that I shouldn't be going to see them, because I should. I tried, you know, to arrange something for Thanksgiving, but ..."

"I know. We're not going there. You can relax."

Katie didn't relax. She felt as if she needed to confide in Rick more than she had before. As he kept driving, she kept going, talking openly about her parents. She told Rick what Julia had said regarding honoring them. She also told him about her conversation with her mom, about leaving a message on Clint's phone, and about how Larry had been in rehab in Bakersfield last summer.

"Why didn't you tell me any of this before?" Rick asked.

"It never came up. My brothers are barely a part of my life. I tried to reach Clint because of Baby Hummer."

"I thought you said your mom called you while you were on duty that Saturday."

"That's right; she did call me."

"Was there a reason?"

Katie remembered. "She said she wanted my address."

"Did she send you something?"

"I don't know. I should check my campus mailbox. I haven't checked it in about a week. She said she had a letter to send me."

"What kind of letter?"

"I have no idea. Probably something for student loans or a credit card promotion."

The traffic was thickening as they slowed down in the center lane.

"I hope there wasn't an accident," Katie said.

"I should have realized we would hit holiday traffic. I thought we were getting away early enough in the day."

"Where are we going?" Katie asked.

Rick gave her a sideways grin. "It's supposed to be a surprise."

"I thought the necklace was a surprise."

"Okay, so I have two surprises. The first was the necklace."

"And the second?"

"Let's just say we're going someplace I've thought about taking you for a long time."

"Oh, a clue! Keep going."

"It's a place I know you really wanted to go to."

"That's not much of a clue. I've wanted to go to a lot of places. Is it ... Morocco?"

Rick laughed. "Not exactly."

"We're heading south. Is it ... Mexico?"

"No, definitely not!"

"What's wrong with Mexico? I think it would be fun to go to Tijuana or Ensenada for the day. We should do that some time. A group of girls on our floor went a few weekends ago to Rosarita Beach."

"We can spend the day at Carlsbad Beach, or better yet, we could drive up to Newport Beach."

"Don't you think it would be fun to go to Mexico, though?"

"No."

"Why not?"

"It's primitive. I can think of other places I'd rather go."

"Like where? Where would you like to go if you could go anywhere in the world?"

"I would go to Aspen."

"Colorado?"

"My family stayed at a resort there one time that was, in my opinion, about as good as it gets. Five-star, ski lift onsite, great views out the windows. I could live there, no problem."

"You could live where it snows? At a ski resort?" Katie never expected Rick to say that.

"That's the first place that came to mind. If we're just dreaming our ideal dreams, then, yes, that's where I would live."

"I had no idea you liked Colorado that much."

Rick nodded. "You and I should go skiing this winter. I only got away once last year. You've been skiing before, haven't you?"

"Only once. With Christy, in high school. I talked her into joining the ski club. We had to sell candy bars to raise money for the trip. I think I ate more than I sold. It's a wonder I fit into my ski clothes."

"What do you think? Are you interested in hitting the slopes again?"

"I'm interested in trying again, but you should be warned that, when I have a couple of boards strapped to my feet and am pushed down an icy slope, well, let's just say all the snow bunnies out there are safe from any serious competition."

"You just didn't have the right ski instructor," Rick said. "When we go, I'll teach you some of the tricks of the sport. You'll do great. Trust me."

Katie paused to create a mental picture of herself from the ski trip in high school. She really was a disaster on skis. Although, if she remembered correctly, the attendant at the ski rental shop had given her skis that were way too long. Maybe it would be different if she had better skis or at least ones that were shorter and therefore more manageable.

"What about you?" Rick asked.

"What about me?"

"Where would you live if you could live anywhere?"

Katie paused. "I think I'd like to have a small apartment someplace where the rent was affordable, and then I'd spend all my money traveling around the world."

Rick laughed.

"I'm serious. There is so much out there to see."

"That's what my brother says. He's set some pretty high goals for us by starting this chain of cafés. If we can hit the right locations at the right time and get in before an area starts to boom, we can make a lot of money. The Arizona store was a setback, but I'm glad now that it didn't work out. Josh is running some specs on other locations. I haven't told you a lot of the details, but we have a ten-year plan that could turn out pretty good for us."

Katie wasn't used to Rick talking about his financial goals. She also hadn't realized that he and Josh planned to stay with the café business for ten years. Rick had his life planned out.

I wonder where he's put me in that ten-year plan?

"By the way," Katie asked, "Josh is going to be at Thanksgiving dinner tomorrow, isn't he?"

"Yes."

"What about Eli?"

"Yes, he's coming, and he said he was going to bring someone."

Katie perked up. "Is he bringing Joseph?"

"I don't remember who he said it was. It could have been Joseph."

"I hope it is."

Rick looked at Katie. "Why did you ask about Josh?"

She was about to reveal her idea of matching up Nicole with Josh but then remembered that Nicole didn't want Katie to say anything so that it wouldn't turn awkward when they met. "I was just wondering. The same way I'm wondering why we're almost to San Diego. Are we taking a trip into our past and visiting your old apartment?"

Rick glanced at Katie again. "I hadn't thought of that, but it's not a bad idea."

"I was kidding. Where are we going, really?"

"San Diego, as you figured out."

"And what are we going to do in San Diego?"

"You'll see."

Katie gave Rick's arm a friendly slug. "You're a big brat with secrets, did you know that? And just for being a brat, I think you should give me another clue."

"You do, do you? Okay, no problem. Here's your clue. This is a redo."

"A what?"

"A redo. You came here once before."

"That's not a very good clue."

"And when you came here, you didn't have a very good time. I always felt bad about that. I was thinking about this place yesterday, and I decided that, if we came here and had a redo of the experience, it might replace the memory with a new, better memory."

Katie thought through what Rick was saying. "The last time I was at this place, were you there too?"

Rick nodded and slid a glance at her.

A wide, sunny smile broke out on her face. "Rick, we're going to the zoo! You're taking me to the San Diego Zoo!"

"Maybe," Rick said slowly. However, the satisfied expression on his face made it clear that Katie had guessed correctly.

"Hey, I take back what I said about your being a brat. You're my hero! I can't believe you're taking me to the zoo. I love the zoo. Except the last time we were there. I hated the zoo that day, and I hated you. Well, not hated you, but my feelings weren't pleasant toward you like they are now. Oh, Rick, this is such a great surprise! You are so wonderful! I love you!"

The "I love you" popped out before Katie had a chance to tame it back to the secret cavern from which it had sprung.

Rick kept looking straight ahead, driving with a fixed grin on his face.

Katie didn't retract her declaration. She wondered if he took it like all the other exuberant comments as a sort of "you're-cool, I-luv-ya'" statement, or if he took it as it was still resounding inside of Katie like a gong. The truth was spoken aloud. Katie loved Rick.

Now it was up to Rick. What would his response be? Was he building Katie into his ten-year plan? Or was he still taking the one-foot-in-front-of-the-other steps in their relationship without yet having walked over that invisible line that ushered him into knowing for certain that he was in love?

Katie wished dearly that she could know the answer right then and there. She may have told Rick earlier that she was a good "waiter," but at the moment, she didn't like having her feelings out there in the space between them and be the one holding her breath, waiting for what Rick would say next.

Five hours after Katie had slipped with her declaration of love for Rick and he still hadn't said anything, she gave up expecting a response. Her preference all along was that Rick would have been the first one to make the all-important declaration. She convinced herself, because of the way it had popped out, that she could brush it off and wait until he was the one to propel their relationship further with his own. No doubt he would plan carefully when he would say the three little words that could change everything for them.

They had arrived at the San Diego Zoo at three o'clock and made their way around to see all of Katie's top choices of animals within a few hours. Katie declared each creature to be her favorite until they moved on to the next exhibit. Then that particular animal moved to the top of her list.

Rick teased her, held her hand, and bought her a hot dog to calm her hunger before their big plans for dinner.

At the panda exhibit, they didn't see much of the animals because they were sleeping. The koalas were drowsing as well. However, the polar bears were active and delightfully sociable that afternoon. One of them swam right up to the glass in the underground viewing room and put his paws and face up to his window on their world. Katie placed her hand on the glass and talked to him. He lingered only a moment before turning his rounded, wide backside to them and swimming off.

Rick liked reading the facts at all the displays. He was especially impressed when he read that the first polar bear had come to the San Diego Zoo in 1917. The poor thing had been kept in a cage. Now the Polar Bear Plunge was the largest polar bear exhibit in the world, and the water was kept at 55 degrees even on San Diego's hottest days.

The gorilla exhibit was a big hit with both of them. They laughed hard and had fun watching the little children marvel at the orangutans swinging and springing around in their habitat. One of the orangutans showed off more than the others. A person standing next to Rick and Katie said, "I think that's the one that paints and has its own web space."

Katie thought the man was joking, but others around them confirmed that the San Diego Zoo orangutans were renowned for their intelligence. Rick found a brochure that explained a Bornean orangutan named Ken Allen had been part of the habitat for twenty-nine years. "Curious Ken Allen" made a name for himself by managing to escape on three occasions and wandering about the zoo, checking in on all the other animals. The zookeepers never could find out how he managed to escape.

Their enjoyable jaunt around the zoo was so different from what they had experienced nearly five years ago when they came for the day with Christy, Todd, and Doug. The five of them had spent the day trying to appear casual and cohesive even though the odd number made for a lopsided grouping. Katie spent most of that day feeling down because Rick was ignoring her after having kissed her the night before in front of the apartment he shared with Doug and Todd. At one point Katie remembered she dissolved into a swamp of tears and angst and was angry at Christy for trying to cheer her up.

This trip to the zoo was indeed a redo, and the fun she and Rick had together this time far surpassed the drama and trauma of the previous zoo excursion.

"Do you think it's because we're older?" Katie asked Rick, as they were strolling toward the exit. "Is that why we had such a better time? Are we able to manage our relationships that much better?"

"I think you are what makes things like this fun," Rick said. "I can't believe you told that little girl when we were watching the flamingos that when they stand on one leg it means they have to go to the bathroom."

Katie laughed. "Did you see her when she was walking away with her mom? She was hopping on one leg."

"We can guess where they were headed."

"What about us?" Katie asked.

"What about us?" Rick took a final sip from the soft drink he had been carrying around since they had stopped at a stand by the reptile exhibit. "Did you want to stop at the restroom too?"

"No. I was trying to ask where are we headed now?" She meant where they were going for dinner, but apparently Rick took the question to be a relationship one.

"I'd say we're headed for more good times. What do you think?"

"More good times, yes, definitely. Anything else you would like to add to that prediction?"

Rick put his arm around her shoulder. "I think we're headed for many more good times for many more days to come. Is that enough, or are you ready for more?"

"More?"

"How much more of a commitment do you need at this point?" Rick's voice was buttery, but his question felt like a needle to Katie.

"I don't necessarily need any more of a commitment. I just know that ..."

"You just know what?"

She wasn't going to blurt out that she was in love with him. Not here. Not at the exit of the zoo. He was giving every sort of hint that he felt the same way, and yet, until he actually said the words, she wasn't going to repeat them.

"I just know that I'm really happy with where we are right now, and I'm glad we took the long way here in the slow lane," she said.

"Me too."

As they drove out of the parking lot, Katie thought about Rick's earlier responses. He was giving Katie every reason to believe she was indeed part of his ten-year plan — and beyond. One day, she believed he would tell her that he loved her.

And I need to wait for that day. I don't want to press him into an emotional corner and hold him hostage until he says it. I need to hear the words when they spring out of his heart, all exuberant and untamed.

"So where are we going now?" Katie asked. This time she added, "Someplace fun to eat, I hope. My hot dog burned off way back at the Polar Bear Plunge. I'm so hungry I think I could eat a polar bear. Although not one of the polar bears we just saw, because they were so cute. And so big! How can a creature that big swim with such agility?"

"I have no idea, but I think you're going to like where we're going to eat since you're so hungry. I'm hungry too."

"Is it someplace we've been before or that you've been to before?"

"No. I found this place online. It had great reviews, and it's different."

"Different, huh?" Katie knew Rick always was interested in finding restaurants that offered "different" cuisine. That's why he had gotten so excited about the Thai restaurant that opened a few months ago near his apartment. He had been talking about a new Indian restaurant that opened in Fallbrook. Katie hoped tonight wasn't the night he wanted to try out that particular restaurant. She wanted to eat a big chunk of meat, not a variety of spicy rice dishes.

Rick drove down a narrow street in the Old Town area of San Diego and found a parking spot on the street, which he said was "slightly miraculous."

Katie spotted a chocolate store across the street. "Do you mind if we stop in there before we eat?"

"Are you looking for some appetizers?" Rick teased.

"No. Well, maybe. Not a bad idea. I wanted to buy something for your mom for tomorrow."

When she had joined Rick's family for Easter, all the other guests had brought beautifully wrapped gifts of candles or specially wrapped fruits. Rick's family was big on gift giving, and Katie didn't want to show up empty-handed this time at his mom's big dinner.

Entering the candy shop, Katie asked Rick, "What does your mom like?"

"She likes anything chocolate."

"Look at these!" Katie pulled a wrapped chocolate turkey on a stick out of the basket on top of the counter. "What about a couple of these?"

Rick didn't look convinced. "You could get an assortment of truffles," he suggested. "You can select the ones you want, and they'll pack them for you."

Katie picked candies from the elite rows of bonbons and truffles, as a young woman with impressive white gloves loaded up a two-pound box assortment. Rick had suggested Katie buy a one-pound or even a half-pound box. Katie wanted to make a good impression so she turned down Rick's suggestion and went for the two-pounder, making sure the top layer was the most delectable-looking chocolates.

The woman behind the counter sealed the beautiful brown box with gold stickers and wrapped it with a wide, gold ribbon. She pushed a few buttons on the high-tech computer screen in front of her and with a smile at Katie said, "That will be $57.82."

Katie didn't move. She didn't blink. For a moment she didn't breathe. The only word that stumbled out of her mouth was, "Dollars?"

"Here." Rick quickly reached for his wallet. "I can put it on my card, if you don't have that much with you. You can pay me back later." With a wink he added, "You're good for the loan. I know where to find you."

"No, I can get it," Katie said stubbornly. She pulled out her debit card, knowing she didn't have enough in her checking account to cover the expense. However, Thursday was Thanksgiving and a bank holiday, and she was pretty sure she could put enough in her account to cover the purchase since her Resident Assistant paycheck was deposited automatically into her savings account every other Friday. All she had to do was remember to transfer the needed amount to her checking account.

When they left the chocolate shop with Katie carrying the expensive treats in a fancy-handled shopping bag, she was still in shock. She had never paid that much for a gift. True, she was frugal and not a big gift giver so she didn't know what the going rate was for such things. But spending nearly sixty dollars for candy blew her mind.

"Ready to eat?" Rick asked.

She nodded and forced a smile. The last thing she wanted to do was give Rick any indication that she wished she hadn't bought the chocolates at all. Or maybe that she should have purchased just a pound, as Rick had suggested.

Note to self: When Rick says go for a pound or even half a pound of anything, listen to the man!

Rick led the way down the street to a charming restaurant that exuded tantalizing barbecue smells. The sign over the entrance read, "Churrascaria."

"It's Brazilian." Rick held the door open for Katie. He pointed to one of the waiters in a gaucho-style uniform who was walking past them with a big chunk of beef on a long skewer. In his other hand he held a long knife.

"They come around to the tables with meat that has been rotating on the barbecue spit. Then they slice off as much as you want while it's still hot."

"As much as I want?" Katie perked up.

"You are hungry, aren't you?"

"Very."

The host seated them at a table by a long, opulent salad bar. "Is that in case you don't want the meat?" Katie asked. "The vegetarian option?"

"No, it's all included."

Katie's eyes grew wide. "All included? How much does dinner cost at this place?"

"It doesn't matter. Just enjoy it. Do you know what you want to drink?"

Katie ordered hot tea, and then together they made their rounds of the spectacular salad bar. The first skewer of meat offered and sliced at their table was chicken wrapped in bacon, followed by thin slices off a skewer of sirloin beef. The flavor was rich and peppery. Katie loved it, and so did Rick. They tried every spit of meat that was brought to their table.

"They have sixteen different kinds of meats," Rick said. "I think we should have started counting because I'm guessing we didn't even make it past a dozen."

"That last one with the garlic was amazing," Katie said. Even though the slices were thin and only one or two at a time, she was full. Her caesar salad and shrimp were still untouched, even though she loved both of them. She couldn't force herself to eat another bite.

"Sierra is still in Brazil, you know, and she told me about eating at places where they bring you more meat than you can eat. I didn't picture this, but I'm sure this is what she was talking about. And just for the record, you can bring me here anytime you want."

Katie had a feeling the bill was more than she had spent on the chocolates. She wanted to make sure Rick knew how much she appreciated the whole day.

They went for a hand-in-hand walk around the neighborhood in an effort to let their dinner settle before starting the long drive back to school.

"You are so good to me, Rick. Thanks for everything today. The zoo, that amazing dinner, and this necklace. You really don't have to be so generous."

"The way I see it, I'm way behind."

"Way behind what?"

"Way behind in thinking up fun things for us to do and going interesting places for dinner. We've been together for almost a year,

Katie. I know, we've been officially dating only a few months, but we did a lot of casual things together for a long time. Most of this past year I've been so focused on the café and on starting up another one with Josh that I feel as if I've fallen behind in my boyfriend duties."

"Boyfriend duties?" Katie laughed. "Hey, if going out with me is a chore or a duty, you are much further behind in our relationship than you realize."

"Okay, so duty was the wrong word. But you know what I mean. I want to focus on you now. I want us to do fun things together. Don't laugh at me, but I made a list. And this was on the list. I wanted to redo the zoo so you would have a good memory of being there with me."

Katie gazed up at Rick with a look of devotion and appreciation. "Mission accomplished, my list-making boyfriend. I now have the hap-happiest zoo memories ever."

"Good." Rick stopped walking. They were in front of a shop that sold bicycles. All the stores were closed, but this was a charming, touristy sort of street, so all the shops were fixed up to look as posh as the chocolate shop. The bicycle store had a window box with bright yellow and blue pansies.

As they stood there, Rick wrapped Katie in his arms. She knew he was about to kiss her. Willingly tilting her chin up to meet his kiss, she closed her eyes. Just before Rick's lips met hers, an unexpected bubble of the garlic-soaked beef that was settling in her stomach rose up and threatened to escape her lips in an unflattering manner.

Katie quickly turned her head and tried to cover up the escaping burp with a fake cough followed immediately by a poorly executed imitation sneeze. Her range of odd sound effects sent Katie into a fit of laughter.

"What's so funny?" Rick asked.

"Nothing. Me! My sneeze! Ha!" Katie tried to straighten her expression and bring the moment back around to the lovely romantic interlude they had almost experienced. "I'm sorry, Rick."

He looked confused.

No way was Katie going to tell him that she almost released a toxic cloud of garlic in his face. Poor guy. He looked so left out of Katie's private joke.

"Come on." He took her by the hand and led her back to the car.

"Are you upset?" she asked.

"Should I be?"

"No. I just … my breath is really garlicky," she said. "I'm sorry I cracked up like that. I didn't mean to ruin the moment."

"I might have some gum in my car."

"Good. I'll take some."

They pulled onto the freeway and headed north, chewing peppermint-scented gum and talking about the zoo and other date ideas Rick had on his list. The mood was good. The traffic was awful, but it gave them the luxury to discuss several topics at length.

An hour into their ride home, Katie suddenly grabbed Rick's arm. "Oh, no! Rick, we have to turn around!"

"What's wrong?"

"The chocolates! I forgot the chocolates! I put the bag under the table at the restaurant, and I forgot it. Rick, we have to go back!"

He wasn't happy. But then, Katie wasn't happy either.

"I would say just forget it and let it go, but that chocolate was a major investment for me, Rick. I have to retrieve it."

"You should have bought a smaller box," he mumbled.

"I know. You were right. I'll pay you for the gas it's going to cost us to go back."

"You don't have to pay me for the gas, Katie. I should have remembered the bag too. I could have reminded you to pick it up before we left."

"I hate it when I do things like this."

"Don't spend the next hour beating yourself up. Here. Use my phone and call the restaurant. They can hold the bag for you at the front so we can just run in and grab it."

"You have their number in here?"

"I put it in when I called them a few days ago. It's in my restaurant list in the address book."

"I don't know anybody who has a restaurant list in his cell phone," Katie muttered as she scrolled down. "Why would you go to all the trouble of putting in phone numbers for restaurants?"

"For moments just like this," Rick said in a flat voice.

"Point taken." Katie found the number and called the restaurant. They said they had her bag and that they would hold it at the front.

It took an hour and fifteen minutes to drive back to the restaurant; then they turned around and drove another two hours in the holiday traffic. Part of the ride they were cordial. Part of it they were chatty and into the rhythm that had kept them both happily buoyant for the earlier part of the day. But when Rick dropped Katie off at Crown Hall after one in the morning, both of them were wiped out.

"I'll come by at eleven tomorrow morning," Rick said.

For a moment, Katie couldn't think of why he was coming by. Then she remembered it was Thanksgiving. Dinner was going to be at two o'clock, but Rick had said they always gathered before noon for appetizers and to watch football or play board games.

"I'll be ready at eleven," Katie said, more as a reminder to her foggy brain than as an answer to Rick. "And Nicole will be with me."

"Good," Rick said.

Katie was about to close the car door when Rick said, "Katie, the bag."

"Oh, the chocolates. I almost forgot them again." She reached for the bag.

"Do you want me to keep them and bring them with me tomorrow?"

"No, I'll remember them. Thanks again, Rick. Really. It was an amazing day. And night. And beginning of the next day. I'm sorry again about forgetting the candy."

"Don't worry about it. Get some sleep. I'll see you in the morning."

Katie waved, and Rick pulled away from the curb. The campus felt strange. Not one student was in view. Even at odd hours of the night, someone was driving in or out of the parking lot or sitting in the lobby. Crown Hall felt like a ghost town.

Using her master key on the front door, Katie schlepped her way down the hall, yawning as she went. No music floated out from under the closed doors along the way. No sounds of someone taking a late-night shower, and no young woman sitting outside of her room hugging her knees, away from the listening ears of her roommate, and talking in whispers on her cell phone.

Katie found it easy to go right to bed. What wasn't easy was waking up the next morning when her alarm went off on her cell phone. She had allowed plenty of time for a long shower to rinse off the final hints of the zoo. But even with plenty of time, Katie was finding it difficult to get ready before eleven.

She shuffled down the vacant hall in her robe and knocked on Nicole's bedroom door, calling out, "Hey, I don't know what to wear. What are you wearing?"

Nicole opened the door and motioned for Katie to come in even though Nicole was on her cell phone. She was dressed, and her sleek, dark hair looked great. Her brown print dress accentuated all the right places in all the right ways. Her earrings and necklace were ideal for the outfit, and even her shoes were the same shade of brown. Nicole was a Thanksgiving feast for the eyes, and Katie was certain that Josh would notice her and be wildly impressed.

Hanging up her phone, Nicole immediately asked, "Am I overdressed?"

"No. And don't even think of changing. You look perfect. Fantastic. Now what can I borrow?"

Nicole laughed. "Anything. What do you want to wear? Pants? A dress?"

"I want to wear a dress. Or a skirt. I think I'm more comfortable in skirts."

"Here, try this one. And if that doesn't work, try this one." Nicole handed Katie an armful of wardrobe options.

It took only six attempts before Katie settled on a winning combination. She went for one of Nicole's black skirts only because it fit better than any of the others, and a green-and-white top with a fun green sweater that looked good with her eyes. The neckline showed off the green necklace Rick had given her as well.

"You need to take me shopping," Katie said. "I would never pick these pieces off the rack, but now that I put them all together, I like this outfit. I like the skirt too."

"You know what? You can have that skirt. I haven't worn it in more than a year. Seriously, take it."

"Thanks. I will. I'm going to run back to my room and pick up my gift for Rick's mom. Then I'll be ready to go."

"What did you buy her?"

"The world's most expensive chocolates."

"I got her a mum. Is that dumb?"

"A dumb mum?" Katie laughed.

"I didn't know what to buy her." Nicole picked up the rust-colored potted plant.

"Those are mums? They look like little daisies. Only brown. Or is that a shade of orange?"

"It's ochre."

"It's what?"

"That's the name of this shade of brown. Ochre."

"Okay, I'll just tell you right now that you and Rick's mom are going to hit it off beautifully. If you say, 'Oh, I like your ochre doodad there,' you won't need a gift to get on her good side. You will shoot to the top of her favorites list by your color-wheel vocabulary alone."

"Fine. But I'm still bringing the chrysanthemums."

"Oooh! Say that word around her too. She knows all the real names for flowers and plants. She's going to love you."

Katie was right. With or without the flowers or the color-wheel lingo, Rick's mom instantly adored Nicole. So did Rick's dad. Josh, however, seemed too engaged in a conversation with Rick's dad to do anything more than say hello. When Rick's dad stepped out of the kitchen to answer the doorbell, Katie tried to find a way to connect Josh and Nicole.

"So, Josh, are you still living in Arizona, or did you move back here when the Tempe café plans didn't go through?"

"I'm in between. The way things are going, I might be back here by Christmas, but it depends on what my girlfriend ends up doing."

"Your girlfriend?" Katie shifted a quick glance at Nicole, who was dunking a baby carrot into the dip bowl. Nicole seemed unaffected by the news that Josh had a girlfriend, but Katie felt as if another apology was due to her friend. First she tried to set up Nicole with Eli and that went nowhere. Now it turned out Josh had a girlfriend.

"Shana applied for a job in San Diego. If she gets it, she'll move here by the end of December. I wouldn't have a reason to stay in Arizona then. Of course, a lot will depend, too, on where we line up the next café venture."

Rick's mom entered the conversation as she filled a wooden bowl with tortilla chips. "I wish Shana could have joined us for Thanksgiving. Please let her know she's welcome for Christmas. You too, Katie, of course. We had such a nice time when you were with us last Christmas.

You're always welcome; I hope you know that. Now that we've moved and are so much closer to Rancho, I'm hoping you'll stop by even if Rick isn't with you. And Nicole, you are always welcome too."

"Thank you," Nicole said. "Are you sure I can't do something to help you with the meal?"

"Not yet. I'll let you know when we get closer to sitting down to eat."

"The table is beautiful, by the way," Nicole said. "Rick showed Katie and me around the house. The dining room is gorgeous. I love the dark wood. Your china is one of my favorite patterns. My aunt has the same one. It's Lenox, isn't it?"

Coming from any other young woman, those compliments might sound like a bunch of fake lines intended to impress. From Nicole, they were sincere. Rick's mom seemed to pick up on that.

"Yes. Did you see the gravy boat that goes with the set? I think that's my favorite piece." She led the way into the dining room, and Nicole followed, eager to chat about the china.

Katie turned to Josh. "I hope the job works out for Shana. I look forward to meeting her."

"You'll like her. She's a lot like your friend." Josh nodded toward the dining room where Nicole was standing with her back to them.

"Nicole is great, isn't she?" Katie knew Josh meant the comment in a positive way, but truthfully she would have liked it better if Josh had said that Shana was a lot like *Katie*. That would have boosted her ratings with Rick's family, and she always felt that was a good thing. Besides, if Josh was going to compare his girlfriend to Nicole, then Katie wished she would have introduced Josh to Nicole before he became involved with Shana.

But she didn't have a chance to get out of sorts over the layers of possibilities in Josh's comment because Rick's dad returned to the kitchen with Eli and Joseph.

Katie greeted Joseph with an unplanned half hug and gave Eli a warm hello. Rick's brother and dad seemed to be a little surprised at the earthy appearance of Rick's roommate. Or maybe it was Joseph's appearance.

Rick, who had been out in the garage looking for some sort of serving bowl for his mom in the collection of unopened boxes, entered at that moment. He introduced Eli, and Eli introduced Joseph. Rick's mom and Nicole returned to the kitchen, and another round of introductions took place with more handshaking and curious glances.

Katie had to admit, Rick should have prepped Eli for the Doyle household dress code. Eli was in jeans and a sweater with a hole in the arm. His hair stuck out from under the beanie he should have removed when he entered the house. Joseph wasn't quite as scruffy-looking as Eli, but his shirt was wrinkled and carried the faint scent of the gas station.

"Please, help yourselves to some appetizers." Rick's mom went to work as the ideal hostess and made sure everyone had something to drink.

Spread across the counter, along with the tortilla chips and fresh-cut vegetable platter, were a fresh fruit salad, French bread with spinach dip, and an assortment of olives, cheese, and gourmet crackers.

"This is a beautiful feast." Joseph took some of the olives and chunks of cheese. "Thank you so much for inviting me to your Thanksgiving dinner."

"There's more to come," Rick said. "This isn't dinner. This is just the warm-up."

Joseph looked incredulous. Katie wondered what it must be like for someone who had grown up in humble surroundings to enter a large and exquisitely decorated home like the Doyles'. What must he think?

True, the cafeteria at Rancho Corona provided an abundant variety of food in assembly-line fashion. But here, all the food was displayed artistically and was accompanied by china plates for the appetizers and crystal goblets for the soft drinks.

Katie looked at Eli. He was staring at Rick's mom as if trying to memorize her appearance. She was a beautiful woman. Tall and dark-haired like Rick. When she was young, she had done some modeling, and when Rick was young, she had sold skincare products. Rick told Katie once that his mother's grandparents used to live in Italy and that he still had relatives there.

Stepping a few feet over to get Eli's attention, Katie gave him the signal they had practiced at the Pizza Doubles Night right before Nicole came downstairs. She scratched her right eyebrow and brushed her hair back.

Eli didn't pick up on the clue.

Katie gave the signal a second time. He still didn't respond. Resorting to a more obvious tactic, Katie reverted to the original "take a picture, it lasts longer" finger frame.

Eli glanced at her, as did everyone else.

Katie quickly pulled her hands apart and did an odd sort of flicking movement, as if some salt or dip from the finger food had gotten on her hands and the frame configuration was part of her method for removing it.

Eli responded to Katie's mime act by stroking his goatee. That was the signal he had given her in the lobby at Crown Hall, so she was pretty sure he was in sync with her now. At least he had stopped staring.

The Doyle family was strong on traditions, and one of those traditions was a board game they played when everyone was together. Katie secretly thought it an odd game, but she had jumped in on previous occasions and knew that she would give the game her best efforts again this time.

The game came with a spinner and pieces to move around the board, but it lacked real competition. It was a "let's talk" game. Whenever a player landed on a blue space, he had to draw one of the question cards and answer the question. If he landed on a red space, he had to think of a question and ask it of the person on his right.

Katie guessed the game was invented by a therapist who was having trouble convincing his own family to interact. Not that Katie knew how a normal, healthy family was supposed to interact at the holidays, but sitting down to prescripted questions felt odd to her.

Nonetheless, while the turkey cooked, the guests sat around a large coffee table in the spacious family room, and Rick took the first spin of the dial. He landed on red and had to ask Nicole a question. He asked her if she was glad that she had come to the Doyle home.

Nicole graciously said, "Yes, I'm very glad to be here. Thanks for asking."

That started the game in a nice, cordial way.

Eli was the first one to draw a question card. He read it aloud. "Describe one of your favorite birthdays."

He stared at the card for an uncomfortably long moment before finally looking up. "I was nine. We were living on the compound in Zambia, and it rained on my birthday."

Everyone waited for the next part of his story. Except for Joseph, who smiled and nodded.

"We hadn't had rain in fourteen months," Eli explained. "When it started to rain, everyone ran out into the open area in front of the medical building. It was like a big party. School was out for the rest of the day. Everyone laughed, danced, and stomped around in the mud. My friends and I had a big mud fight, and my mother made a cake. My father gave me a small flashlight he used to always keep in his pocket. I still have the flashlight. That was definitely my favorite birthday."

The rest of the group sat still for a moment in hushed contemplation. It was Josh's turn next. He spun the arrow and landed on a blue square. His question was, "Where do you hope to live five years from now?"

"You guys already know the answer to this one." Josh gazed at his parents and Rick. "My goal is to be a millionaire by the time I'm thirty-five."

"But where do you want to live five years from now?" Nicole prodded.

"Hawaii. Although I think it might take me closer to ten years to get there, the way things are going. The Tempe project was a setback, but if we can swing this next deal by the end of the year, I think we might be back on track. I have the preliminary paperwork in motion, and we meet with the builder on Tuesday, so —"

"Wait," Katie interrupted. "You guys found another property to develop? I didn't know you had found something already."

Josh nodded and gave Rick an irritated glance, as if Rick should have been the one to give Katie the details.

"We have two specs going. I'm sure Rick will tell you about them."

Rick shot a glare back at Josh as he said, "It's still preliminary. One is in Redlands, and the other is east of San Diego. Both sites are a few hours' drive from here."

"And both are being offered way below market," Josh added. "If these two work out, it will definitely make the loss of the Tempe site worth it. We'll be able to double our efforts and our profits."

Rick's dad jumped into the dialogue. "We'll know more after we meet with the builder Tuesday. Now, whose turn is it?"

Katie had a sinking feeling. All the time Rick had talked about spending with her might well be redirected after that meeting on Tuesday. He could easily go back on the same sort of schedule he had when he and Josh were trying to pull everything together to build the café in Tempe.

Josh said he wanted to close the deal by the end of the year. That meant things could change quickly for Rick and Katie. She wasn't sure how she felt about that. A small echo inside was telling her the reason she found it so easy to tumble into love with Rick was because of the sense of security she felt after he expressed his affection for her with kisses as well as being more available for them to spend time together. How would she feel when he wasn't so available?

Rick's mom was taking her turn and answering a question about her feelings whenever she went to the dentist. While she described her aversion to long needles, Katie floated out of the conversation and tried to imagine how things might be between her and Rick for the rest of the semester, the rest of the year, the next ten years, and the rest of her life.

Pulling herself back to the present, Katie realized that part of loving Rick meant entering into his life at whatever level was appropriate for that stage of their relationship. If she really loved him, which she knew she did, then she would need to enter into his goals and the pace at which he intended to accomplish those goals. Being with Rick the rest of her life would always mean financial plans, career objectives, and long hours of work.

She wasn't afraid of such a life. It was just different from the one she had lived and certainly different from how she had imagined her life would be.

The only part she knew she would have to work at would be the money part. Buying the chocolates for Rick's mom had been a small taste of the level his family lived at. When Katie and Nicole had entered the kitchen earlier and presented Rick's mom with the mum and the candy, she had expressed equal appreciation for both gifts. She gave Katie a hug to thank her for the big box of candy and then said, "There's never any point in trying to diet around the holidays, is there?"

It was a friendly comment and delivered lightheartedly. But now that Katie thought about it, she realized the expensive chocolates might go untouched by Rick's mom altogether. Katie knew she would have to develop a new sense of understanding for all things pertaining to money. Especially gift giving to the Doyle family members. She liked challenges. This would be one she believed she could conquer.

"Katie's turn." Rick turned the spinner toward her.

She pulled her thoughts back into the game and spun a five. Her token landed on a red space and she had to ask Joseph a question. Without thinking of how her question might sound, she pulled her inspiration from the little trail her thoughts had just journeyed.

"If you had a million dollars, what would you do with it?"

"That's always a good question," Rick's dad said.

Joseph didn't appear to have the same appreciation for the question that Rick's dad did. He stammered a bit, as if the thought had never occurred to him. After a moment he answered, "I would bring my wife and daughter here to live with me."

The group fell into another stunned silence.

"Your daughter?" Katie asked. "I only saw the photo of your wife. I didn't know you had a daughter as well."

"She was only three months old when I left Ghana, and we didn't have the opportunity to take photos of her."

Rick shifted uncomfortably. "How can you stand to be away from them?"

"Some days are easier than others. When I hear from them and know that they are well, it gives me courage to continue and finish my course. My wife understands what I am trying to accomplish here with my schooling. She knows it will be for the good of our people, and so she says her sacrifice is a small one."

The conversation rolled on as Joseph explained how, when his grandfather was a village chief, a missionary from the US had come and told them about Christ. Joseph's grandfather believed, and as a result, most of the people in the village came to Christ. Since then, the village grew to surprising numbers and enjoyed good health and a steady supply of clean water. Joseph's father was now the chief, and Joseph was selected as the one to go to college on a scholarship provided by the mission organization that first made contact with his village. Joseph's career plan was to return to his village as a pastor as well as a teacher at the school.

The contrast in life goals between Joseph and Josh was stunning.

"I'm sorry you, your wife, and your daughter are separated during this time," Rick's mom said. "When was the last time you saw them?"

"Twenty-three months and two weeks ago."

Rick's mom let out a feathery sigh that expressed what Katie was feeling and what she guessed the rest of them were feeling as well.

"What you're doing, Joseph, is very commendable. I know the Lord will bless you and your wife for your great sacrifices."

"The Lord has already blessed us. Abundantly." Joseph's expression was peaceful. Katie wished right then that she had a million dollars so Joseph could be reunited with his family during the final seventeen months that he would be at school.

"Whose turn is next?" Josh asked.

Katie didn't feel like playing anymore. Rick must have felt the same because he said, "What about our annual walk around the block?"

Katie had heard about this Doyle tradition last Christmas. The family always went for a walk while the turkey was in its final hour in the oven. They returned to a fragrant-smelling home and had worked up an appetite in the process.

"Good timing, Rick," his mom said. "Yes, how about a walk? Is everyone ready to work up an appetite?"

Rick's dad was the first to stand. The others followed and gathered at the front door. Katie noticed that Rick's mom had stayed in the kitchen.

"Isn't your mom coming?"

"No, she usually works on the mashed potatoes and green beans while we walk."

"I'll stay and help." Nicole gave Katie's arm a squeeze. "These shoes aren't the best for walking. I would prefer to stay."

"Just make sure you leave a few lumps in the mashed potatoes," Katie said. "That's how Rick likes them. Slightly lumpy."

"Got it. Slightly lumpy."

As they left the house, Katie fell into step with Joseph. "What is your daughter's name?"

"We named her Hope."

Katie felt her heart turning more tender toward Joseph and his wife, Shiloh. Even their daughter's name was a reflection of their shared aspirations for their village and their people. "I wish there was a way they could join you here. The three of you should be together."

"That was our original plan. We both prepared the necessary forms and visas, but all did not go as we wanted. It is okay. We are certainly inside of God's plan. He has many thoughts we do not understand."

The group walked down the wide street of the new housing development. All the landscaping was fresh and green, and all the trees were young. Most of the houses were occupied; yet the neighborhood had that sleepy, just-woke-up sort of feel to it. It was a baby community and one destined to grow strong.

Rick sidled up to Katie and took her hand. Drawing her a few paces back from the others, he said, "Are you okay?"

"Yeah, I'm just thinking about Joseph. I wish he could bring his family here."

"I know what you mean. It's times like this I wish I were a millionaire so I could make stuff like that happen. Sometimes I buck up against Josh's goals to make a lot of money. Then I hear someone like Joseph express a need, and I wish I could just write the check."

"I know," Katie said.

"It helps me remember why I agreed to go after this café franchise project with Josh and put so much effort into it. If we can make a success of it, we're in a great position to do a lot of good financially for other people."

Katie was glad Rick said what he did at that moment. Inside the house her thoughts had teeter-tottered to one side of the equation, thinking that the lifelong pursuit of wealth was a wicked goal in light of Joseph's single-hearted focus on obtaining training so he could go back to Ghana and teach others. Inside of Rick's comment she saw a balance. The world needed wealthy believers who gave generously. As Joseph had just said, maybe God did have many thoughts we don't understand.

Rick gave Katie's hand a squeeze. "When I asked a minute ago if you were okay, I was referring to the news about the two new cafés. How are you processing all that?"

When Katie had heard the news, she had formulated the first lines of what she wanted to say: "Why didn't you tell me yesterday? We were together all day and almost all night, and we talked for hours. Yet you never brought it up. Why?"

However, now that she had had some time to put things in a clearer perspective, she was thinking of Shiloh and the sacrifice she was making with their little girl, Hope, so Joseph could accomplish his goal. To Katie, that seemed like a more beautiful picture of real love than the possessive, feeling left out, accusatory approach she originally was going to take with Rick.

With that renewed sense of appreciation for what Josh and Rick were trying to accomplish long-term, Katie had a different answer to his question. "I would have liked to have heard the update from you, but I think I can understand why you wanted to avoid the topic yesterday. It was our fun day. Well, fun except for when I forgot the candy."

"Don't worry about that, Katie. It all worked out."

"I guess. I should have gone with the half pound, like you suggested. I learned a lot, though. And I learned a few things from Joseph in that game, which, by the way, I've always bashed as being a stupid game, but now I think I can understand why your family likes it. Anyway, my thought on the whole café deal is that you should go for it. Whatever opportunities God brings to you guys and however things come together or when they come together, I think you should go after your dreams and goals. This is what you want to do. You don't have to report back to me at every turn, although the more you do tell me, the less likely it is that I'll end up blurting out embarrassing declarations in front of your family."

Rick smiled. "You're the best, Katie. You know that? You're so good for me."

Katie looked up at him. They had straggled far enough behind the others that no one could hear what they were saying. Rick seemed just a tiny hop away from uttering the three powerful words that had once again risen to the surface of Katie's heart. She dearly wanted to speak them aloud. The statement on the end of her tongue was, "The reason you think I'm so good for you is because I love you, Rick Doyle."

She kept her words inside and waited for Rick to make the declaration she couldn't help but believe was on the edge of his lips. They stopped walking. Rick looked into Katie's eyes. She met his gaze, expectant, ready to hear those life-changing words.

So what did he say?" Nicole was on the edge of her bed late that Thanksgiving night, listening to Katie's summary of what had gone on between her and Rick during the walk. Katie was settled on the air mattress on Nicole's floor, having spent the past hour bringing her up-to-date on Katie's relationship with Rick.

"He said, 'You look gorgeous today.'"

"And?" Nicole prompted.

"That was it. He kissed me quick and light, and we walked fast to catch up with the others. When he was within earshot of his dad, he said, 'I'm missing Max right about now.' And then he, his brother, and his dad went into a long dialogue about Max, which I think was good and healing for the Doyle men."

"I'm sorry. You lost me. Who is Max?"

"Max was their dog. He was a great dog. Huge, slobbery old dog. I loved him. They had him for, I don't know, fifteen years or something. Rick was taking care of Max last summer when his parents moved out of their other house, and the old boy never made it to move into the new house."

"Did Rick ever come back to the topic of your relationship?" Nicole asked.

"No. You were there the rest of the day. We didn't talk privately after that."

"It was a wonderful day. What a meal! That woman knows how to cook. And decorate. Did you see their master bedroom and bathroom? Of course you did. You were right beside me when we took the tour. I'm telling you, Katie, I've never seen such a beautiful home. I can't believe they've only been in the house for a few months."

"They are an amazing family. In terms of ambition and class, they are polar opposites of my parents. If Rick and I ever do get married, I'm really nervous about his parents meeting mine."

"Get married? Is that what you just said?"

"Yeah, I guess I did, didn't I?"

"Do you think you guys are going to get married?" Nicole settled in under her covers. "I mean, have you talked about marriage yet?"

"No. Like I told you, we haven't even gotten to where we're saying 'I love you.' Sometimes, like today, I could see it. I could picture myself adjusting, adapting, and fitting in with his life and his goals. Then other times I . . ." Katie felt her throat tightening. "Other times I think about people like Eli and Joseph, and I feel like I gravitate more to that simple sort of life. You know? Like Eli saying that his favorite birthday was when it rained and they danced in the mud."

Katie giggled at the mental image of a bunch of children tussling in the mud while jubilant adults laughed and raised their faces to the pouring rain. "It's a great image, isn't it?" she continued. "What a beautiful, simple way to celebrate. I bet not one person in the whole compound owned a china gravy boat. No, I bet not one person in the whole compound had even *seen* a china gravy boat. Well, except for maybe Eli's parents before they went to Africa."

Nicole looked like she was about to protest Katie's statement, so Katie quickly added, "I mean, it's not that there's anything wrong with china and gravy boats and all of it. I loved Thanksgiving today with the toasts in the crystal goblets, the beautiful flowers strewn down the center of the table, and all the little figurines of the turkeys, pilgrims, and Indians. But, I don't know, you'll have to tell me, Nicole. Can a person like me come to appreciate and eventually fit in with such high-class people and celebrations? Or will I always be drawn to mud fights rather than gold-plated salad forks?"

"Katie, I firmly believe you can do whatever you set your heart and mind to do. You fit in like one of the family today."

"Really?"

"Yes."

"I didn't seem like the visiting hillbilly cousin?"

"No, not at all. The Doyles love you. That was clear."

"They loved you too. All except Josh, of course, who decided to go and get a girlfriend when I wasn't looking! Sorry about that. I'm glad you told me not to say anything ahead of time, because I didn't. Although, once again, it would have been nice if the Rickster would have told me his brother had a girlfriend."

"By the way," Nicole said, "what was that box thing you were doing with your fingers when we first got there?"

"I was making a picture frame. As in, 'take a picture, it lasts longer.' It was a signal for Eli. He stares."

"I noticed."

"He doesn't realize how intense his gaze is. So before the pizza night I tried to set up a signal with him, but he apparently forgot it."

"It's a pretty obvious signal, don't you think?"

Katie laughed. "Yeah. I came up with a much subtler one, but when he didn't respond to it, I went for the big 'duh' signal."

Nicole laughed. "Poor Eli. No, actually, not poor Eli. I'm starting to see why you like him. I saw a different side of him today, and I think he's intriguing."

"Oooh! Good! Does that mean you might give him another chance? We'll be with him all day tomorrow when we paint their apartment, so you could let him know you're interested."

"Whoa! Stop this buggy right there, missy!"

Katie cracked up. "What did you just say?"

"It's a line my dad used to say to my sister and me whenever we got rowdy. What I was trying to say is that I am *not* interested. Do you hear me? N-O-T, not interested in Eli. I was only saying that he doesn't set me on edge anymore. I don't mind being in the same room with him. That's all."

"Well," Katie said playfully, "that's a start."

"Don't you even go down that trail, Katie Weldon, or I'll be forced to engage you in a full-out pillow war, and to be honest, I'm way too tired. What time is it?"

"Almost two."

"That's it for me. What time are we going over to Rick and Eli's?"

"You said we would be there at eight o'clock."

"I did?"

"Yes, you did. Eight o'clock, Nicole! What were you thinking?"

"I was thinking we would go to bed before midnight. Should we text them and say we're coming at nine or ten instead?"

"Not a good idea," Katie said. "Remember how Rick told us he was going to cook breakfast? Well, he's definitely an early bird, and trust me, his omelets are worth getting up for."

"Should I set the alarm for 6:30 then?" Nicole asked.

"Are you crazy? Set it for 7:40. That will give us plenty of time. We just have to pull on jeans and T-shirts and find some bandanas for our hair. We're going to be painting, remember?"

"I know, but I like to take a shower in the morning to wake up."

"Suit yourself. Don't wake me until 7:40. I can be ready in ten minutes, and it takes ten minutes to drive there."

Nicole set the alarm but didn't tell Katie what time she was setting it for. It went off at 6:50 the next morning, allowing Nicole a full hour to shower and get ready while Katie tried to catch a few more winks and nods. It was pointless. She shuffled down the vacant hallway to her room where she did as she had predicted the night before, donning a pair of jeans, an old T-shirt that she had worn a year ago on a Mexico outreach trip, and a blue bandana. As soon as she washed her face and brushed her teeth, she was ready to go.

Katie returned to Nicole's room and found her putting on mascara.

"Yo, Miss America! Workday means you don't have to look adorable. Besides, you look adorable without any assistance."

"I just feel funny not putting on a little makeup. There, that's all I was going to do anyhow. I'm ready."

They walked through the empty dorm, and Katie said, "This is almost creepy, isn't it? I forgot how cavernous and quiet this place can be when everyone leaves. Thanks, by the way, for working my shift for the checkout Wednesday."

"No problem. We're a good team, Katie."

"Yes, we are. Teamwork is the only way to go. I have a feeling that will be the theme of this day too. I'll warn you now that Rick is a hard worker. Once he gets on task, whatever it might be, watch out! The man is a machine."

The first task Rick took on that morning was creating omelets that would impress the most particular food critic. Nicole and Katie weren't even close to being in the food-critic category. They also weren't even close to being hungry after all they had eaten the day before. Rick looked a little hurt after both of them ate only a third of their massive omelets. When they both said they wanted to keep them in the refrigerator to eat later, Rick looked pacified.

Nicole went to work in Rick's kitchen, cleaning up just as she had done the day before when she was the first to help Rick's mom with the dishes after their Thanksgiving dinner.

"What about some more coffee for everyone?" Rick asked. "I'm going to make some fresh."

"Do you have any tea?" Katie asked.

Eli, who had been quietly chowing down his omelet at the kitchen table, spoke up. "I have Nairobi chai and also some black tea from the plantation I told you about."

"Oh, that's right, you have tea from Africa. Fantastic! I want to see this stuff. Do they cut the leaves after they dry them?"

"I have no idea."

"I might be able to tell by looking at them. Where do you keep the good stuff?"

While Katie and Eli huddled over yellow tins of finely chopped tea leaves, Nicole and Rick worked side-by-side washing dishes while their coffee brewed in Rick's stainless steel high-end coffeemaker.

Katie decided to try the Nairobi chai first, even though she told Eli she wasn't a fan of tea made from leaves that were chopped down to fine nubs, the way this chai was. "I think I already know I'm going to like the Kenyan black tea better, although I'm always willing to try new things. Look at the texture of these leaves in the black tea. Man, these are primo. They unfurl so nicely in the boiling water. They have to have room to open up and swirl around to release the best flavor. That's why teapots and loose leaves are, in my opinion, the best way to go. Tea leaves this nice can get cramped in a teabag. Although, most teabags don't use leaves this large or this fresh. One place I researched in India had a report filed against them. The report said that after they packed the best tea as loose leaf and put it in canisters, they swept the floor and put all the leftovers into teabags."

"That can't be true," Nicole said. "Can it? I drink tea from teabags all the time. Tell me it's not true."

"Like I said, it was written up in a report. Could have been an urban legend sort of report. I don't know. All I'm saying is that if you can get leaves this fantastic, keep them loose, and use a filter."

Over his shoulder, from his dishwashing spot at the sink, Rick said, "Katie, I've missed hearing you get into all your tea talk."

"My tea talk?"

"You haven't gotten excited about tea leaves for a long time. I'm just saying it's nice to hear you excited about your passion again."

Katie thought about Rick's statement as Eli brewed the Nairobi chai. Was tea her passion? She didn't feel energized talking about tea the way she used to. Nor did she have any interest in trying to once again create her own tea blends. To her, the love of tea had been a happy interest in her life, and yes, maybe it could have been considered a passion for a brief time. But it was definitely a time that had passed. She liked tea and all things related to tea. But she knew she would rather talk about where a tea came from and what life was like for the people who ran the plantation than talk about the tea itself.

An idea came to her. She had a paper due next week on the influence of technology in uniting people from different parts of the world through a shared interest. This was perfect. She could write about the tea plantation in Kenya and how they moved their product to other parts of the world.

Katie grilled Eli on what he knew about the plantation, as Rick and Nicole moved into the living room and started the painting project by taping the baseboards and around the doorframe.

Eli wrote down the link to the plantation website and said the tea could be ordered online. He talked about his friends who owned the plantation and how they had endured drought, government restrictions, and infringement from neighboring landowners. "A lot of the challenge for them has come from their being Kenyan. They're not part of the original European colonists who owned the land up until the seventies. Their father was an extraordinary man. He was a doctor, educated in England. Thanks to his money, they were able to purchase the plantation and run it as a fair-trade business. I think it will be easier for their children than it has been for them. Although, who knows with all the political unrest in Africa. The future isn't like a beacon of shining light for Africa. The future is more like a glimmer of light that comes and goes."

Eli held out the prepared cup of Nairobi chai to Katie. "Have a sip."

She blew on the rim of the mug, fully aware that Eli was staring at her. His intensity was bothering her less and less. Taking a small sip, she pressed her lips together and swallowed.

"Wow."

"Do you like it?"

"I don't know."

"It's different, isn't it?"

"It doesn't really taste like tea. It's definitely a chai beverage. Without the milk, it would really be overpowering, wouldn't it?"

"I drink mine with lots of sugar, the way most Kenyans do. And I do mean lots of sugar."

"Where's your sugar?" Katie took the box of granulated sugar that Eli pulled from out of the cupboard and sprinkled some into the mug.

"More," Eli said.

"Really?"

"If you want to try it the way we drink it, yes. More."

Katie poured more sugar. Then, at Eli's nod, she poured a little more. Going for a spoon, she stirred the still-steaming beverage. "It's going to taste like hummingbird food."

She took another sip, and this time her eyes opened wide. "That completely changes the taste. Wow, this is potent stuff. Do you ever drink it cold?"

"I've never tried."

"Let's make some more and put it in the fridge. It would make a good drink for later when we're sick of painting."

Eli started to do as Katie suggested. He was only a foot away from her when he turned and said, "Katie, I wanted to thank you."

"For what?"

"For trying."

"I don't mind trying your tea at all. I still want to taste the black, but maybe later. I'm going to drink this first now that I have it all sugared up. I have a feeling it's going to get me amped up to super-painting speed in about sixty seconds."

"I meant trying to fix me up with Nicole," he said in a low voice. "I appreciate your trying."

"Well, hey, I hope you don't feel bad about things not, you know ... turning out or whatever. I'm just happy that all of us can hang out like this. If there's one thing I've learned over the years, it's that good friends are like gold when you don't have family around."

Eli nodded. He rubbed the side of his neck and looked away from Katie for a moment. She noticed that he was rubbing the side where the backwards, L-shaped scar was located. One day she would ask him how he got the scar. But not today.

"So did you guys buy the paint already?" Katie asked.

"No, Rick was still trying to decide on the color."

"Come in and have a look," Rick called back. "We're checking out the samples right now."

Katie and Eli joined the other two as Nicole was standing by the wall holding up small strips of paper that had sample colors within the same hue.

"I'm thinking the brown one looks good," Rick said.

"It'll make the room dark, won't it?" Katie asked.

"You could go with this more buttery shade of brown." Nicole held up a different strip of color. "This one at the top. It's called 'Caramel Café Au Lait.'"

"I like it," Rick said. "What do you guys think? Eli?"

"Looks good to me."

"I like the name," Katie said taking on a pose like a Mexican hat dancer. "Caramel Coffee Olé!"

Rick laughed. "It's not Spanish. It's French, right, Nicole?"

"It sounds like 'olé,' but you're right, Rick. It's the French term for 'with milk.' 'Au lait.'"

"Okay. Olé for the au lait! Who wants to go to the paint store?"

Rick looked at Nicole. "I'll drive," he said.

"I'll go," Nicole offered.

Katie was going to offer to go too but realized that would leave Eli alone with the rest of the room to prep. She had such a soft spot in her heart for being the leftover that she said, "I'll stay here and finish getting the room ready. Be sure to buy some of those rollers with the long handles. It'll make the painting go faster."

"We'll be back." Rick stood by the front door, holding it open for Nicole. He positioned himself in such a way that she had to slip underneath his extended arm to exit. As she went under the Rick bridge, he offered her a warm smile, and she smiled back.

Katie stood for a moment after they were gone and stared at the space they had both just occupied. The scene was familiar. Rick used to do that in high school. He would stand across from a door as he held it open so that the girl who was exiting would have to come under his covering. Why did he do that now? Why did he smile at Nicole? Why did she smile back?

If any of their behavior had seemed unusual to Eli, he didn't give any indication. He was already at work, moving a chair toward the center of the room so they would have more room to paint without the chair being in the way.

Katie brushed off her impression of Rick and Nicole exchanging a flirting moment and put her attention to the task at hand. "Do you have any African music?" she asked.

"Some."

"We should have music to work to." Katie went to work with the roll of tape along the baseboards while Eli got the music going. The room soon filled with wonderful, rich sounds coming from exotic voices.

Eli opened all the windows and covered the furniture in the center of the room with a torn sheet and his old green sleeping bag. Katie smiled at the bookcase. She knew how secure it felt to be covered by that wonderful, weighty sleeping bag. The thin November morning sun peered in on them through the open window and shed a fair blessing on the moment.

Katie looked at Eli, who was removing the electric light sockets. He didn't seem to notice that she was staring at him. It didn't matter. Katie wasn't trying to get his attention. She had a boyfriend, after all. Unlike her boyfriend, she wasn't given to flirting just for the fun of flirting. She felt happy in this music-infused, light-filled moment and wanted to share the sensation with a friend.

"Eli?"

"Yeah?" He didn't take his eyes off the task.

"It's a beautiful day, isn't it?"

"Yes, it is." He still didn't look at her.

Katie turned back to her taping task. She felt deeply, warmly happy but couldn't explain why. It didn't matter. Her heart felt full. She decided it was simply one of the side effects of knowing she was in love.

The four hard-working painters stood back to admire their work after the first wall was finished.

"Great color choice," Katie said.

"The black frames on your pictures are going to really look good," Nicole added. She had set up a paint station in the kitchen and had transformed all Rick's frames with inky brushstrokes while Eli, Rick, and Katie started rolling.

"I feel like we're on one of those decorator reality shows," Katie said. "The host of the TV show should walk through the door right about now and tell us if we beat the other team."

"What other team?" Eli asked.

"Have you ever seen those decorating shows?"

"I don't think I have."

"They usually have some sort of competition going to make it interesting while people are painting each other's homes or changing their neighbor's furniture," Nicole explained.

"Changing their neighbor's furniture for what?"

"It's hard to explain," Nicole said. "You'll have to watch one of the home makeover shows sometime."

"Our only competition here," Katie said, "is who managed to get the least amount of paint on them, and I think we will all agree that would be Nicole."

"You haven't seen my hands. The tips of my fingers are black from trying to do little touchups on the frames."

"You know," Rick said, pulling the green sleeping bag off the top of the bookcase. "What if we painted this black too?"

"We would need more paint," Nicole said.

"Easily done," Rick said. "I have to go over to the café and sign off on a few things. Would you guys be okay continuing here while I run over? I'll bring back some more paint and a pizza."

The three willing volunteers agreed to the arrangement and kept painting while Rick left. Katie called Christy and Todd to see if they were home and wanted to come over to admire the work. Since both of them had the day off, they were still in Newport Beach at Christy's aunt and uncle's house.

"We went for a long walk on the beach this morning," Christy said. "You wouldn't believe how much both of us needed this little break! It feels like we haven't had any time to do leisurely things like this since our honeymoon. How's your weekend? Is it quiet in the dorms?"

"It's creepy quiet in the dorms. But I'm not there right now. Nicole and I are helping Eli and Rick paint their living room."

"You're kidding."

"No, it looks great. Wait till you see it. How long are you guys staying at Bob and Marti's?"

"We'll be here most of tomorrow. Todd has to be back for Sunday morning, of course, but we don't have anything going on tomorrow. Aunt Marti wants to go shopping tomorrow, but Todd and I might take off early and drive down the Coast Highway if the weather stays nice. I really want to see Doug and Tracy, and tomorrow might be our only chance for a while. Can you believe that baby Daniel is already five months old? I haven't seen him for weeks. I'm sure he's changed a lot."

"Five months. Wow. Time is going fast."

"Are you ready for another shocker, as far as time going by quickly?"

"What's the shocker?"

"Can you believe that in a few weeks it will be one year since Todd proposed to me? That means it's also one year since you and Rick started hanging out together. Remember? It was Friday before Christmas vacation, and all of us went to the Dove's Nest because it had recently opened. But none of us knew Rick was going to be there."

"A year," Katie repeated. "That was a very fast year."

"No kidding. I think the four of us should plan to do something to celebrate, don't you? We could find something to do that doesn't cost a lot. I'd say we could go to the Dove's Nest, but I don't think that would be very enjoyable for Rick."

"I'll ask him if he has any ideas. Hang on just a minute." Katie stepped outside the apartment, leaving Eli and Nicole to keep working while she finished her call to Christy with a little privacy. Taking the walkway toward Christy and Todd's apartment, Katie waited until she thought her voice would no longer carry through the open windows of Rick and Eli's apartment before she said, "You'll never guess where Rick took me on Wednesday afternoon."

"The zoo."

"How did you know?"

"He came down the night before and asked me if I thought it was a good idea since the last time we were there we all felt so much tension between us."

"And you told him it would be a good idea?"

"Yes." Christy paused on her end of the cell phone. "What? Are you telling me it wasn't a good idea?"

"It was a fantastic idea. I loved it! We had so much fun. We went to a Brazilian restaurant for dinner in San Diego, and it was amazing, all you can eat. The only bad part of the date was the traffic and that I left something at the restaurant so we had to go back. But aside from that, it was the best date ever. Thanks for telling him it was a good idea."

"I'm so glad you guys had fun. What happened with the ... you know."

"Is somebody close enough to hear you?" Katie asked.

"Yes." Christy said it enthusiastically, as if she were agreeing wholeheartedly with something Katie had said.

"Okay. I'll guess. You want to know what happened with Eli at Thanksgiving dinner yesterday at the Doyles'?"

"No, but if you want to tell me, I definitely want to hear. I had a different question for you."

"Oh, you want to know what happened with the I-love-you part."

"Exactly."

"He hasn't said the words to me yet, and I'm fine with waiting. I really am."

"That sounds wise."

Katie stopped in front of Todd and Christy's apartment door. "Hey, it's a good thing I walked down here. You guys have a box on your doorstep."

"We do? Who is it from?"

"Service Center – something. I can't read the last word."

"Oh, that's the part for our microwave. Or it could be the replacement for our doorbell. It should have been delivered to the apartment manager. Could you leave the box at Rick's apartment? We'll have the manager install whatever it is next week."

"Is your microwave really broken?"

"Yes."

"I hope it wasn't the popcorn."

"I think the microwave was on its way to retirement before you put your popcorn in, but the fire probably didn't help."

"Why didn't you tell me? I'll pay for the repair, Christy. I'm sorry about that."

"Don't worry about it. Hey, could you do me one more favor since you're right there?"

"Sure."

"You know the night you were over, and I got up and opened the door?"

"And Mr. Jitters ran inside your apartment? Yes, I remember."

"Good. And do you remember where I put the thing outside?" Christy talked in cryptic language.

"You mean the bowl of cat food?"

"Exactly. Could you check on that?"

Katie leaned down and looked behind the bushes. "The bowl is here. It's empty."

"Okay."

"Chris, why are still feeding that cat? It's such a mangy fur bag. You're only encouraging it, you know."

Christy didn't answer.

"Okay, well, you can tell me later if you want. But if you're trying to keep this a secret from Todd, I think that's not a good idea. You should tell him. I mean, I haven't been to marriage counseling like you guys, but it seems to me that even small situations like this should be discussed between married couples, and they shouldn't keep anything from each other."

"I know," Christy said softly.

"Okay, well, we can talk about that later when you guys get home. Say hi to Bob and Marti for me and Doug and Tracy, if you end up seeing them."

"I will. But wait. You said earlier that you thought I was going to ask about Eli going to Thanksgiving at the Doyles. What happened there?"

"Nothing. It was great. Nicole came, and so did Joseph. The meal was fantastic. Everybody had a really good time. The only shocker, well, except for Joseph being a little overwhelmed with the Doyles' gorgeous home and the ridiculous abundance of food, was a small announcement by Josh that he has a line on two more properties for new cafés. At least both of them are within a few hours' drive of here."

"I hope the deal goes through for Rick and Josh's sake, but I know that could potentially mean you and Rick go back to commuter-dater mode."

"Yeah, that's what I'm thinking it might end up becoming again. The thing is, I'm going to be swamped for the next month starting on Sunday when the students return to the dorm. After that, I have a very full final semester. If Rick ends up being on the go all the time during the next six months or so, well, I'm going to be just as busy."

"You have such a great attitude, Katie. I look back on so many stretches Todd and I went through, and to be honest, I know I complained far, far too much. We had it good in many ways. I didn't appreciate all we had."

Katie took Christy's words to heart as she walked back to Rick's apartment with the box under her arm. She wanted to be more deliberate about appreciating Rick and their times together. This had been a good day, and they still had the evening and some of Saturday to be together before Katie had to go back on duty. She intended to make the most of the time they had.

Her objectives were accomplished nicely that afternoon, as they finished off painting the room and the bookcase. They were ready for the pizza Rick had brought back from the Dove's Nest, even though the four of them being gathered together once again around a pizza after the Pizza Doubles Night made for some odd comments. All in all they meshed much better this time than they had a week earlier.

"What do you think?" Rick said as they cleaned up the painting equipment. "Should we move the furniture back or let it dry overnight?"

"I think you should let it dry," Katie said.

"That's what I think too. We might as well go do something. Do you want to see a movie?"

"I'd love to," Katie said. "Anything particular you guys want to see?"

The four of them discussed potential options and decided to take Nicole's car since it was the one with the most room. As Nicole backed her car out of the apartment parking area, she hit a bump and stopped the car.

"You guys don't have speed bumps, do you?"

"No, what was that?" Eli asked. He and Katie were in the backseat since Rick had the longest legs and took the front seat for the extra space. Eli looked out the back window. "Pull up, Nicole. I'll get out to see what it was."

Katie climbed out of the car too. She had a not-so-good feeling that she knew what Nicole had hit. She was right. "Mr. Jitters," Katie mumbled as she and Eli examined the mass of black fur in the eerie red glow of Nicole's taillights.

Nicole turned off the engine, and she and Rick came to see what Katie and Eli were staring at. "Oh, no! Did I kill it?"

"I can't believe this old cat is still around," Rick said. "It's been wandering the apartment complex for weeks."

Eli reached down compassionately and pressed his hand to Mr. Jitters' abdomen. "You didn't kill it, Nicole."

"It's still alive? We should find a vet," she said.

"No, the cat is dead, but you didn't kill it. The carcass is cold. It's been here awhile."

"We should dispose of it," Rick suggested. "I'll go back to the apartment and bring a trash bag."

"What are going to do?" Katie asked. "I don't think we can throw it in the dumpster, can we?"

"I have a shovel," Eli said. "We can bury it."

"Where?" Nicole asked.

"We could drive out somewhere and—"

"To the desert!" Katie exclaimed.

The group fell into a lengthy discussion about whether they should drive to the desert. Nicole and Rick weren't in favor of the idea. They were more interested in going to the movies. Katie liked the idea of skipping the movies and going out to bury Mr. Jitters under a canopy of stars. That show would be better than anything they would see in the theater. Eli's vote was also for the stars.

Nicole made the suggestion that broke the deadlock. "What if we tell your apartment manager? I mean, it isn't your cat. I wasn't actually the one who killed it. Wouldn't your manager want to know about dead animals in the parking area?"

The four of them split up. Eli went back to the apartment to wash his hands, Rick and Katie went to talk to the manager, and Nicole moved her car and waited for the others.

"Christy had a soft spot for that cat," Katie said as she and Rick approached the manager's apartment.

"Was she the one who was feeding it?"

"Who says Christy was feeding Mr. Jitters?" Katie said, trying to play coy.

"Someone was feeding the feral thing. I had a feeling it was Christy. Her years at the pet shop made her tender toward animals, didn't it?"

"I think so."

The manager answered Rick's knock. Rick explained the situation and the older, balding man said to leave the cat where it was. He would take care of it.

They were about to leave when Katie said, "Oh, and one other thing. A box arrived for Todd and Christy. It's at Rick's apartment. If it's a part for the microwave, I have to tell you that I might have been the one who broke it. Not on purpose, of course, but I put some popcorn in it, and the popcorn caught on fire. The problem was most likely the popcorn, but in case the fire had something to do with the microwave no longer working, I'll pay for the damage."

The apartment manager tilted his head and gave Katie a curious look. "What is your name?"

"I'm Katie Weldon. I'm Rick's girlfriend."

The manager looked at Rick as if he were surprised to think that Rick had a girlfriend. "Well, Katie Weldon, I'll have a look at the microwave, and if I decide the fire caused the damage, then I'll send you the bill through Rick."

"Okay. Thanks."

They headed back to the parking lot, and Rick said in a low voice, "Why did you tell him all that?"

"Because. It was the right thing to do."

"Katie, he's going to send you the bill. You don't know the guy. Do you know what I had to go through just to get clearance to paint our living room? You don't go around asking people who manage run-down apartments to invoice you for repairs. We can do improvements like the painting at our own expense but—"

"Okay, got it." Katie didn't want this to escalate into one of their irritating arguments. "I thought I was doing the honorable thing."

"Honorable, fine, but taking responsibility wasn't necessary. It's the same as if we told Nicole she killed the cat when really the cat was already dead and just happened to be in the road when she drove over it."

"Okay. I got your point."

They were back at the car now. Katie was ready to slip into the backseat, go to the movies, and drop the discussion. Rick had one more point.

"It's not as if you have the money to volunteer to pay for things like that, Katie."

She wished she could have kept her untamed lips shut, but before she could stop the words, Katie blurted out, "Well, I didn't have sixty bucks to pay for the box of chocolates for your mom, either, but that was the right thing to do. Not that she's even going to enjoy the chocolates. She made some comment about being on a diet."

"My mom is always on a diet. Don't take this to such an extreme, Katie. Let it rest."

"Fine."

"Fine."

Eli was back in the car with Nicole. They had overheard the last part of Rick and Katie's spat.

"Sorry," Katie mumbled to Rick before she got into the car.

"Me too," he mumbled back.

"Is everything okay?" Nicole asked.

"The manager said he would take care of the cat," Rick said, taking the front seat again. "Let's go. We can probably still make the 7:15 show."

The four of them drove in silence. Katie hated this. She hated feeling stifled. Having such a stupid argument with Rick was definitely stifling not only their relationship but also the atmosphere with their friends. Everything had been going great all day. Eli and Nicole were getting along just fine. Katie enjoyed trying Eli's tea from Africa and listening to his music. Rick was happy with the results of their hard work. She didn't want to be the reason for the silence in the car.

"So, what about tomorrow?" Katie asked in an effort to move the mood back into an airier place. "Do you have to work all day, Rick?"

"Yes."

"Okay. Well, would you like Nicole and me to come over and help Eli move the furniture back and hang the pictures?"

"It's up to you guys."

Now Katie was mad. She was trying. Why couldn't Rick try to keep the conversation going and head back to a lighthearted tempo?

He stayed in his sullen mood for much longer than Katie thought he should have. Fortunately, they walked right into the theater and found fairly decent seats all together in spite of so many people being there that night. The previews started right away so there wasn't much need to talk. Rick and Eli were in the outside seats, and Nicole and Katie were next to each other in the middle.

Halfway through the film, after a scene that had everyone in the theater laughing, Rick reached over and took Katie's hand. She was still feeling on the edge of exasperation toward him and wanted to wiggle her hand away. But holding hands had always been a good thing for them, and she hoped that staying connected to Rick this way would help her to feel as if she was still connected with him at the heart level.

How can it be possible to feel so certain that I am deeply in love with this man, and then we have a ridiculous disagreement, and I feel oceans away from him?

Katie thought of how Christy used to tell her things like this as Christy and Todd were living in their dating and engagement season. In those times, Katie found it hard to understand why Christy and

Todd would fight about matters that seemed so insignificant. Now she was the one experiencing that same sort of complicated relationship, and she saw how small issues could escalate when a person had such a huge emotional investment in another individual.

The thought that kept Katie buoyant was that she knew Christy and Todd still had moments like this. Just holding onto that thought gave Katie a sense of normalcy. Maybe she and Rick were right where most couples found themselves when they were falling in love.

She felt her fingers relaxing in Rick's hand. He seemed to feel the release of tension because he gave her hand a squeeze. She squeezed back. Letting out a long, low breath, Katie thought of how much more complicated this relationship was than she would have ever expected.

Why doesn't love make things easier? Am I trying too hard? Am I more in love with Rick than he is with me? Could it be time for us to have another DTR? If it is, do I have to be the one to initiate it?

Katie couldn't remember how long it had been since she and Rick had one of their "Define The Relationship" conversations. She knew she didn't want to be the one to declare her feelings for him first. Yet she didn't want her heart to deepen its roots in the relationship if the emotional investment she and Rick had with each other was lopsided. Why couldn't they be at the same place, at the same time, emotionally and relationally?

Trying hard to let go of her unsettling thoughts, Katie pulled herself into the present and let the movie lull her into a calmer place. For now, she told herself, it was enough to just be with Rick. The specific details that she was eager to learn about their relationship would come to the surface eventually.

Neither of them said anything about their tiff when they left the theater, and Nicole didn't bring it up after she and Katie returned to the dorm. The plan was to sleep as late as they could and then give Eli a call to let him know they were coming over. Eli had duty on campus at six o'clock Saturday evening, and Rick said he would be back to the apartment at about that time.

Katie gave herself over to a deep, restorative sleep that lasted unin-
terrupted until almost noon. When she finally went down the hall to
take a shower and to see if Nicole was up, she heard one of the showers
running. "That you, Nicole?"

"Yep."

"When did you wake up?"

"About twenty minutes ago."

"Me too. Pretty nice not to have to get up for anything, wasn't it?"

"Luxurious! Although I woke up wishing we had brought the rest
of Rick's omelets back so we could have eaten them now."

"They're probably waiting for us in Rick's fridge. I can be ready
in about twenty minutes."

"I'll try to go fast," Nicole called over the rush of water now running in Katie's shower stall.

About forty minutes later the two of them were on their way to the
apartment when Nicole said, "Katie, I have to tell you something."

"Okay."

"I'm fine with going back over to the apartment today and finishing things up, but if you don't mind, I don't want to spend the whole
day there."

"All right."

When Nicole didn't add a further explanation for her choice,
Katie asked, "Is it Eli? Does he still make you uncomfortable? Because
yesterday it seemed you guys were getting along great."

"I'm okay being around Eli. I'm not attracted to him or eager to
spend a lot more time with him or anything, but you're right about
him. He is a unique and intriguing guy. I misjudged him at first."

"So, if it's not Eli, is it something else I should know about?"

Nicole hesitated.

"I mean, I know last night got kind of tense after the whole Mr.
Jitters episode and the talk with the manager and everything. I hope
you didn't feel uncomfortable because of the way Rick and I were acting around each other."

"It wasn't you, Katie. It's just that the four of us were together on Thursday all day and then all day yesterday and now ..."

"You're right. I'm monopolizing your whole weekend. I didn't even ask you if you wanted to come back today, did I? This is your break, and here I am, taking over your free time and—"

"It's not like that, Katie. The painting and decorating have been fun. I love doing stuff like that, as you know. It's just that I have some homework I need to finish today, and I wanted to do a little shopping at some of the sales this weekend and ... I don't know. I just think it's better if I'm not around you, Rick, and Eli all evening as if we're a couple of couples, you know?"

Katie nodded. "I understand. Believe me, I understand. Do you want to just drop me off, and then I could have Rick take me back to the dorms later?"

"No, I'll help with the furniture and pictures and everything. And the rest of my omelet is waiting for me, right? I mean, I do have my priorities somewhat in order. Free food. I'm there!"

The two friends laughed together and went on to enjoy their day-old-yet-nonetheless-delicious omelets and pulling everything in order at Rick and Eli's apartment. The finished results were impressive. The color warmed the room. Nicole's idea of painting all the frames black made a huge difference.

Rick had one large, framed print. It was an enlarged custom print of a photo his dad had taken in Italy of a costal village as viewed from the deep blue Mediterranean Sea. All the brightly colored houses that clung to the rocky cliffs now looked even more dramatic inside the painted frame. The picture was what Nicole called the "themed focal piece" of the room, and she hung it so that your eye went to it when you entered the apartment.

The other four, smaller, framed pictures were also photos. One was of Rick's family with Max, all hanging out in the backyard of their old home in Escondido when Max was a puppy. Another photo was of Rick in all his high school quarterback glory, wearing his Kelley

High football uniform and striking a power pose. The other two were photos Rick's dad had taken, and both were sunsets.

All the colors in the room blended beautifully. Nicole was pleased, and while she was there, the three of them got along great. However, when Nicole left, Eli and Katie looked at each other awkwardly, as if they hadn't realized they would be alone for a few hours until Rick returned from work. Katie didn't expect to feel as off guard and flittery as she did.

"You hungry? I am. Sort of," she said.

Why am I reverting to my old, monosyllabic ways now that I'm alone with Eli?

"I could make some tea for us," he suggested. "You haven't tried the Kenyan black yet."

"Yes. Right. Good. Okay."

Katie sat down on the couch and made her lips close before another chopped word slipped out. Picking up the remote control, she turned on the television and flipped through until she found a program that seemed just right.

"It's one of those home makeover shows, Eli. Now you can see what I was talking about earlier. And it's a marathon so there's going to be one show after another."

"Good," he replied from the kitchen.

It took a few minutes for him to return to the living room and present Katie with a mug of steaming Kenyan tea. "I added milk and just a little sugar."

Katie took a sip. "Oh, now this is good. Very good."

"It must be those long leaves you were admiring yesterday. This is good tea." Looking at the television with Katie he said, "Explain to me what these people are doing with the sledgehammers."

Katie introduced Eli to the American pastime of redecorating and remodeling homes while Eli introduced her to Kenyan black tea and made poignant comments on the contrast between the wealth in the US and the want in Africa. He didn't make his comments in a way that made Katie feel guilty for living with a roof over her head that didn't leak, but Eli's observations were eye-opening for her.

At one point Eli was quietly telling her about how he and his father would go every day into the slums and dumps outside of Kenya to deliver clean water to as many people as they could. Eli depicted the horrific living conditions with compassion and tender descriptions of the specific people. He talked about how hard it was to leave that life, come to Rancho Corona, and try to fall in step with a different rhythm of life.

The way Eli unfolded his story was like the unwrapping of a gift. The gift was his life, his story. He kept it wrapped up and tucked away; yet today he opened that gift and offered it to Katie.

His compassion touched her so deeply that she cried.

And that was how Rick found them when he walked into the apartment, seated beside each other on the couch with tears running down Katie's cheeks.

What happened?" Rick asked, going to Katie's side and placing his hand on her shoulder.

"Africa!" Katie blurted through her tear-dabbled lips. "Eli was telling me about Africa."

Rick let go of her shoulder. "Oh, I thought something was really wrong."

"Something is really wrong," Katie said. "Something is wrong with us as a people and something is horribly wrong with our world when millions are dying, suffering, and going hungry and thirsty while we spend our money on paint and chocolates!"

Rick turned an accusatory glance at Eli. "What did you tell her?"

Eli headed for the kitchen with their empty tea mugs. "I just told what my life was like before I came here."

Rick took Eli's place on the couch and put his arm around Katie. She leaned against his shoulder and finished out her tears. Eli returned from the kitchen and handed her a paper towel.

"Thanks. Sorry, you guys. I guess I just never think about the rest of the world, you know? You made it seem so normal, Eli. So real. People really do live in horrible conditions. Disease is out of control. They don't even have fresh water to drink. I mean, how basic is that?"

"That's what my dad does now," Eli said. "I told you how the organization he works for digs wells and locates clean water even in remote locations. You would have to know my dad to understand his devotion. He loves Africa. He accomplishes the work of three men. He does a lot more now since ..."

Eli didn't finish his sentence. Katie assumed that Eli's returning to the States had made a difference in his father's productivity. She knew that Rick's parents did a lot more after Josh and Rick were out of the house. They started the Dove's Nest and the accompanying bookstore, The Ark, after their sons were independent.

"Rick, I have an idea." Her tears were gone. She was a woman on a mission. "What if the Dove's Nest sent money to Africa for clean water? You could put a box out on the counter by the register to collect donations. Or you could decide that every time someone ordered a pizza that all the profit would go to Africa. You could put a sign up. I bet people would contribute. Even if it was just their loose change, think how much could be collected by the end of a month. I mean, the problems around the world are huge. We have to do something. We have to start somewhere. Why not do this one thing? As a café, I mean. You could be known as the restaurant that cares about the rest of the world."

Rick's head had begun to nod at about her third sentence. As she ramped up her presentation, he raised his hand like a stop sign. "I'm with you. Yes, why not? We can do this."

Katie clapped her hands and turned to Eli. "You can connect us with the organization your dad works for, right? Maybe they have brochures or something."

"I can do that." Eli rubbed the side of his neck, as he grinned slightly. It was an expression Katie hadn't seen on him before. "This is good."

"Yes," Rick agreed. "Good idea, Katie. I'll take if from here. This is something I've wanted to do for a while, but I didn't know exactly what to do or how to start."

"You know," Eli said as he extended a look of appreciation at Katie, "I needed this."

"Needed what?" Katie asked.

"I needed to talk about home. About Africa. Since I've been here, I haven't really opened up about what my life is like, or rather what my life was like before I came here. I think I was in culture shock for the first few months. Then all I wanted to do was forget, you know? I've seen a lot I want to forget."

Katie and Rick quietly watched as a wave of emotion washed over Eli's face. "If you could do this, Rick, if you could collect even a little bit of money and send it on, it would make such a difference. You have no idea."

Katie leaned forward. "We could do a fund-raiser as well. As a floor or as a dorm. Why couldn't Crown Hall collect spare change or sponsor a car wash or something? I'm going to work on this, Eli."

He drew in a deep breath. "Thanks, you guys. I appreciate this. I think the hardest thing for me since I've been here has been trying to figure out what to do with my story. My history. All that I've seen and experienced. None of it fits here. I haven't really trusted anyone except Todd and Joseph."

"What do you mean, 'trusted'?" Katie asked.

"Maybe 'entrusted' is a better way of saying it. I haven't entrusted myself or my story to anyone beyond Todd and Joseph. I'm not trying to sound like a victim. I hope that's not what you're hearing."

"No, go on," Rick said.

Eli let out another deep breath. "The way I see it, I managed to find a way to fit into the bubble at Rancho. I do my job, I take my classes, I eat and sleep. But life here is so different. It's a bubble to me. I'm insulated. As long as I'm in the bubble, I don't think much about everything I've lived before I came here. That needs to change. I need to find a way to merge the two worlds."

Rick nodded his understanding. Katie continued to lean forward to encourage Eli to keep talking.

"So, thanks, Katie, for listening to me and for coming up with the idea for gathering contributions. I think this is what I've needed to bring my two worlds together."

Katie gave Eli a compassionate grin. Once again she told herself that she had misjudged Goatee Guy from the start. She hadn't given him the grace and space necessary to be himself.

For the rest of the weekend, Katie thought about the things Eli had talked about. When she saw Christy at church on Sunday, she told her about the conversation with Eli and the fund-raising ideas she and Rick were working on.

"I'm sure Todd could set up something with the youth group," Christy said. "Car washes are always good fund-raisers. And what about The Ark? If Rick puts out contribution boxes or something like that on the café side, he should place them on the bookstore side as well."

"I'll tell him that. Good thinking, Chris. This is going to be so good for everyone."

"I think so too," Christy said, as the two of them headed for the church parking lot. Christy was going to give Katie a ride back to campus before returning to church to pick up Todd.

"Speaking of cars and parking areas and running over things and ...," Katie said slowly.

"Did you get Baby Hummer repaired?"

"No, she's been dismantled, I'm sure, by now. I should have a check in my mailbox for all the parts. I don't know how much it's going to be, and I haven't stopped by for my mail for a while, but I'm hoping it's at least enough to cover my tuition. My savings is already g-o-n-e."

"What about buying a new car?"

"I'm going to have to remain a ride beggar for a while, it seems. You, Nicole, and Rick have all been so nice about giving me rides. Thank you."

"Anytime. Well, at least, anytime I have the car. I sympathize with your situation, Katie, because sharing a car with Todd has been growing into a bigger challenge than when we first got married. We're trying to figure out how we can buy another one."

"Let me know if you find a two-for-one special. Although, I don't know how I can buy even the most inexpensive car at this point. I don't even know how I'm going to pay for next semester."

"Well, maybe the check for the parts for Baby Hummer will be more than you think. You did say that Baby Hummer fell into the vintage category. Maybe her guts went for a high price."

"Speaking of guts," Katie said, climbing into Todd and Christy's Volvo and buckling up her seatbelt. "And back to my previous hints with the car and the parking lot and the running over things ... I think it falls to me to tell you that Mr. Jitters is no longer with us. He went to ... wherever mangy, scary felines like him go when they die."

"I know," Christy said, sticking out her lower lip. "Poor Mr. Jitters."

"How did you find out?"

"I heard it from Mr. Yeager, our apartment manager. He came over last night, by the way, to look inside our microwave."

"Oh, I was going to tell you about that too. I offered to pay for the repair."

"That's what he said. But, Katie, how are you going to pay for it if you don't even have enough for tuition?"

"That's what Rick said. I'll tell you what I told him. I don't know how I'm going to pay for it. I just want to do the right thing."

"I appreciate that, but I honestly don't think it was entirely the popcorn that messed up our microwave. It's old and never worked well from the time we moved in. I told our manager that. I told him the microwave was just like our doorbell, which still doesn't work, by the way. The part that came in the box was the new doorbell. Mr. Yeager put it in last night, and the new one doesn't work, so it must be a wiring problem. It could be the same problem is messing up the doorbell and the microwave."

"Okay, lesson learned. I don't need to be so eager to try to make things right in the entire universe."

"Not the entire universe," Christy echoed. "Stick with the fund-raisers for clean water for Africa. That is a problem you can work toward solving."

Christy dropped Katie off in front of Crown Hall, and the two of them decided to connect again for lunch later in the week. A number of students were coming and going from the open doors of Crown Hall. It was good to feel the dormitory once again breathing students in and out. Life was returning.

Katie noticed that Jordan, one of the RAs from the guys' floor, was in the office checking in two returning students. Katie went around through the door and joined him inside the office. She stretched out on the couch and closed her eyes for a few minutes. This was a good place. Rancho Corona might be a bubble, as Eli had said the day before, but it was a beautiful bubble and a place where Katie was free to be herself more than she ever had been at home while growing up. She loved this place and these people.

"When are you on duty?" Jordan asked Katie.

She opened one eye and said, "Three. Unless you want me to start sooner. Do you want a break?"

"You don't mind starting early?"

"No. Nicole covered for me during checkout on Wednesday, so I guess I feel like I should double up for someone else today."

"Nice. I'll take you up on that if you're serious," Jordan said.

"I'm serious."

"Thanks, Katie. I owe you."

"No, you don't. Well, I actually shouldn't say that, should I? I'm sure I'll need help eventually for something." She slid into the warmed chair and took a look at the list on the computer screen, as Jordan picked up his backpack and left the office. Not even a third of the students had checked back in yet. The rest would undoubtedly come in a big clump.

Katie looked at the clock and wondered why she had been so quick to jump in. She hadn't had lunch yet, and now she was commit-ted to staying on duty for the next six hours instead of four.

She hoped that Nicole, in her sweet and caring way, would think to bring Katie something to eat.

Three hours into Katie's shift, she had checked in only fourteen students, and Nicole hadn't come by. She was starving and decided to give Rick an SOS call. When he answered, she said, "Food! Must have food!"

"Katie?"

She laughed. "Of course it's me. Who else would call you and say, 'Food! Must have food'?"

"It didn't sound like you."

"That's because I'm famished. I'm faint with hunger. What are you doing right now? Is there any chance you can bring me something to eat? I'm on duty at the front deck, and I have to stay here for two more hours."

"I'm afraid it would take me about two hours to get there."

"Where are you?"

"San Diego. We're looking at the potential café location Josh found. I don't know why we came this afternoon. The traffic you and I sat in last Wednesday afternoon is all backed up once again. I can call you when we get closer and see if you're still desperate."

"I will be desperate. Even if I managed to scrounge some food in the next few hours, I'll still be desperate to see you."

"That's a good one, Katie. I'll call you later."

"Wait! How does the property look?"

"Pretty good. It's an old tire store that used to be on the edge of town but now that two big housing developments are going in, the location is ideal. No other developers wanted to touch it so the price is good."

"Why didn't anyone else want it?"

"It still smells like tires inside. Josh says we can get rid of the smell. He's thinking we should go for a soda shop theme with this one because one of the housing developments is for residents over the age of fifty-five. The soda shop might be nostalgic for them. We're still in the brainstorming stage."

"Sounds like it might be more fun than the Tempe store. You could get Nicole to help with the decorating."

"My mom suggested the same thing. She came down with Dad, Josh, and me."

"I should let you go if all of you are in the car right now."

"It's okay. Josh is talking to Shana. He's trying to persuade her to move here now even if she doesn't get the job. Josh is definitely moving back."

Katie had a tiny inkling that if Josh moved back but Shana didn't, it might be the end of their short relationship and thereby give Nicole a second chance with him. She kept her thoughts to herself and told Rick she had to go because some students were arriving and she had to get back to work.

During the last two hours of Katie's shift the stream of returning students barely let up. She forgot about food until Nicole breathlessly dashed into the office. "You would not believe the traffic! Katie, I intended to be back sooner, but I was sitting on the freeway going nowhere."

"Did you bring food?" Katie looked inquisitively into Nicole's shopping bags.

"I have leftover Santa Fe chopped salad. Do you want it? I'm sure I can find a fork somewhere in here."

"I would love it! Here, trade places with me. I know where the forks are." Katie scarfed down the warmed-from-the-inside-of-the-car salad while Nicole picked up her duties at the desk.

When they hit a brief lull, Katie said, "What did you do all day?"

"Are you ready for this?" Nicole's smooth skin turned a peachy shade of pink. "I went to church this morning with Julia, and Phil was there."

"Who?"

Nicole lowered her voice. "Phillip Sett. Remember?"

"Oh! Right, the feel-upset guy. Did you go to lunch with him?"

"I did. He said he wanted to make up for not being able to go to the Pizza Doubles Night."

"Impressive!"

"There's more. We went to lunch in Oceanside at a darling beachfront restaurant. Then we sat in traffic all the way back."

"Sounds like you had a good time."

"It was nice. Not stupendous. Nice. The nicest part was that he asked me, you know?"

"Yes, I know. I definitely know what you mean."

The next round of students arrived, and Katie stayed on for an hour after her shift ended just to help Nicole. Julia came by and asked Katie if they could set up an appointment on Monday afternoon. Katie wrote herself a note and stuck it in her purse.

When she went looking for the note after class the next day, she couldn't find it. She was pretty sure Julia said to meet her in her apartment at four o'clock. Since Katie had a little extra time, she circled back to the campus mailboxes and opened her box. Three letters were waiting for her and one postcard reminder that her student parking permit fees were due December 1.

"Well, that's one expense I won't have to worry about."

She hoped one of the envelopes held the check for Baby Hummer's parts. Hopefully, it was enough money to get her through at least the next month. She knew she could pick up extra hours back at the Dove's Nest during Christmas break and that would cover her expenses for January. After that Katie had no idea where the needed funds would come from. She wasn't worried, though. God always had provided just enough. Never too much, never too little. Always just enough. She whispered a little prayer of thanks for the way God always took care of her.

Checking the return address on the first envelope, Katie knew it was the awaited check. She slid her thumbnail under the flap as she walked back to Crown Hall and pulled out the enclosed check. She stopped in her tracks.

"You have to be kidding me!"

Several students turned to look at her. Katie pulled her tirade back to an interior rant. *What is going on? This isn't even enough to cover a week of expenses. Did you see this, God? Did they rip me off or what? I can't believe this. I'm going to call those guys and tell them their little joke is not funny. They better pay me the full amount or else.*

Instantly motivated, Katie reached for her phone and made the call to the number on the top of the check. She picked up her pace as she walked back to Crown Hall and debated with the mechanic in a voice that was loud enough for anyone nearby to hear. "You paid me peanuts! You can't possibly tell me this is the full amount. You said Baby Hummer was vintage. Classic. Is this all she was worth?"

"I'm afraid so. Not many of the parts were salvageable once we tested them. Did you look at the itemized list inside the envelope? You can see exactly what parts we were able to sell and the price we received for them. We took our commission off the top, and that's listed too."

Katie didn't respond.

"You still there?" the mechanic asked.

"Yeah, I'm still here. I'm sorry I yelled at you. I'm just bummed."

"I understand."

"I know. Thanks. I do appreciate your sending the check right away."

"No problem."

Katie hung up feeling awful for the way she went off on the poor guy. It could be that he had ripped her off in some way, but what could she do? The part that embarrassed her the most was the realization that right before she opened the envelope she was sweetly thanking God for always providing. Two seconds after her expectations weren't met, she was yelling at God and at other people as if life was suddenly unfair to her.

Drawing in a deep breath, Katie entered Crown Hall and headed for Julia's apartment. Instead of riding in the elevator, she decided to take the stairs to burn off some steam. When she tapped on the side of the partly opened door, Julia appeared with her cell phone to her ear.

She motioned for Katie to come in and then slid back into her room and closed the door.

Katie could hear only muffled echoes of Julia's conversation and quickly decided it wasn't her business whom Julia was talking to. She looked back at the envelopes in her hand and stuck out her tongue at the skimpy check.

There. That was her last negative thought on the matter, she decided. God knew what he was doing even if Katie didn't. What would be the purpose of trusting God if everything came automatically and easily? Katie told herself to be thankful. It was a good exercise for her heart—a heart that was too easily sidetracked.

"Thanks," Katie whispered into the stillness of Julia's apartment. On the wall surrounding Katie were various photos of Julia in different locations around the world. On one of Katie's visits, Julia had described where each picture was taken.

Next to the door was a beautifully framed plaque hung at eye level with a saying in Maori, the language of the indigenous people of New Zealand. The first time Katie saw the words *He aha te mea nui? He tangata! He tangata! He tangata!*, she had asked Julia what they meant. Julia told her it was an ancient riddle of the indigenous people of New Zealand. The first line was a question: "What is the greatest thing?" The second line was the answer: "It is people! It is people! It is people!"

Katie thought about the significance of that saying in light of what had been going on in her life. Had not God richly blessed her with what was most important? People. People. People.

"Thanks," she whispered again to God. This time her gratefulness carried much more sincerity.

Katie tucked the check back into the envelope, and since Julia was still on the phone, she decided to open the other two letters. The next one was from her bank, notifying her that when her debit card request went through for the chocolates, her funds were insufficient, and she had been charged an overdraft fee.

She stared at the notice. Her RA paycheck should have been automatically deposited on Friday. She had no idea the transaction she made on her debit card on Wednesday would go through that same day. Didn't banks take holidays on Thanksgiving anymore?

Despite the letter, Katie didn't scream at God or shake the notice toward the heavens. This time she clenched her teeth together and felt her anger imploding instead of exploding. This was her doing. She knew it was her stubbornness and pride that had prompted her to buy the chocolates even though they were too expensive and even though Rick had offered to loan her the money until Friday.

She couldn't blame anyone but herself.

Refusing to enter into the mess emotionally, Katie pulled out the next letter in hopes that it brought good news. At the very least, she hoped it was an advertisement. Coupons for a dollar off on her next pizza would be nice.

The return address, however, caused her hopes to plummet. The letter was from her mother.

Katie chose not to open the letter. Not there. Not in the mood she was in.

Stuffing all the letters into her shoulder bag, Katie crossed and uncrossed her legs. She flipped her hair behind her ears and nibbled on her thumbnail.

When Julia didn't appear, Katie couldn't stand it any longer. She dug her hand into her bag and pulled out the letter with her parents' home address hand-printed in the top left corner. The envelope was thick, and when Katie turned it over, a sticky note was affixed to the back. It was the note she couldn't find earlier. In her handwriting was the time she was supposed to meet with Julia—4:30. She was early. No wonder Julia wasn't available when she showed up.

Katie considered leaving and coming back later. But where would she go for ten minutes? Gazing down at her mother's handwriting on the envelope, Katie decided to open the letter.

Inside was another envelope. It was addressed to Katie and sealed. That's when she remembered her mom's phone call several weeks ago requesting her address. Now her curiosity was piqued. The letter wasn't actually from her mother. It was from someone named "Nathaniel Brubaker, Attny." The return address listed Joplin, MO, as the city and state it was from. Now she was confused. She didn't know anyone in "MO," whatever state that was.

Carefully opening the single-sheet letter printed on white, water-marked stationery, Katie noticed the words after Nathaniel Brubaker's name on the letterhead. "Attorney at Law."

Why would a lawyer send me a letter? Did I violate some law in the state of 'Mo' without even knowing it?

Katie quickly scanned the letter and then read the final line, "Please contact me at your earliest convenience to settle this."

"Settle what?" Katie said aloud.

She was just reading the letter a second time more carefully when Julia entered from the bedroom.

"Sorry to keep you waiting."

"I was early," Katie said without looking up from the letter.

"Everything okay?"

"I don't know." She handed the letter to Julia. "Can you tell me what this means?"

As Julia read, her eyes grew wide. She looked at Katie and said, "Your aunt Mabel passed away."

"I know. She died last summer. Or maybe it was last spring. And I think she was my great aunt. So why are they telling me now?"

Julia was rereading the letter with her lips moving silently. "I think she left you something in her will. Mr. Brubaker will discuss the details with you when you call him."

"I hope she left me her car. I could use a car. Although, she probably had an old-lady car that's in worse shape than Baby Hummer was. And how would I get to wherever this is to pick it up? What state is MO, anyhow?"

"Missouri."

"Then why don't they use the first two letters of MI?"

"I think that's the abbreviation for Mississippi. No, actually, Mississippi is MS. MI must be Michigan."

"That explains why I always get those states messed up. I never had a clear idea of where my relatives were from."

"Do you want to call Mr. Brubaker? With the time change he's probably not in, but you could leave a message."

"Sure. I guess." Katie pulled out her cell phone and dialed the number listed on the letterhead. A recorded message came on giving the office hours and asking her to leave a message. Katie stated her name, her cell phone number, and for good measure, her mailing address at Rancho.

"Let me know what he says when he calls you," Julia said.

"I will."

"So how was Thanksgiving weekend for you, and how's everything going?"

Katie and Julia spent the next half hour catching up. Katie didn't have a lot to report except some of the happy details of the zoo date last Wednesday, the good time with Rick's family, and then painting his apartment. Katie skimmed over the specifics and went on to talk about how she wanted to do a fund-raiser for clean water for Africa, and some of the ideas she had for how the whole dorm could participate.

"We'll bring this up at our next staff meeting," Julia said. "You have the meeting on your calendar, don't you? It's this Friday at three."

"I'll be there. Do you want me to bring information on the organization Eli's dad works for?"

"Yes. If you want, you could email everyone before the meeting and send them a link, if there's a website they can look at ahead of time."

"I'll do that."

"Now." Julia leaned forward and looked intensely at Katie. "I need to give you some direction on your position."

"Okay."

"During the past few weeks, several women on your floor have come to me saying they haven't felt you've been available to them."

"What?"

"Just hear me out, Katie. As you remember from training, your role is not to be a mother to these women and you're not to attempt to be everyone's best friend. So I realize they might be expecting more of you than is required. I also know it's a challenge to find the right balance. I'm not worried that you're not doing your job or you're not trying to be available. You have classes too, as well as a budding social life. So don't take this as any sort of reprimand from me. This is only information for you to process and see how you might remedy some of the gaps."

"Who was complaining?"

"I don't think it matters. I really don't. I listened to what they had to say and assured them that I would speak with you."

"Oh, yeah? And exactly what did these anonymous women have to say?"

"Katie, you're coming across defensively. You need to take this as helpful direction and not as an accusation. What they said was that they went by your room a number of times, but you weren't in."

"So they went to talk with Nicole, right? We're a tag team. Or did Nicole receive the same complaint?"

"They did go see Nicole, and no, they didn't have a complaint against her."

"I don't see how any of them could expect me to be waiting around in my room all the time. How could I do that? I can't be there every time they want to talk about their problems."

"Katie."

"I mean, what do they think I'm doing? I'm not trying to ignore anyone."

"Katie!" Julia's voice was firmer this time. "You're still taking offense at this. Hold what I said out here, away from you. Examine this objectively. You can't take everything so personally in this position."

Katie tried hard to pull her emotions into a more neutral level. "Sorry." She let out a long breath. "So, what am I supposed to do?"

"I think a couple of actions could help. You can put a time-in-and-out clock on a message board by your door."

"I already have a message board by my door."

"I know you do. What I'm suggesting is that you add whatever system you prefer that will let people know where you are if you're not in your room or what time you'll be back. You've seen some of the handmade dials the other RAs have. Or you can use cards that say when you're in class or when you're in the cafeteria or studying. Then just be sure to leave a time when you'll be back. You can work out whatever system you want. All you have to do is find a way to communicate your availability more clearly to the women on the floor."

"Okay."

"Are you all right with that?"

"Yeah, I'll come up with something. I'll find out where Nicole got her fancy little in-and-out magnetic board with the tiles for class and studying and whatever else." To herself, Katie thought, *Not that I can afford to buy one right now . . .*

"I have one other suggestion," Julia said. "You can set up a regular time each week when you make the rounds. I know that Nicole did this last year, but I don't know if she's started this year. The two of you could go together or separately. All you have to do is stop by everyone's room and say hello. It doesn't have to be a lengthy visit, and it's not supposed to be a time to pry their life stories out but rather just a chance to touch base with everyone."

"Okay, I'll talk to Nicole about that too."

"Oh, and I suggest you take a notebook with you on your room calls. Inevitably you'll receive a bunch of requests for things like a burned-out lightbulb or a complaint about a missing bottle of shampoo they left in the shower."

"Notebook. Got it."

"Thanks, Katie," Julia said with a smile. "I appreciate your taking this as constructive suggestions rather than as criticism."

"That's something I need to work on."

"I'm sure you're finding that being an RA is providing you with the opportunity to do just that."

"Exactly."

Katie returned to her room before heading out to the cafeteria for dinner. Something ancient and rebellious inside her made her walk right past each of the rooms and ignore every woman on the floor all the way to her room at the end. She agreed with Julia that she should be more deliberate about connecting with the women. But because some unnamed woman or two or maybe more had gone and "tattled" on her, Katie want to pull back from all of them rather than make the efforts she had promised she would.

Once inside her room, Katie threw her pillow at the wall and let out a "*Grrr!*"

"Chill out," she told herself as she paced. "This is your job. You're getting paid room and board for this. Take that as your performance review. Relax. You have some areas to improve in, that's all. Give into it. Don't fight."

Her brief therapy session worked. She stopped pacing the floor and let Julia's advice settle over her. Just then, her cell phone rang. It was Rick.

Katie's greeting was, "How in the world do you put up with me?"

"Katie?"

"Yes, of course it's me. Why do you keep asking if it's me when I call? That's what my mother does, and it drives me crazy. You can at least read the caller ID in case you don't recognize my voice for some strange reason."

"I called at a bad time, didn't I?"

Katie couldn't tell if he sounded impatient or sympathetic. With Rick sometimes it was hard to tell the difference.

"I'm okay," she said, not at all interested in repeating Julia's conversation to anyone.

"Are you sure?"

Katie sighed, and then on a whim, she spilled her guts to Rick. She managed to do it in an abbreviated manner and summarized by saying, "So I guess I'm going to have to put more effort into the one-on-one part of my position between now and Christmas break."

"That might be a good thing," Rick said.

"I know. It's what I need to do. I shouldn't have such a bad attitude."

"No, I meant it might be a good thing that your job is going to require more of you in the next few weeks because I'm in the same place. My job is going to require a lot from me too."

Katie scowled from the edge of her bed and was glad Rick couldn't see her face. "What's going on?" She tried to keep the question sounding much lighter than it felt inside her.

"We bought the San Diego property today. At least we started the process. We're committed. It's going to be huge, Katie! This is what Josh and I were waiting for. We still can't believe God opened this door so quickly after the Arizona property fell through. Until Josh packs up his stuff and moves here, I'm going to be working round the clock."

"Wow." Katie tried to sound a little enthusiastic for Rick's sake. "So, our golden moment of actually going out on normal dates has come to an end."

"Our dating hasn't come to an end."

"I meant the luxury of going to the zoo for the day like we did last week. That's the golden part that's going to have to end."

"Not end, Katie. Just go on hold. We can still meet up for dinner and maybe a movie now and then. You do understand what a fantastic opportunity this is and how I have to jump in and move on it, don't you?"

"Yes. I understand. Of course I understand. This is what you do. Sorry I'm sounding grouchy about this. Deep down I'm very happy for you, Josh, and your parents and for the sad, abandoned tire store that will soon become a happy little sock hop."

"We're not taking it quite that far."

"But, Rick, I would be lying if I didn't say I was bummed. I liked having time with you last week, even if it was only for a few days."

"I know. So did I. Listen, I don't know when I'll get to see you this week because I have a couple of trips I have to make to San Diego."

"Hopefully without all the traffic this time."

"Yes, hopefully without all the traffic. But I will be home next Sunday, so let's set that as our day together, okay? If you have duty, try to switch with Nicole. If you have homework, try to do it all before Sunday. That way we can have the whole day together."

"Okay." A tiny bit of the rebellious side of Katie made her feel like saying, "Why do I have to be the one to make all the adjustments and bend my life to your schedule?"

But she didn't say that. She remembered Christy commenting a few months ago about how she never expected married life to be so much about bending her life to fit into Todd's. Christy also said Todd was doing the same thing. He had to adjust his schedule daily just to work out their transportation needs with only one car between them.

That thought made Katie remember her disappointing check from the parts garage as well as the other two significant letters. She decided not to say anything to Rick about the letters. By the time she would see him next Sunday she would have more information from the lawyer. She also knew it would be of no value to bring up the expensive chocolates yet another time.

They talked a few more minutes, and then Rick said he had to go.

Katie hung up and thought how Rick was going to need the same sort of in-and-out calendar she would be hanging by her door. Maybe she could find two-for-the-price-of-one at Bargain Barn, her favorite place to shop. He could put it up by his office door at the Dove's Nest, and if she couldn't reach him by cell phone, at least Carlos or one of the other employees at the Dove's Nest could check his calendar and tell her when he would be back.

Imagining that scenario prompted Katie to calm down her feelings about what Julia had said. If some of the girls on her floor — especially some of the lower classmen — felt a sense of loss and maybe even abandonment when they couldn't find Katie, she now understood more sympathetically how they felt. She didn't like falling into that thin-emotions place, where she had been many times before in her life when it came to Rick.

She was a strong woman. She could handle this. All of it.

Leaving her room and heading for the cafeteria, Katie determined not to feel sorry for herself over Rick's upcoming busy schedule. She also determined that she would make a generous effort to show kindness to all the women on her floor every chance she got, beginning now.

At every open door, Katie popped her head in and said a cheery hello. Everyone she passed on her walk to the cafeteria, she greeted by name. That was, the people she actually knew by name. When she arrived at the cafeteria, Eli was in line two people ahead of her.

"Hey, Eli!"

He turned around and gave her a great smile and came back to join her in line. "I emailed my dad. You wouldn't believe how excited he was about the idea of us doing some fund-raisers. It gets pretty bleak over there, and I think he was in a deep rut at the moment. This was like medicine for him."

Katie stuck with Eli through the cafeteria line, and the two of them ate together at a table by the window that only had two chairs. Even after they finished eating, they kept going with ideas for fund-raisers. Eli told Katie more stories about times he went with his dad into remote villages to do the preparatory work before sending in a team to drill a well.

He described a horrible problem one village had with a parasite in the water that burrowed under the skin and left the children and adults with painful bumps under their skin where the parasites had taken up residence.

Katie shivered at the description and was glad she was finished eating.

"You won't believe this, Katie, but within two months after the new well was dug and the people no longer had to drink from the contaminated stream, the parasites went away. The people were healed by the clean water they were drinking and using for cooking and wash-ing. It transformed the village."

"You have to tell that story," Katie said.

"Where?"

"Here, at chapel." Katie's eyes grew larger. "Yes, that's it! At chapel. We have speakers all the time who come and tell us what's happening in various parts of the world, but Eli, you're here. And you've seen all this and experienced it. Would you speak at chapel sometime?"

He shrugged. "I guess. What would I say?"

"Just what you've been telling me. Tell your stories. I know people on the chapel committee. I'll talk to them tomorrow. Eli, this is so cool! We could start a fund-raising project that the entire university could participate in!"

Katie's enthusiasm didn't diminish as the evening went on. She and Eli kept talking until the cafeteria closed down. Then they walked over to the Java Jungle, an on-campus coffee shop, and kept talking until after nine.

"I really have to go," Eli said. "I'm on duty at midnight, and I have a paper to write that's due tomorrow."

"Let's set a time to meet tomorrow," Katie suggested. "What's your cell number? I don't think I have it."

They made plans to meet on Tuesday. Eli suggested the fountain at the center of campus. At first Katie said yes. Then she paused and said, "Let's meet at the Java Jungle instead." The fountain was a special place for her since she and Rick had shared some fun picnic lunches there as well as a few water fights. It felt funny thinking of starting some new memory in that place with Eli.

By the time they met at the Java Jungle on Tuesday, Katie was brimming with updates. She was waiting for Eli when Julia stepped into the small coffee hangout and waved at Katie.

Katie motioned her over and was about to tell her the newest vision for Eli's speaking in chapel when her cell phone rang.

Katie didn't recognize the number and assumed it was Eli. She answered it by saying, "You will not believe all the good things that are about to happen!"

After a pause, a woman said, "Katie Weldon, please."

"Oh. Yes, this is Katie."

"Please hold for Mr. Brubaker."

Katie covered the mouthpiece and looked up at Julia. "It's the lawyer," she whispered.

Julia pointed to the door. "You should take it outside where you can hear better."

"Will you come with me, Julia? I might need you."

The two of them stepped outside and walked over to a bench that was across from the main student community building and backed up to the brick wall of Dishner Hall, the music department. This was about as soundproof as they would find outside.

"Ms. Weldon?" The voice on the other end was low and somber.

"Yes?"

"You responded to my letter regarding Mabel Overton."

"Yes."

"I am handling Mrs. Overton's estate. She had a specific request in her will that we find all of her relatives who are attending college."

"Mr. Brubaker? I'm going to put you on speaker phone."

"Will anyone be able to hear our conversation?"

Katie looked around. "Only my RD. My resident director. I want her to hear what you have to say because she was with me when I opened your letter and she's with me now. I just want her to listen so she can tell me if I need to do anything that I don't catch while you talk. Does that make sense? I've never spoken to a lawyer before, and to be honest, I'm nervous."

"No cause to be nervous. Go ahead and put me on speaker."

Katie held the cell phone between them and looked around again to make sure no other students were near. They still were isolated in their out-of-the-way location.

"Okay," she said. "The coast is clear. I mean, you can go ahead with what you were saying."

Mr. Brubaker described how Katie's great aunt wanted to find all her relatives who were attending college because that was something she had dearly wanted to do but never was able to. The lawyer had conducted an extensive search, and Katie was the only direct relative who was attending college or had expressed an interest in going to college.

Katie glanced at Julia. She had no idea why any of that should matter to her deceased great aunt.

Then Mr. Brubaker made Mabel's intentions clear. "As the sole university student, you are entitled to the entire sum of her estate."

Katie raised her eyebrows and kept looking at Julia. This was good news! Maybe her great aunt had left her enough to cover the rest of her tuition after she cashed the check for Baby Hummer's parts.

"Would you like to know the amount of your appropriation?" he asked.

"The amount? Sure."

Mr. Brubaker said the amount, and Katie promptly dropped her cell phone.

Julia scooped up the phone. "Thank you, Mr. Brubaker. Katie is a little stunned at the moment."

"Understandable. Her great aunt purchased a small amount of stock in an oil company back in the forties. With oil prices today, I'd say it paid out nicely."

"Yes," Julia agreed.

"Mr. Brubaker, are you sure about all this?" Katie said, finding her voice. "Things like this happen in the movies but not in real life."

"Oh, they happen in real life every day, Ms. Weldon. Trust me. Now, I have your address there at Rancho Corona, so I will be sending the final paperwork to you at that address unless you would like me to send it elsewhere."

"No, here would be fine."

"Good day, then."

"Wait! Mr. Brubaker?"

"Yes?"

"Does anyone else know about this? My parents or any other relatives?"

"No. You may do what you wish with the information and the money."

"Okay. Thank you."

"You're welcome. Have a nice day."

Katie hung up her cell phone and stared at Julia. "Have a nice day? Did he just say 'have a nice day'?"

Julia grinned. "Wow, Katie."

"Tell me the amount again."

Julia repeated it as Katie invisibly drew the numbers in the air with her finger. "That's a whole lot of numbers in front of the decimal point. And nice numbers too, don't you think? Nice, big, fatty numbers. Julia, this is insane! Slap me awake, will you? This can't be happening."

Julia slid her arm around Katie's shoulders and gave her a tight hug. "It appears to be real, Katie. No joke. Did you pray for financial aid or something?"

Katie laughed. She laughed and laughed until tears ran down her face. Once she had her voice back she said, "Julia. What am I going to do with all this money?"

"You're going to take your time, you're going to pray ..."

"Right. Of course. God wouldn't have done this if he didn't have a reason. Do you think he has a plan for this money? Of course he has a plan. Do you think ... do you think he has a dream? A dream for something that could happen, and he wants to use this money to make it happen?"

"Why don't you ask him?"

"Yeah, of course. Why can't I think of these things? I'll ask him. Do you want to pray with me?"

"Of course."

For the next five minutes Katie and Julia bowed their heads on the bench on the side of Dishner Hall and prayed together. Both of them thanked God for this unexpected and extravagant gift. Julia asked God to give Katie wisdom.

Katie concluded their spontaneous prayer with, "Father, what about you? Do you have any dreams that you want to use this money for? Because you can have it. I know it's yours already, but if you're sending it my way so that I'll use it in some way that will make your kingdom come and your will be done on earth as it is in heaven, then I'll do it. Just tell me what you want. Amen."

"Amen," Julia echoed.

Katie opened her eyes and looked at Julia, feeling a little more stabilized. "This is wild."

"God is wild," Julia said. "He rarely does what we think he's going to do."

Katie nodded. A few feathery thoughts about Rick and where their relationship was headed came fluttering over her. She wasn't sure why. She would have thought that the money would be all she could think about after receiving such stunning news.

"Julia, may I ask you a wacko question?"

"Okay."

"Whatever happened with Trent?"

Julia looked startled. "What do you mean what happened with him?"

"You said you didn't marry him, so I just wondered what happened. I mean, if you don't mind telling me. My thoughts are all over the place, and I guess I'm trying to figure out my whole life now in one view, and I wondered about you and love and marriage and the future."

Julia took a long moment before saying, "I ..." She didn't go any further. With a tranquil expression returning, she said, "You know what, Katie? I will make you a promise. I promise I will tell you about Trent one day. I haven't told many people, but I will tell you. Not today, but one day."

"Okay, I'll wait. I'm a good waiter. Well, not really. It's kind of a joke Rick and I have. I don't know why I can't stop thinking about Rick! Do you think I'm losing my mind? I feel like I am. I feel like I'm on overload."

"Why don't you go back to your room and be by yourself for a while? You can let all this sink in and pray some more and get your bearings. I'll be around, if you need to talk any more."

"Thanks." Katie walked back to Crown Hall in a daze, although one persistent thought stayed in her mind. By the time she was at the dorm's door, she felt that singular thought had been seared on her brain. That thought led her to an important decision. She entered the lobby and decided, *I'm not going to tell anyone about the inheritance. Not Rick or Christy or Nicole or anyone. Only Julia needs to know for now. If I tell too many people, it will be confusing to know what I should do next.*

Trying to remember her new approach of greeting everyone along the way, Katie stopped for a few minutes to chat mindlessly with three different girls. When she entered her room, she closed the door and stood with her back against it.

This isn't real. This isn't happening. What if Julia hadn't been with me? I would have freaked out. I'd probably be running around campus right now screaming and telling everyone.

She drew in a breath.

This is better. Just you and me, Lord. Just you and me.

For about twenty minutes, Katie lay on her bed, staring at the ceiling. Her cell phone rang, but she let it ring. Whoever it was, she couldn't talk right now. She was thinking. Meditating. What was her next step?

Her tuition payment was due next week. She would use the money to pay that, of course. Not just for this next payment but for the rest of the year. She would pay off all her school bills. That was what Aunt

Mabel wanted, wasn't it? That way Katie could graduate in May without any student loans and without any debt.

Never in a million years would she have guessed that God would do this sort of thing. She had told him when she started college that she trusted him to get her through, but even in her wildest imaginings, this was never the way she thought he would do it.

"Thank you," Katie whispered. "Thank you, thank you, thank you!"

She thought of all her friends who were struggling to find ways to pay for their tuition. Why couldn't she help them out? Anonymously. Julia could direct her in how to make a silent donation. Why not? She could contribute to Joseph's tuition and Eli's.

"Eli!" Katie shot up and scrambled for her phone. "I left the Java Jungle and never went back to meet him!"

Katie checked and saw that she had three messages from him. Quickly dialing his number, she got his voice mail. "Eli, I am so, so sorry. Something came up. I umm ... well, just call me later. Maybe we can meet for dinner or something."

She reached for a spiral notebook off her desk and remembered that she hadn't done her reading yet for her class that evening. The reading would have to wait another twenty minutes or so. Katie needed to put her flood of thoughts down on paper before her mind started to scramble again.

She scribbled down all the students she knew who were working to pay for their tuition. The list grew, and Katie became discouraged. If she tried to pay for tuition for everyone on the list, all the money would be gone before she reached the end of the list.

Scratching out that list, she started over. Eli was at the top of the list. She had no idea how his tuition was being covered. Julia could help her find out. Joseph was next on the list. As she wrote his name, she thought of the game they had played on Thanksgiving. Joseph's answer to what he would do if he had a million dollars was to bring Shiloh and Hope here to be with him at Rancho Corona.

A lovely smile grew on Katie's face. She could do that. She could make that possible. Actually, God was the one who could and was making it possible.

Katie started a new list. The header was "God's Dreams." The first thing on the list was "Shiloh and Hope move to Rancho." When she wrote the last "o," she added a happy little curl at the top of the "o." Then, for fun, she added eyes and a big smile inside the "o" in Shiloh and in Hope and in Rancho. Three happy faces.

"What else?" Katie asked aloud. "What else do you want to do with this ridiculous chunk of change?"

Right on the top of her thoughts was the fund-raiser project for clean water for Africa. She wrote that down. If she made a big contribution, that wouldn't mean the fund-raiser was off. It just meant more money would be added.

Katie was too excited to wait and ask what else God wanted on his list of dreams. She called Julia and asked her to come down to her room. "I need help."

"Are you okay?" Julia asked.

"I am way beyond okay. I am jubilant."

"Oh, dear!" Julia said with a laugh. "I'll be right down."

What started that afternoon in Katie's room between Julia and Katie stayed in that room and between Julia and Katie. It was the most delicious sort of secret ever.

After Katie outlined for Julia how she wanted to break up the money, Julia nodded and then said, "You forgot one rather important thing."

"What? Tithing?"

"No, I think you have the tithing quadrupled with what you want to direct to the clean water project. The one thing you forgot was yourself."

"I have my tuition covered. It's in this column right here."

"Katie, what about a car?"

"Oh, yeah. I could use one of those."

"Ya' think?" Julia said playfully. "I can't believe you didn't come up with that at the top of the list. You thought of everyone but yourself."

"Not exactly. I just forgot about my transportation deficiency. I think it's because everyone has been so nice about toting me around. I haven't missed my car as much as I thought I would."

"You still need to buy one."

"I know. I don't need a new car, but something dependable would be great. This could be fun! I could pay with cash!"

The paperwork arrived on Thursday, and Julia helped Katie go over the specifics to make sure she had responded to every question asked of her and signed every place she was required to sign.

As they were driving back from the shipping store from which they sent the papers back via FedEx overnight, Julia helped Katie to decide out how much she would put in savings, how much she would transfer to checking, and how much she needed to hold out for taxes. Another amount needed to be placed into a long-term savings account where it would earn higher interest and be available to Katie after she graduated. Katie wasn't convinced about the after-graduation savings certificate, but Julia pointed out that the sum would allow Katie to move into an apartment.

"And if I don't need to get my own apartment after I graduate?" Katie said, alluding to the possibility that she might be like Christy and get married right after graduation.

"Then I would say you will have all the money you need for a knockout wedding dress as well as a reception that will wow all your friends and family."

"And I won't have to ask my parents for a dime," Katie said, pensively. That was the moment she realized how much her life had changed. Not just because of the money but because she really was independent.

With that in mind, Katie added another savings account to the list. This one was for her parents. "You told me the best thing I could do was to honor my father and mother. I don't want to tell them about this money for all the obvious reasons, but I do want to put some aside for them in case they have medical problems or retirement expenses they can't cover."

Julia nodded her agreement. "This is good, Katie. Very good. You're being a good manager of what God has given you."

"Well, he hasn't given it to me yet. I still have the feeling that this is one of those I'll-believe-it-when-I-see-it sort of moments."

Katie backed out of her proposed lunch date with Christy later that week, stating honestly that she had way too much to do. She was dying to tell Christy, but she knew if she told Christy, Christy would want to tell Todd, and if Todd knew, then he would tell Eli and, of course, Rick, and then there would be no stopping the news. Everyone would know, and the secretiveness of the giving would be spoiled.

For that reason she also avoided long conversations with Nicole. Her conversations on the phone with Rick were all about his adventures in San Diego and how he always left the new building smelling of rubber tires. When he told her on the phone Friday night that he was sorry, but he wouldn't be able to keep their date on Sunday, Katie was barely ruffled.

"I've had so much going on here you wouldn't even believe it."

"You're not upset?"

"No. I'm eager to see you, but I can wait. I'm a good waiter."

Rick chuckled. "You are, Katie. You're the best. I . . ."

A small grin grew on Katie's face as she sat in the noisy cafeteria with her cell phone pressed to her ear. "Yes, you started to say something . . ."

"I appreciate you more than you'll ever know," he said.

"Chicken!"

"What?"

Katie knew it wasn't a good idea to badger Rick into saying he loved her. She quickly redirected her declaration. "We're having chicken tonight. I'm in the cafeteria."

"I can hear that. I should let you go."

"Okay, but call me later when you can."

"I will. I always do."

"I know." Katie closed her phone and carried her tray over to the window table where she and Eli had sat Monday night when she came up with the idea of his speaking in chapel. She took her plate and drink off the tray since it was such a small table and put the tray against the window. She did have chicken on her plate. The last thing she ever wanted to do was to lie to Rick. In a small way she felt unsettled since she hadn't told him about the inheritance.

At the same time, she knew it was the right decision. The more she thought about it, the more right it felt to keep everything as it was—a splendid little secret between her and God. Clearly God had sent Julia along for the needed support. It was no coincidence, Katie was sure, that she had opened the first letter when she was sitting on the couch in Julia's apartment. It was also no coincidence that Julia had stepped into the Java Jungle just minutes before Katie received the call back from the lawyer.

Katie offered a prayer of thanks over her Friday night cafeteria chicken and ate by herself. She thought about all the homework she needed to catch up on over the weekend. She also tried to figure out when she would have time to go look for a car, and when she would have time to meet Christy for lunch.

When she thought of Christy, she thought of two things. Poor ol' Mr. Jitters and Todd and Christy's one-car dilemma. Pulling out the small notebook she now carried with her ever since Julia suggested she keep one handy on her dorm room visits, Katie wrote herself a note: T and C—Cat and Car. She put the note on the page where she was keeping a list of what she was calling her "Fairy Godmother" list. If she could bless someone in an anonymous way with the extra money that was going to go into her savings account, their name and the specific gift went on the Fairy Godmother list. It didn't mean she would follow through with all the flighty notions on that list, but it was certainly fun to think about how she might buy Christy and Todd an extra car or a pet.

Katie pensively chewed the tough piece of chicken and decided to cross the "cat" off the list for Christy. She already knew that one wouldn't be viewed by Todd as a blessing. The car, though, might be a possibility. She didn't know how it might happen and how she would keep it anonymous, but she had time. The money hadn't arrived yet. When it did, she could put it away and wait until just the right moment to activate her Fairy Godmother list.

The check arrived on Thursday, three weeks before Christmas. Katie opened her mailbox and saw the envelope. It took every molecule of restraint within her to simply reach for the envelope and slide it into her shoulder bag without letting out a wild screech of jubilation. She hotfooted it back to Crown Hall, dialing Julia on the way.

"Hi," Katie said calmly. "It's me, Katie. Um, you know how you said if I ever needed a ride that I could ask you for one?"

"Yes."

"Well, I wonder if you would be available to drive me to the bank this afternoon."

"Oh, the bank. The bank! Yes! Wow! Already? Okay. Yes. I'd be honored to drive you to the bank."

"Good. I'm almost to Crown Hall right now."

"I'll meet you in the lobby."

The two of them kept up the calm façade as they connected by the front door.

"Are you ready to go, then?" Julia asked.

"Yes. Thanks for doing this for me."

"It's no problem, Katie. Anytime."

Then, because she couldn't help but add a little curlicue to the moment, Katie said, "I do hope I'll be able to somehow buy a car pretty soon, but until then, I really appreciate the ride."

Julia glanced around. It didn't seem that anyone had heard Katie's comment. No matter. The two of them knew all the hidden meanings. As soon as they slipped into Julia's car, Katie opened the envelope.

"My hands are shaking!" Carefully pulling the significant piece of paper out of the envelope, Katie laid it in her lap and stared.

"Is it as you expected?" Julia asked.

"Down to the penny. Wow. What a lot of beautiful, beautiful fat and happy numbers. Look at them all lined up like wishes. So many wishes are going to come true as a result of these unsuspecting numbers. I feel like singing!"

As Julia drove to the bank, both of them sang. It was kind of silly and spontaneous, but at the same time, it seemed the most natural thing to do. It was an act of worship.

Once they arrived at the bank, though, they both moved into being all business. That was easy to do because of the preliminary work Julia had done. She had prearranged an appointment with the bank manager and had called as soon as Katie called her. That allowed the two of them to sit in the manager's office and conduct the transaction privately.

It took nearly an hour before everything was completed. They were nearly finished with the details on the account Katie wanted to use for the fund-raiser when the manager said, "Am I to understand that the majority of these funds are going to charity?"

Katie explained about the fund-raiser plans and Eli's connection to the project. "He's going to speak at chapel tomorrow," Katie said. "You're welcome to come hear him, if you'd like."

The manager sat back and folded his hands, his expression contemplative. "I'm not able to come to the chapel," he said. "But I'd like our branch to participate in the fund-raiser. Would you be able to provide information for us?"

"Of course." Katie and Julia exchanged surprised glances.

He tipped his big leather chair forward and, looking at Katie, said, "I've never seen anything like this. You are an inspirational young woman. To have this kind of money at your disposal and to choose to put so much of it toward this cause is profoundly moving."

Katie didn't know what to say.

"I've decided I will be making a personal contribution of three thousand dollars to the fund. My contribution will show up in the account by the end of this month."

"Thank you!" Katie rose and reached out to shake his hand. "Thank you so much!"

"No, thank you for your impressive example. I've been in banking for two decades, and I've never seen this sort of dedication. Especially in someone so young. May I ask you how you reached this decision?"

Katie looked at Julia and back at the bank manager. "We just prayed about it. I asked God if he had any dreams that he wanted to fulfill with the money, and then I started to make a list."

"Well, again, thank you for your example, Ms. Weldon. You are a credit to your God and to your university." He rose and opened the door of his office.

As Katie and Julia stepped out, the clients waiting to meet with the manager next came toward them.

"Rick, Josh! Hey!" Katie rushed forward and gave Rick a huge hug. "I can't believe you guys are here."

"We're here for our business loan," Josh said. "So wish us well."

"I take it these young men are friends of yours," the manager said.

"This is my boyfriend, Rick Doyle, and his brother, Josh."

"Is everything okay?" Rick asked Katie. He said it quietly, but Katie was pretty sure the manager and Julia could hear him. "You're not overdrawn, are you? Because if you are . . ."

The manager covered his mouth as a cough seemed to suddenly overtake him.

"No, everything is great. Julia offered to give me a ride. I had to put some of my finances in order." She turned and gave the manager a sly smile. "We were able to work out everything."

"Well, if you need a ride again, just call me. I didn't know you were coming here today."

"I didn't know either. It just worked out that way." Katie turned to Julia. "Have you guys met yet? Rick and Josh, this is Julia, the resident director of my dorm."

They exchanged polite hellos. The manager then invited Rick and Josh into his office.

"If it helps," Katie said to the bank manager with a playful grin, "I'd be willing to vouch for those two."

"Thanks, Katie girl," Josh responded with an equally playful pat on her shoulder. "I'm sure that means a lot coming from a college student who doesn't even own a car at the moment. Not sure what kind of collateral you could offer us, but thanks for the vote of confidence."

Josh's comment bugged her, but Katie brushed it off and offered a calm smile to the bank manager. The office door closed behind the two brothers, and Katie debated whether she wanted to wait until they were finished and get a ride back to Rancho with them, or go back now with Julia. She opted for going back with Julia, and the two of them drove through Archie's Burgers on the way to campus.

"We'll have two chocolate milkshakes," Julia said.

"Small, medium, or large?" the voice in the drive-through box asked.

"Large!" Katie yelled back. "Definitely large! We're celebrating!"

When they drove up to the window, Katie handed Julia a twenty-dollar bill. "I've always wanted to do this. Give her the twenty and then say, 'Keep the change.'"

Julia did as Katie asked, and by the look on the young woman's face, they had just made her day.

Slurping and smiling and sighing, Julia and Katie took their time driving back to Rancho.

"That was fun," Julia said, as she parked her car and the two of them sat in the parking lot cooling off in the afterglow of all that had happened.

"It was very fun," Katie agreed. "And don't worry about my toss-ing twenty-dollar bills around campus and raising suspicions. I've thought a lot about it, and I know I have to play it cool. I will. And one more thing. I've thought about this a lot too, so I hope you'll honor my exhaustive efforts of the brain. I want to pay you for your consulting." Katie pulled out one of her new checkbooks and started to write a check.

"Now, before you protest," Katie quickly inserted, "just know that I don't want to hear any rebuttals from you. I want to give this money as a thank you for all your help. What you do with it is up to you. But you have to take it."

Julia didn't resist. She cried and said thank you and hugged Katie.

Katie asked, "Do you think you have time to take the cashier's check over to student services?"

"The one for Joseph?"

"Yeah, I can't wait to put all the steps into motion. If there's any way Shiloh and Hope can get here before Christmas, it would be incredible."

Julia had taken all the necessary steps to arrange for Joseph's wife and daughter to move here. All that was needed was the check. Then Joseph would be notified, the flights would be finalized, and every-thing wonderful for their family would be set in motion. No one knew who was making this contribution. Julia had done an excellent job of keeping Katie's confidences.

Eli's tuition had been covered, but Joseph's tuition was already covered by a scholarship. All Katie was paying for was the travel expenses and housing for Joseph and his family until he graduated.

Katie returned to her room while Julia carried out the next steps at student services. Several women greeted Katie as she walked down the hall, and she stopped to chat with two of them before going into her room and closing the door. She still didn't have an in-and-out calendar on her message board, but she had begun writing down "Be Back" and a projected time of return whenever she left her room. The stop-and-chat technique she was using every time she went up or down the hall seemed to be helping in terms of how the women greeted her when they saw her. Things were looking up in every area of Katie's life.

She was almost to her room when Rick called.

"We got the loan." He sounded thrilled and surprised.

"That's great!"

"You don't understand, Katie. We received enough to open both cafés. The one in Redlands and the one in San Diego."

"What café in Redlands? I thought that was just a spec?"

"It was, but with this kind of funding, Josh and I can do both. We need to go out to celebrate. What are you doing right now? Do you want to meet us at the Thai Palace? Oh, wait. Josh just said he doesn't have time to do a sit-down dinner. I'm going to drop him off at his car at the Dove's Nest, and then I'll go over to the Thai Palace and pick up some food. We can eat at my place. Can you grab a ride?"

"Yeah, I'm sure I can bum a ride off someone. I'll see you in half an hour."

"Make it forty-five minutes."

Katie went through the rounds of her usual free rides. Julia was taking Talitha and her roommate out to dinner for Talitha's birthday. Nicole wasn't picking up her calls. Three of Katie's other possible generous friends with wheels all had plans, and none of them was heading toward Rick's apartment.

She tried Christy as a long shot, but she was working an evening shift for someone who was sick and Todd had the car and was in a meeting.

"Okay. So I guess I do need a car."

She didn't want to call Rick back and make him pick her up. On a whim, Katie called a cab company. She didn't even know taxis were available, but when she tracked one down and made the call, she asked to be picked up at the front entrance to Rancho Corona so that as few people as possible would see her getting into a cab.

Jogging her way across campus, Katie reached the front entrance and waited for the cab to arrive. She realized what a bad idea it was to stand at the entrance because several students noticed her as they drove onto campus and stopped to ask if she was okay. She told them she was waiting for someone, which she was. She just didn't know that someone.

The next car that exited Rancho stopped. It was a beat-up white Camry. "Katie!"

"Hey, Eli. Are you going home?"

"Yes."

"Why didn't I think to call you? I need a ride to your apartment."

"Sure, hop in."

"Wait just a second." Katie quickly made a call to the cab company to cancel her request. She wanted to do it away from Eli so he wouldn't hear her make the call.

Once she was in the car, Eli said, "Would you mind if we make one detour?"

"Of course not."

"Good. My car needs petrol, and I have something to drop off for Joseph."

"Oh, sure. Okay. How is Joseph?"

"He's doing okay, I guess."

"What about you?" Katie asked. "Are you ready for your presentation in chapel tomorrow?"

"I think so. Thanks for setting up everything."

"You're welcome. It was easy."

"I saw all the flyers that were printed and the donation boxes. They look good."

"Nicole did all that. She's amazing with that sort of thing. You'll never guess what happened today."

"What?"

Katie thought of all that had happened and forced her lips to form only a small grin. "I had to go to the bank, and I ended up talking to the bank manager. He said we could put flyers and donation boxes there at the bank."

"Really? That's amazing."

"I know. God is doing something much bigger than I ever expected." Katie looked out the front windshield and noticed that Eli still had the dried floral halo hanging from his rearview mirror. "You know, you really should throw that thing away, Eli."

"Why?"

"It's dead."

"No," he said, shooting her a fairly fierce glance. "It's not dead. It reminds me to pray."

"For what?"

He hesitated. "For you. For several people, but one of them is you."

"Me? What do you pray for me?"

"I pray that God will bless you."

Katie didn't mean to, but she laughed aloud and then quickly covered her mouth. "That is so cool. Really. Thank you. I think you can stop now."

"Why?"

She was going to say that God had blessed her so much that she didn't need any more prayers sent to heaven on her behalf. Quickly retracting her thought in case it might arouse suspicion, Katie simply said, "Actually, no. Keep praying. I'm sorry I laughed. That's really kind of you, Eli. Thank you. Yes, keep praying for me. I always need prayer."

With a sideways grin, he said, "That's what I thought. That's why I decided to add you to my list." He pulled down the sun visor on his side of the car and revealed a worn index card that had a list of names on it. Katie saw that her name was indeed on the list. So was Rick's.

"Thank you," Katie said sincerely. "Really, Eli, thank you."

They pulled into the gas station where Joseph worked, and Eli got out to pump the gas. Joseph apparently noticed him from his spot behind the counter inside the convenience store because as soon as Joseph realized it was Eli, he blasted out the front door with a huge grin on his face.

"Eli, she's coming! They are coming! You will not believe!" Slapping his hands together and then lifting them to the heavens, Joseph looked up and laughed with the wild abandon of a crazed man.

Eli rushed over and put his hand on Joseph's shoulder. People in the cars and waiting inside the convenience store stared at them. Katie bit her lower lip to keep from crying or laughing or in any way giving away a clue that she knew why Joseph was dancing around and ranting in what must have seemed to be a nonsensical way to Eli.

As Katie watched from her spot in the car with the window down, Joseph told Eli about the phone call he had received and how it was a dream he had stopped dreaming long ago. Shiloh and Hope were coming to live with him. Then Joseph cried. Eli helped him back into the convenience store and got him back behind the counter so he could help the line of people waiting for him.

Katie decided to finish pumping the gas and then took the squeegee and washed Eli's car windows. All the while, she fought back her own tears, as she watched Eli talking to the people inside the store and point to Joseph, who was still beaming from ear to ear.

All of the customers started to smile. Katie watched as each of them shook Joseph's hand and left the store grinning.

"That's incredible," one customer said as he walked past Katie. "Did you hear what happened? I thought the guy was having a nervous breakdown when he ran out here. Turns out his wife and daughter are going to be reunited with him after several years. Touches you right here, doesn't it?"

Katie nodded, trying hard not to cry.

"Gives you hope for the world, you know? Good things still happen, don't they?"

"I like to call them God things," Katie said.

The man nodded slowly and returned to his car. When Eli came back out, he was smiling like crazy. "Do you want to go in and say hi to Joseph? He has some amazing news."

Katie felt torn. She didn't know how she would react if she looked at Joseph or heard his news face-to-face. She was worried she might "crack."

"Why don't you tell me his news on our way back to the apartment? Joseph looks a little busy in there at the moment."

Eli reluctantly agreed. He started up the car. "Hey, thanks for washing the windows."

"Sure. So, what's Joseph's news?"

Eli choked up as he told Katie. She choked up as she heard him tell her. All she could say in response was, "Wow!"

"Ruth at student services told Joseph everything had been arranged by an anonymous donor. Can you imagine? It's probably someone who supports the mission association that has done work in their area for a number of years."

Katie gave a noncommittal, "Hmm."

All the way to the apartment, Eli talked. This was new for him. He practiced part of what he was going to say in chapel and told Katie about the last email he received from his dad. As he chatted on, Katie watched his expressions and thought of what a huge amount of Eli's personality had been hidden away until recently. She also noticed the scar on his neck. It was in the shape of a backward L. With a private sense of regret, Katie remembered how when she first met Eli she silently decided the "L" stood for "Loser." How wrong she had been. If anyone else at Rancho had similar first impressions about Eli, those thoughts would be dramatically changed tomorrow morning when he spoke at chapel.

They arrived at the apartment only a few minutes after Rick had returned with a fragrant assortment of his favorite Thai food in little white boxes. As soon as Rick saw Katie enter with Eli, a shadow came over his face.

"I should have asked if you were going to be home for dinner," Rick said to Eli. "I would have brought more food."

"Don't worry about it. Actually, I'm not staying. I'm on my way out. I just had to pick up some books, and Katie needed a ride so it worked out."

"Are you sure?" Rick said.

"Yeah, I'm good." Eli smiled. "I'm real good."

"Thanks for the ride," Katie said.

"Anytime. Just call me."

"Okay, thanks."

Rick opened up the boxes he had unpacked on the kitchen table. Katie went to the cupboard and pulled out some plates. She found a bottle of mineral water in the refrigerator and took two glasses from the cupboard. Pouring the bubbly water into the glasses, she handed one to Rick and said, "Here's to you and Josh for obtaining the loan."

They clinked glasses and took a sip.

"Ahh," Rick said. "Vintage year. Nice sparkling aftertaste. I hope you don't mind that I got mostly spicy ones."

Katie made a face, but Rick didn't see her. She didn't care for the spicier dishes. As a matter of fact, she wasn't as big a fan of Thai food as Rick was. She preferred Casa de Pedro any day.

Eli walked past them on his way to the front door. "I'll see you guys later."

"See you in chapel tomorrow," Katie said. "I'll be the one in the front row smiling."

"Thanks." Eli gave her a warm grin and left.

"You know what I love?" Rick said a moment after Eli left the apartment.

"Me?" Katie ventured.

Rick sidestepped Katie's response by looking away. "I set myself up for that one, didn't I?"

"What were you going to say?"

"I was going to say that I love the way you're getting along with my roommate. I appreciate it. It makes things better around here, you know?" He kept his gaze averted and pulled noodles from the largest white box with a serving spoon.

"Rick." Katie put her hand on his and stopped his movement before he dove in for a second helping. "Look at me."

Rick looked at Katie.

Without pausing to think through what she was about to say, Katie said, "I wasn't going to do this, but ..."

"I know what you're going to say." Rick put down the spoon and lifted his hand to smooth her hair back from her temples.

"Do you?" For Katie the question had a double meaning. She was asking Rick, "Do you love me?" But she knew it could also be interpreted as, "Do you know what I was going to say?" Either way, their conversation was headed for the declaration Katie had been thinking about ever since that afternoon at the Dove's Nest when she looked at Rick across the sea of field trip students.

Rick looked into Katie's eyes. He smiled a slight smile and ran his thumb across her cheek. Drawing close, he kissed her.

As they drew apart, Katie had the sense that everything she wanted to know about Rick's feelings toward her had just been expressed in that kiss. Yet she still wanted words. She wanted "the" words.

Searching his eyes, she asked again, "Do you?" Only this time, her eyes alone asked the question.

Rick put his arms around Katie and pulled her close in a hug. Whispering into her ear so that his breath sent tiny quivers up and down the hair on her neck, he spoke her name. "Katie. I want you to listen to me and take in what I'm going to say."

She tried to pull back so she could watch his face as he spoke, but Rick gently held her close.

"One of the agreements I made with myself when I got my heart right with the Lord was that I wouldn't tell a woman I loved her until the next words out of my mouth would be a proposal."

Katie swallowed and felt her eyes misting over.

"I'm not quite there yet. Do you understand what I'm saying?"

She nodded her head, knowing he could feel the movement.

"Almost," Rick whispered. "Almost."

Katie nodded again.

Rick released his hold, and Katie withdrew far enough so she could read his eyes. She saw in his warm gaze every assurance that she needed for the time being.

He dipped his chin, and he kept looking at her, raising his eyebrows slightly as if inviting her to respond.

"I'm a good waiter," Katie said softly.

Rick grinned. "Yes, you are."

"And you're a very good waiter."

"Yes, I am," Rick agreed.

"What you're alluding to is far too important to decide on a whim," Katie said.

"Yes, it is."

"I can live with 'almost ever after.'" She smiled at him.

"Almost ever after," Rick repeated. Then he added, "For now."

"For now," Katie echoed.

They drew together at the same moment and gave each other a kiss that was equal to any fairy-tale kiss that ever accompanied a story of "almost ever after."

Dear Peculiar Treasure,

While I was writing this story, I saw something in Katie's imaginary life that I also see in mine and perhaps you see in yours. We never quite know what will happen next, do we? Life is a beautiful mystery. God, who is the author and finisher of our faith, is writing the story of our lives. He puts in all the twists and turns of the plot at just the right moment. Some chapters of our lives are full of suspense. Others are packed with humor. Some chapters make it seem as if our whole story is an epic tale of love, and then we turn a page and suddenly we're in the middle of an unsolved mystery or a page-turning suspense thriller. We all have tragic chapters in our lives. We just don't know when the pain will slip into our stories. Nor do we see the surprises that come at just the right moment to fill us with wonder and hope for what's next.

One of the life surprises for me while writing this book was participating in a project our church launched called Advent Conspiracy (www.adventconspiracy.org). We were able to raise a crazy amount of money to dig wells that provide clean drinking water in overlooked places of the world. I imagined Katie jumping in to assist with an organization such as Blood:Water Mission (www.bloodwatermission.com) or Living Water International (www.water.cc).

The verse Katie heard in the song while watching the stars dance in the heavens is from Micah 6:8. That verse applies to each of us in our life stories. What does God require of us? To act justly, love mercy, and walk humbly with God.

Your life is a glorious, one-of-a-kind, complex, and expertly crafted God-tale. He did not create you "on a whim." He knew you from before you were born and has ordered every breath you take before you even take it. You are his "Peculiar Treasure." My prayer for each of you is that you would embrace each page, each paragraph, of your story, with wonder. May you live expectantly and joyfully knowing that the One who spins the stars in space holds your heart in his hands. Trust him for whatever is about to happen next.

With a humble heart,

Robin Jones Gunn

Please come by for a visit at www.robingunn.com and sign up for Robin's Nest Newsletter in order to receive updates on future releases.

Peculiar Treasures

Robin Jones Gunn,
Bestselling Author
of the Christy Miller Series

Katie Weldon catches more than just the bouquet at the wedding of her best friend, Christy Miller. She also snags a job offer that launches her into an adventure she never imagined.

Katie eagerly accepts the job as resident assistant at Rancho Corona University only to find herself in a community of conflict. She thought this was where God wanted her, but how can God use her—love her—when everything is falling apart? Especially with her boyfriend, Rick.

Katie turns to the women in her life for solace. In the safety of their love and encouragement she finally allows herself to spill her heart about her relationship with Rick. But even their advice can't postpone the decision Katie must face, a decision that will define who she is and the woman she's becoming.

The first book in the Katie Weldon Series, *Peculiar Treasures* follows Katie as she struggles to believe that God can love her, faults and all.

Softcover: 978-0-310-27656-2

Pick up a copy today at your favorite bookstore!

More Fun

with Christy, Todd, & Katie

As Christy, Katie, and Todd head into the tumultuous years of college, each must make life-changing decisions about life, love, and God. From a whirlwind trip abroad to an engagement surprise to a beautiful wedding, the path ahead for these three friends will see both happy and hard times.

With important decisions on the line and fun memories to be made, you won't want to miss a single adventure with your favorite friends.

CHRISTY AND TODD:
THE COLLEGE YEARS
Until Tomorrow, As You Wish, I Promise

ROBIN JONES GUNN

Christy & Todd

The COLLEGE YEARS

DON'T FORGET WHERE IT ALL STARTED...

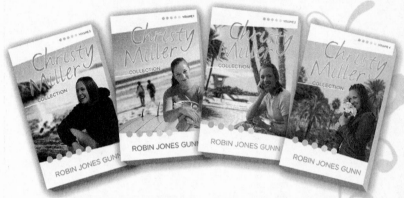

Christy Miller Collection, Volume 1 (Books 1-3)
Christy Miller Collection, Volume 2 (Books 4-6)
Christy Miller Collection, Volume 3 (Books 7-9)
Christy Miller Collection, Volume 4 (Books 10-12)

Sierra Jensen Collection, Volume 1 (Books 1-3)
Sierra Jensen Collection, Volume 2 (Books 4-6)
Sierra Jensen Collection, Volume 3 (Books 7-9)
Sierra Jensen Collection, Volume 4 (Books 10-12)

MULTNOMAH BOOKS

Share Your Thoughts

With the Author: Your comments will be forwarded to
the author when you send them to *zauthor@zondervan.com*.

With Zondervan: Submit your review of this book
by writing to *zreview@zondervan.com*.

Free Online Resources at
www.zondervan.com/hello

 Zondervan AuthorTracker: Be notified whenever your
favorite authors publish new books, go on tour, or post
an update about what's happening in their lives.

 Daily Bible Verses and Devotions: Enrich your life
with daily Bible verses or devotions that help you start
every morning focused on God.

 Free Email Publications: Sign up for newsletters on
fiction, Christian living, church ministry, parenting, and
more.

 Zondervan Bible Search: Find and compare
Bible passages in a variety of translations at
www.zondervanbiblesearch.com.

 Other Benefits: Register yourself to receive online
benefits like coupons and special offers, or to participate
in research.